MANTIES IN A TWIST

THE SUBS CLUB
BOOK III

J.A. ROCK

Rock

Riptide Publishing
PO Box 1537
Burnsville, NC 28714
www.riptidepublishing.com

Cover art: Kanaxa, kanaxa.com
Editor: Delphine Dryden, delphinedryden.com/editing
Layout: L.C. Chase, lcchase.com/design.htm

ISBN: 978-1-62649-348-3

First edition
April, 2016

Also available in ebook:
ISBN: 978-1-62649-347-6

MANTIES IN A TWIST

THE SUBS CLUB
BOOK III

J.A. ROCK

For Cleveland

TABLE OF CONTENTS

Chapter 1 1
Chapter 2 21
Chapter 3 39
Chapter 4 59
Chapter 5 71
Chapter 6 87
Chapter 7 95
Chapter 8 113
Chapter 9 125
Chapter 10 139
Chapter 11 157
Chapter 12 179
Chapter 13 195
Chapter 14 215
Chapter 15 235
Chapter 16 253

ONE

"Behold." Amanda stepped back from the wall where she'd just hung Ryan's and my newest amazerbeam piece of art.

Ryan and me, we couldn't even talk for a minute, that's how glorious this painting was.

It was of a hare dressed in a black and gold shirt with puffy sleeves, like from Shakespeare times, and a floppy cap and striped pants. The hare had a gold watch in his pocket and a serious look, and was just a generally very regal and well-dressed rabbit. The background was a sky blue that really made the brown fur pop.

"You're so talented." Ryan had this voice that was sort of like Boots, the monkey from *Dora the Explorer*. It was, I mean, a *little* deeper than that, but not much. He was super short—almost legit midget short, and I got that maybe midget wasn't the right word anymore, but you know what I mean. He spoke really aggressively though, so you still took him seriously even though he sounded like a cartoon. "It goes perfectly with the walls."

Amanda frowned at the painting. "It took forever to get the eyes right."

Amanda was one of Ryan's friends from high school. Ryan actually had tons of friends from way back, which was cool. Because I was, like, *intensely* close with my friends Miles, Gould, and Dave, and I liked having a boyfriend who understood the concept of friends you go way back with.

"It's huhhhh-mazing." I admired the detail work on the well-dressed hare's puffy sleeves. "The guys are gonna shit when they see it." Okay, Dave would think it was cool. Miles would think it was dumb. And Gould probably wouldn't say anything, but he'd give me that look, the one that was like a thumbs-up with his eyes.

Ryan turned to me. "We should figure out when we're doing the housewarming party."

"Let's do it Saturday."

He put his hands on his hips, which for some reason made him look even shorter. "We don't have curtains yet."

"So we'll hit up Triple B later." I was always down for Bed Bath & Beyond.

He smiled. Dave thought Ryan's smile was demonic, but I thought it was cute: his lips pulled back a little bit, and the edges of his top and bottom teeth met, and I could see where he kind of looked like a doll that had come to life. But why did a doll coming to life have to be a bad thing?

"You really wanna go again?" he asked.

"Always." I high-fived him. This guy and I, we'd been making Bed Bath & Beyond our bitch. We'd gotten like four gift cards from his parents and three from mine, and had blown through almost all of them. We'd bought a vegetable spiralizer, organic shams for the sofa, a Pasta Boat, and a Mighty Blaster garden hose nozzle that Ryan rigged so it would go on our shower. He was really handy, as long as he had a step stool.

We kissed. I squeezed him and lifted him off the floor, and we went at it until Amanda cleared her throat. "Um, so can I do my laundry now?"

I set him down.

Ryan stepped back. "Of course. I'll show you the laundry room."

We had a laundry room.

We had basically a house. I mean, it was an apartment, but it was the whole second floor of a house. We were on the opposite side of town from Dave and Gould, which kinda sucked—my old place had been really close to them. But it was closer to the Green Kitchen, where I worked. Maybe now that I had more space, I could get the guys to come over instead of always going to them.

Ryan and Amanda headed to the back of the house. That was the deal: she'd paint us a picture of a well-dressed hare, and in exchange, she could do her laundry for free at our apartment whenever she wanted. I glanced at the hare again. We'd wanted a unique painting, and had been trying to decide between a hare and a megalodon, which were my and Ryan's favorite animals, respectively. I was glad we'd gone with the hare, because you could make a hare look classy, but that was harder to do with a megalodon.

I went to the kitchen and got, like, weirdly, nonsexually excited by the contact paper in the silverware drawer when I opened it to get a spoon. We'd done that. We'd scrubbed and decorated this whole place, with some help from our friends. Like, I'm talking painted the bathroom, set fire to a pile of dead earwigs we found behind the fridge—which almost did not go well, so if you're thinking of trying it, maybe do it outside—and put knobs on the closet doors and picked out bedding that complemented the walls.

I wasn't a master of introspection, but I figured my happiness was about more than contact paper or the square footage or even the well-dressed hare.

I finally felt like a grown-up.

My friends considered me the least mature member of the circle—probably on the basis of the number of fart jokes per hangout session. And because I did stuff like trying to put Dawn in the dishwasher when I ran out of actual dish detergent. I know, forgive me for thinking something called dish soap could be put in something called the *dishwasher*. But now I was living with a guy I loved, and I knew how to do stuff like wash windows with vinegar and newspapers and clean the baseboards. I was a fucking *adult*.

I grabbed some animal crackers and a jar of peanut butter from the cabinet and went to the table.

My phone made a lightsaber sound. I took it out of my pocket and checked. Text from Dave: *Hey, buddy. Wanna come with Maya and me laterz for location scouting?*

For a few seconds I didn't know what he was talking about, so I texted *What are you talking about?* and then I realized he probably meant the kink fair, and then he was like, *The kink fair*. It was cool he was asking me, even though I figured it was mostly because Miles was getting ready to bring a kid into his life, and Gould was working. I wasn't really anyone's first choice to handle club business.

Basically, last year, my friends and me had formed the Subs Club, an online group where submissives and bottoms could talk about stuff like BDSM safety and watching out for doms who sucked.

We'd started it because our other best friend, Hal, got killed a couple of years ago by a dom named Bill Henson who didn't know what the fuck he was doing.

I bit the head off a hippo. Animal cracker dust got on my screen as I thought about how to reply.

The club had run into some trouble at first, because we'd kinda violated the privacy of a bunch of local doms by reviewing them on our site. So we'd taken down the review blog and started a discussion forum called the Sounding Board. But a few months ago, Dave had decided we should take the Subs Club on the road. We'd given a talk about safe BDSM at a local college, and then Dave wanted to host a kink fair in the spring and make it free to the public. So he'd asked an all-female kink group called Finger Bang if they'd help us plan it. Maya, who was in the Subs Club *and* Finger Bang, was kind of being a liaison.

I texted back: *In like flynn.*

I opened the peanut butter and started dipping my animal crackers in it.

Then I remembered something.

I texted Dave again. *Shit sorry forgot Ry and I are going to look at curtains.*

I waited, but Dave didn't write back.

Ryan returned a few minutes later and stole a camel from me, and we made out a little more.

"So Trips B tonight? For real?" I had to work the next two days, but I'd totally find time to put the curtains up if it meant our place would look awesome for Saturday.

"You bet." He bit my lower lip and held on, but then I stood, which meant he either had to release me or do tiptoes. He chose tiptoes. Dude never gives up.

We stared at each other for a moment and laughed, and then he let go and went to the fridge to check the Capri Sun sitch. I got out my phone.

He rummaged in the fridge. "We're out of Pacific Cooler."

"Yeah, dude." I started a text to my mom. "We should hit up Giant Eagle after curtains."

He straightened, letting the fridge door fall shut. "Did you ever find your Giant Eags card?"

"It was in the washing machine. Looks okay, though."

I texted Mom that the housewarming party was set for Saturday. She wrote back that she'd be there, and then I got this, like, intensely mommish text that she was proud of me, with lots of exclamation points.

It was nice to have one person who was a hundred percent on board with my choice to move in with Ryan, since all my friends had been like, *Too soon, man*. Ryan and I had only known each other four months, and I guess they all figured I hadn't thought this through. But when I'd told Mom, she'd said it was great that I was always willing to take risks and try new things. Which I wasn't even sure was true, seeing as how I'd pretty much lived in the same place and done the same things my whole life, except for when I went to college for a hot minute. And even then, I'd picked a school an hour away.

Mom also texted that my dad would be visiting town next Tuesday through Thursday. Which was random. Dad lived in Oregon, and he hadn't come here to visit in years—always paid for me to fly out and see him. He and Mom got along okay, but not great, and he and I were . . . I mean, I missed him, but not to the point where I couldn't wait until Christmas to see him.

Ryan came over to the table with a strawberry-kiwi Cap Sun. "You look very serious."

I glanced up. "My dad's coming to town."

"I thought he never came here."

I focused on the screen again. "Yeah. The last time was, like, four years ago."

"When's he coming?"

"Tuesday." I hovered my thumbs over the keyboard. "Think I should invite him to see me play?"

I was playing at Pitch, a local bar, on Wednesday night. Mostly covers, but I was thinking of debuting a couple of original songs too.

"Yeah." Ryan peeled the straw off the side of the foil packet. "I don't know your dad. But he'd probably love to see you play."

"Well, now you'll get to meet him." Ryan and my mom were already ridick in love, and I figured my dad would probably like Ryan a lot too. My dad loved anyone who knew how to jerry-rig stuff. And Ryan was nothing if not a jerry-rigger.

"Cool." He stabbed the straw into the foil and took a sip. "This tastes like car air freshener."

Amanda came into the kitchen, and we hung out with her for another hour and a half while she waited for her laundry to finish. Between the three of us, we ate basically all the snacks in the house. By the time she peaced out, Ryan and I were in too much of a food coma for Bed Bath & Beyond.

"How about we take our pants off instead?" Ryan was already unzipping his jeans.

I groaned and undid mine too. Slid them down and stepped out of them. "This feels sooo much better."

"Your boxers have a hole in the back."

I glanced down over my shoulder. "That's on purpose. It's my easy-access hole." I stripped off my shirt too, because it was hot as balls. I rubbed the hair on my stomach to make it fuzz up.

He walked behind me and put his arms around me. His chin didn't even reach my shoulder, and his tiny hands laced over my abs. He was a friggin' adorable doll who'd come to life, and nothing was going to stop me from thinking that, even if I didn't say it out loud.

His size had taken a little getting used to. I was six four and still had my jock muscles from high school. I'd tried a million times to explain to Ryan how much I loved his tininess, but he was sensitive about it, so it was hard to find ways of, like, expressing my enthusiasm that didn't sound insulting. For instance, I'd learned not to say, "It's like when you have a Chihuahua and you're always afraid you're gonna accidentally sit on it." Which I'd *meant* as a compliment, because Chihuahuas are cute as fuck and tough little assholes, but Ryan had kind of been like, *"Hey, bend over and we'll see if you feel like sitting on anything ever again."*

So I kept my admiration secret. I loved that he looked sort of frail, like those ghost kids in *The Others* who can't go into the sunlight, but was actually so fierce that he surprised me sometimes with his strength. I loved that I submitted to him even though he couldn't have physically overpowered me. I felt like his fucking dragon on a chain. I'd do anything he told me, but also I'd murder anyone who tried to hurt him.

He kissed my shoulder. "Let's pass out on the couch for a while, then I'll access your hole."

He was all romantic-as-tits like that. I put my hands over his and squeezed. "Love you."

I'd said "I love you" to him for the first time a couple of weeks ago, and he'd said it back like it was no big thing. My friends all made this huge deal out of *When's too soon to say that shit?* But I didn't care. I didn't think you had to wait a certain amount of time to love somebody. You could love him right away and then change your mind later if he turned out to be a dick. And if you knew you loved him, why not tell him?

"Love you too." He hip-bumped me toward the living room. We waddled side by side, heading for the couch.

He stopped. "Oh shit. Look."

I turned to him, then glanced at the floor where he was looking.

There was a pair of red lace panties on the carpet, a dryer sheet clinging to them.

"Huh." I wasn't sure what to do.

He poked them with his toe. "Amanda must have dropped them."

"We can give them back to her at the housewarming thing."

We stared at the panties. I didn't know much about girls' underwear, but these looked *nice*. Deep red and not too frilly, and the patterns in the lace were, like, intricate. I got a little hypnotized by them, and my stomach tightened, which was either something to do with sexual feelings or with a whole package of Chips Ahoy.

Ryan reached down and grabbed them. "I'll just . . ."

I didn't want him to take them away yet. "Are those Victoria's Secret or something?"

"Uh . . ." He checked the label. "I don't know. They're like a French name?"

"Can I touch them?"

He looked at me like maybe I had a guy-with-the-lotion-in-*Silence-of-the-Lambs* past I wasn't telling him about. "You want to touch my friend's panties?"

"You're touching them right now," I pointed out.

He handed them to me.

"They're big." I stretched them between my fingers.

I kept waiting for Ryan to be like, *Seriously, enough perving on my friend's panties*. But he was just gazing at the red lace in my hands like he was under some kind of spell too. "Those would look hot on you."

I jolted. *Hot on* me*?*

That was . . . I didn't . . . I wasn't . . . These weren't even . . .

We stared at each other for a moment, and then it was like an eighties power ballad started to play, and suddenly my boxers were off and I was pulling on the panties. And Ryan was on his knees all, like, making me turn around for him and squeezing the parts of my ass that were hanging out the back of the lace. And then he pulled my dick over the waistband and put it in his mouth, and that's all I remember.

We woke two hours later on the floor, disoriented and covered in jizz.

Ryan lifted his head. "What happened?"

I looked at my dick, on which hung the shredded remains of the red lace panties. "Either an angry hamster was in these panties . . ."

"Or you looked so hot in them I tried to tear them off you so I could get more of your dick down my throat."

We made eye contact, and I swallowed.

"I think it was the second one."

He nodded. "Me too."

"It was so fucking hot."

"The way you *look* in them—"

"And the way they feel . . ."

He rose onto his knees. Crawled over and straddled me. "I want you to get a pair."

I grinned and sat up. "Seriously?"

He nodded and splayed a hand on my chest, pushing me back down. "I want you to wear them *a lot*."

"Fuck, yes."

"I want you to wear an actual dress."

"Uh, okay."

He tugged my chest hair and leaned down to kiss across my collarbone. "And I want you to wear the panties underneath the dress."

"Yeah?" He was blowing my *mind*.

"Yeah." He ran his hand over my crotch. "And then I want to lift your skirt up and pull your panties down."

I tilted my head back, panting. I was gonna come just thinking about this. "*Yes.*"

"Then I want to stick my fingers in your cunt."

We both froze.

I lifted my head and stared at him. He stared back.

I frowned. "I, uh . . . don't have . . ."

His face turned pink. "I know. I just got carried away."

"You shouldn't use that word."

"I know. Can we just drop it?"

I didn't say anything else. Just let him pull me up and spin me around and push me against the ottoman. I folded my arms and rested my chin on them as he ran his hands up and down my back. All I could think about now was panties. And dresses. And . . .

"Then I want to stick my fingers in your—"

"Tonight," he whispered, kissing the back of my neck and pressing his dick against my ass, "we're gonna go shopping."

I had a feeling he didn't mean for curtains.

Later we were lying on the couch naked, watching *The Return of the King*. Ryan was curled under one of my arms, and I was messing around on my phone.

Ryan shifted to look up at me. "Do you have to text? We're watching a movie."

I glanced at the TV screen. "We've seen this a hundred times. Dave and I are talking about the housewarming party."

We were actually playing this game we'd invented where you picked two random things that belonged to the other person and said you were gonna come all over them. Dave had threatened to come all over my slippers and thighs. I'd told him I was gonna come all over his couscous and lamp. Then he'd threatened my Kindle and wig. Now I was looking around the room for ideas.

Gonna come all over your afghan and lint, I typed.

"You guys text all day, every day." Ryan dug his elbow into my side. "Let's watch."

"Sure." I sent my text and set the phone aside, yawning. Tried to focus on the movie. "Legolas always states the obvious."

"I know. You say that every time."

"'The horses are restless and the men are quiet.'"

"Shut up."

I rested my chin on the top of his head. Glanced across the room at my laptop. "Did we seriously just spend two hundred and fifty dollars on Etsy?"

"It's for a good cause."

I grinned. I was really fucking excited about the clothes we'd bought. This, like, fifties dress with flowers on it. A garter belt and stockings. Four pairs of lace underwear made by that French place Amanda's underwear was from. A bra. I guess I was nervous too. I didn't know if I'd really look good in women's clothes. And was this just about wearing a dress, or did Ryan want me to do makeup and stuff? Because I would probably look like a zombie drag queen if I wore eyeshadow.

He turned his head and kissed between two of my ribs. I squeezed him tighter.

"Do you feel a special kinship with the hobbits? Because you're so short?"

"Kamen."

I made sure to sound real freaking innocent when I replied, "What?"

He slapped my chest, not taking his eyes from the screen. "Watch yourself."

I was getting hard looking at his tiny bird shoulders, the curve of his back. I didn't even think he realized how often he did this to me: I looked at him or smelled him or heard his voice, and suddenly all I wanted to do was fuck. Like, if he knew the actual number of times I'd be willing to fuck per day, he'd be scared.

"I just feel like we could start going around with you on my shoulders. Like *Freak the Mighty*."

"One more short joke. Just one . . ."

I laughed. "Okay. Okay." I snuggled closer. "I'm done."

We watched in silence for a few more minutes.

"What about with dwarves? Do you relate to the—"

"I'm for real gonna take you over my knee if you don't stop."

I always felt a little weird when he said things like that. I got that he was kidding around. Just, for whatever reason, it hurt my feelings when he threatened punishment for real stuff, even as a joke.

The first time I'd met him, he'd spanked me. I'd made some dig about how he was too small to be a dom, and he'd volunteered to show me how someone his size could dominate someone my size. It had been really fucking hot, but mostly because I'd liked *him*—not because I'd *loved* being spanked. I got turned on by guys pulling rank the same way I got turned on by basically everything. But, I dunno.

If I were gonna therapize myself, I'd say this hang-up came from my childhood. Because people hardly ever criticized me when I was growing up. I don't mean I'm so awesome there was nothing to criticize. But my mom loved everything I did, and teachers thought I was dumb but charming, and I was really good at sports. So now it was weird to me when some dom was like, *You're not doing this right*, or *You talk back too much*, or whatever the fuck. I liked BDSM, but I wanted it to be fun, and where was the fun if someone was always gonna tell you what you were doing wrong? Even if it was just a game?

Plus with Ryan, I wouldn't purposely do anything to disappoint that fucker, ever. Except call him short.

He and I hadn't actually done much dom/sub stuff yet. We'd spent the first few months of our relationship dating and having mostly regular sex, except for some bondage-y moments, and then the move had taken up a lot of our energy. Only in the past couple of weeks had we really started getting our freak on, but we still hadn't hit on the exact kind of thing we wanted.

I nuzzled him. "I'm just playing."

Ryan gripped my hair and shook my head gently. "I know."

I looked at him for a few seconds. "Can we not do the punishing thing?"

He glanced at me. "What punishing thing?"

I grabbed the remote and muted the movie. "I get that punishing a sub is, like, part of being a dom. But I don't like it. Even when you're just joking about it. It hurts my feelings."

He sat up, frowning. "Really?"

"Kinda." I was pretty embarrassed all at once.

He studied me a moment more, then grinned, scrubbing my scalp with his knuckles. "Aww. Kamen. I didn't know that."

I grinned and tried to bite him. "Don't make fun of me."

"I'm not making fun of you."

"Well, I do have feelings. I'm not just some big, dumb buffoon."

"Hey. You know I don't think that."

I knew *he* didn't. "Everyone else kinda does, though."

He pulled me closer. "They don't matter."

I twisted my neck to stare up at him. "Is that okay?" I asked finally. "Will it make you feel, like, not dominant enough if you don't get to punish me?"

"Well, I never actually *do* punish you when I say stuff like that, so clearly I'll survive without bending you to my will."

"One time you spanked me for not keeping my head down when I was kneeling."

"That wasn't meant to be serious."

"I know! It was fun. But maybe I'd rather just . . . not."

He kissed my cheek. "Sorry. I had no idea."

"I just kinda figured it out now."

"You can have whatever you want." He ran a hand up my chest.

We watched the movie with the automatic captions on for a few minutes.

He tapped my shoulder with one finger. "Maybe you could earn rewards instead."

"Huh?"

"If I tell you to do something. Instead of punishing you if you don't do it right, I'd give you good things when you *do* get it right."

My mouth hung open slightly. "Like what kind of things?" Everything that came to mind had hot sauce on it. If I could get spicy wings for giving an awesome blowjob or whatever, my life would be pretty much the ultimate.

"Hmm." He pretended to think. "I'm not sure what you like." He ran his fingers up my thigh.

I wriggled a little, knocking a sham to the floor.

He gripped my dick. Stroked slowly.

"Do you like this?" He was smirking. "I forget."

I whimpered and nodded, lifting my hips.

"And you'd probably like it, too, if I did this." He scooted onto the ottoman on all fours, and then bent and put my dick down his throat like a fuckin' boss.

My head tipped back, and I made this sound that was kind of like when you choke on soda and it comes out your nose a little bit.

He pulled his mouth off my dick and gazed at me mock-seriously. "You'd like that?"

"Mm-hmm." My voice was high and tight. My hips were kinda doing their own thing, and my dick bumped his chin.

He sat back. Picked up my right foot, pressed his thumbs into the instep, and massaged. "And this?"

Oh God. Foot rubs were my favorite thing *in the world.*

Besides wings.

I groaned.

"And I know you love putting your tongue in my ass."

I pressed my legs together and arched my back. "Don't . . ." My thighs quivered as he swept one hand up to cup between my legs. He made circles on my balls with his thumb, and I moaned again.

"What's the matter? You *don't* like rimming me?"

More than wings. More than wings, I liked eating his ass. And he knew it.

He stopped touching me. "I can think of something else you *really* like."

He reached for one of our organic shams, and I watched in shock as he ripped the gold cord off the border. "Our shams!"

"It's fine. We've still got one more gift card." He pushed me onto my back and wound the cord around my wrists.

Oh fuck.

He tied the rope and let go. "You know what to do."

I got in my favorite position, arms over my head and knees against my chest, and stared up at him. He stroked my sides with his fingertips, which gave me that kind of *whoa* tingly feeling like when I used to stand on ice cubes with my bare feet to see how long they'd take to melt.

"Okay, please, please, please . . ." I whispered as he trailed one finger through my crack.

He brushed my hole, and I tensed, grunting. Tried to shift to get his finger there again.

He grinned smugly. "There we go. There's lots of things I can give you when you're good."

"Ryan . . ."

He leaned forward, one hand by my shoulder. "But you have to earn them." Normally, around other people, he spoke kind of loud and fast, like he was talking in shouty caps. He also sent emails and texts in literal shouty caps. But when it was just him and me, his voice got all low and soft in a way that made me basically giddy.

I'll earn them. Oh my God, I'll fucking earn them.

"How?" I closed my eyes and swallowed as he skimmed my hole again.

"First . . ." He did a finger-circle around my belly button, making my stomach suck in. I pulled against the sham cord around my wrists, but it didn't give. "I want to know where you put those panties."

I tried to bring my knees closer to my chest. "On the floor. Behind us."

He got up and went around to the back of the couch. Returned with the ripped panties. He climbed back onto the cushions and said, "Open your mouth."

Oh my God. *This* dude.

I opened my mouth, and he stuffed the panties in there. They smelled like cum, and the lace was rough against my tongue.

"You gonna be a good girl for me?" He said it kinda nervous, like he wasn't sure I'd still be into the girl stuff.

But I was totally into it.

I nodded, making a soft sound into the lace. Stretched my arms high above my head and spread my legs as wide as I could, given couch wideness limitations and such.

He stroked my sides again, then my stomach. I was breathing hard as he kissed just below my belly button. "You gorgeous, gorgeous fucker." He pinched both my nipples until I gasped. "I just want to suck these tits all night."

I spat the panties out before I could even think. "Fuck my cunt."

He let go of my nipples. The spit-soaked panties rested on my collarbone.

We stared at each other.

I raised my brows slightly.

His jaw twitched.

I let out a long breath and laughed. "That word just keeps popping out when we're doing things like this."

He nodded. "So maybe we should . . . let ourselves say it."

It was a girl word. And not a nice girl word. But it was so fucking hot. I'd always lived my life very, like, just do what feels good and don't worry about what people think. But over the past few years, my friends had gotten me to consider how the things that felt good to me could hurt other people in ways I didn't even realize.

But Ryan and I were alone. Who was "cunt" gonna hurt?

"Touch my cunt," I whispered.

The smile he gave me was huge and magnificent. It was like the Chrysler Building of smiles. He picked up the panties and pushed them back into my mouth.

My dick jerked as I bit down.

"Wait, hold on." He took the panties out of my mouth and replaced them with his fingers. "Get 'em as wet as you want 'em."

I sucked, getting them real slobbery. Then I licked between them until I could tell it was making him crazy. I beejed the fuck out of his fingers, and his dick was standing straight out by the time I was done.

He withdrew his hand and stuck the panties back in my mouth. He put his wet middle finger against my hole, circled, and then started pushing it in. I wanted to maybe warn him that the Chips Ahoy was creating a situation down in sector twelve, but the fingering felt really good and my mouth was full of panties, so I let it happen.

Wouldn't be the first time I'd farted on his fingers.

I tightened up at first, because I loved doing that: you made it hurt like fuck for a few seconds, and then you relaxed suddenly and whatever was on its way up there just shot in and nailed your prostate and it was literally the best.

He worked his ring finger in too and slid both fingers out, then in again, leaning forward between my raised legs to kiss me. Then he moved his mouth lower, and sucked my, uh . . . tits. He worked on one nipple first, sucking and licking and scraping it with his stubble. Then he switched sides, and I got to feel the ache of the first one, the wetness left by his mouth, while he moved on to the other one.

He wasn't great at multitasking, and his fingers weren't really moving inside me. So I rolled my hips, trying to get that going again while he went all Master of the Imaginary Boob Sucking Universe on me.

He pressed down on my hip and scissored his fingers inside me. "You hot little bitch," he whispered against my chest.

Okayokayokayokay . . . More bad girl words. But I loved it. And being called "little" by someone a hundred times smaller than me was the absolute shit.

He bit my right nipple and pulled up with his teeth. At the same time, he started rubbing my prostate really fast. I grabbed the sham. He used his thumb and forefinger to stroke my taint as he thrust.

"Tight fucking bitch. I love fingering your cunt."

Who even *said* shit like that? But Ryan was, like, Philip Seymour Hoffman–committed to this role. I bit the lace until my jaw ached. His fingers moved back and forth, stretching me. Then he started grinding his dick against my ass.

I couldn't really describe what happened. I sort of imagined I was a woman, but sort of didn't. Like, it was hard for me to ignore that I had giant muscles, plus body hair, plus a dick. But then I closed my eyes and started imagining that I had giant breasts, and that my ass was a cunt, which sounds weird, but it was really working for me. I moaned around the panties.

"You wet little slut."

I opened my eyes and came in his face.

He stopped and wiped his cheek with his free hand. "Seriously?"

I spat the panties out again, heaving. Let my legs drop. "Ssss . . . so fucking . . . hot."

He smiled like he was kinda embarrassed but mostly proud of himself. He still had a little cum on his cheek. "I know."

He pulled his fingers out of my ass, untied me with his other hand, and went to the bathroom.

I listened to him wash his hands. He came back in, face and hands dripping water. He jumped back on the couch between my legs. He was hard. I tried to move my foot so I could press down on his dick and then watch it spring up again, which was generally a great thing to do with boners. But I missed.

"You liked that?" he asked.

I sat up most of the way, letting the panties fall to the floor. "Yeah. Did you?"

He nodded. "I did."

I glanced at the panties. "It doesn't mean we're weird."

"No. It doesn't mean I wish you were a girl."

Whoa. That had never even occurred to me.

I scratched my neck. "Have you ever had sex with a girl?"

"No. Have you?"

I shook my head. "Maybe we should ask Gould."

"Ask Gould what?"

"He has sex with girls. We should ask him how they like to do it. And then we can do it that way. If we want to keep doing stuff like this. With panties."

Ryan frowned. "Girls probably like to do it a lot of different ways."

"Yeah, but maybe there's some special way a lot of them like doing it that we could learn about. And then I'd feel even more like a girl."

He nodded again, more slowly. "So you're, like—*into* this?"

"Dude, I jizzed in your face because of how much I like being called a girl." I paused. "Also, I think we're supposed to call them women, because of equality."

His phone buzzed on the ottoman. He groaned as it buzzed twice more. "Ohhhh *fuck*." He rolled his eyes toward the phone. Groped at the ottoman but couldn't reach it. He let his arm fall and flopped back so that we were lying with our heads on opposite ends of the couch, his legs on top of mine.

I leaned over, got the phone, and handed it to him. Half watched Gollum climb Mount Doom in pursuit of the hobbits while Ryan swiped his screen. "Mmm. Amanda thinks that just because she gave us the painting, we're at her beck and call."

"Huh?"

"She wants us to dog sit Collingsworth. For a *month*."

"Collingsworth!" I looked away from the TV. "The dog butler!" Amanda had this awesome English bulldog/Neapolitan mastiff mix whose head was seriously the size of a microwave. Not a tiny college-dorm microwave either, but one of those giant fuckers that you mount under your cabinets and that are the perfect height for if you were ever fighting a burglar and wanted to, like, open the microwave and shove the burglar's head in and hit the Popcorn button and say, in an Arnold Schwarzenegger voice, *Looks like you're about to become Orville Deadenbacher.* Which Dave told me wouldn't work because microwaves don't microwave if the door is open.

Anyway, Collingsworth was the greatest dog ever, and Amanda had trained him to bring her cans of beer, so he was totally a dog butler. "When?"

"Two weeks from now. Is a month too long?"

"No! The only thing that could make our life together more perfect is a dog." I noticed him frowning at the phone. "Why do you look mad?"

"Oh—" He shook his head. "Whatever. My mom. They definitely can't make it to the party Saturday. Which I figured. That's a long drive, and my dad's back starts freaking out if he's in the car for more than thirty minutes, so—"

"Aww. Hey, we'll go up there soon, okay?" Ryan was super close with his family, but they lived three hours away. I'd met his parents a couple of months ago when they'd come for a visit, and his dad's back had been giving him all kinds of trouble. "And we'll send them pictures of the well-dressed hare and the new curtains and stuff."

Ryan nodded and set his phone back on the ottoman. "Wish they lived closer."

"Me too. Your family's the best."

He looked at me. "My mom still talks about watching you eat all those croutons. She thought it was hilarious."

"I do love 'tons."

He stared at me for a moment, then smiled. "I love you tons."

"Oh my God. You nerd. I love you even more tons. Like, as many tons as a megalodon weighs."

"Shut up. That's too much love."

I glanced around. "We have a house."

"We have a thing that cuts vegetables into spirals."

"We're gonna have a juicer."

"When?"

"Soon."

"And a dog. We're gonna have a dog."

"And curtains."

He nudged my thigh with his heel. "We're champions."

"There can be only one champion." I hooked my legs around his, and we leg-battled for a few seconds, while on-screen Mount Doom erupted.

CHAPTER TWO

Our housewarming party was amazigasmitastic. People brought so much food, and gift cards, and also random nonstick cookware from Target. I'd made burgers and Ryan had baked brownies. The weather was perfect, and I basically was crushing it for the first half an hour. And then I started really *looking* at how many people were there, and it was like, whoa. All these people were celebrating that Ryan and I lived in this place together, and if it didn't work out between Ryan and me, would these people be mad they'd given us nonstick cookware?

Which was dumb to even think, because things were definitely working out between Ryan and me. To a freakish extent.

I picked up an empty plate from the living room and headed for the kitchen. Ended up in the bathroom because for a second I'd gotten confused and thought I was in my old place. Dave was in the kitchen, picking sesame seeds off his burger bun. I rushed him and pretended to break the plate over his head.

"Heyyyy," he said, swatting at me.

"What's up?" I set the plate in the sink.

He flicked a sesame seed onto the counter. "Good party, except for your bun choice. Were sesame seeds Ryan's idea?"

"Uhhh, we just bought whatever was cheapest."

He took his plate and turned to me. "How's it going? Feels like we haven't seen you in forever."

It didn't really seem like that long to me, but maybe he was right. I'd had sex with Ryan instead of scouting kink fair locations, and I'd had to miss the last Subs Club meeting because it was Ryan's and my four-month anniversary, and before that I'd had to say no to a couple of offers to do shit with the guys because of moving-related stuff.

"Yeah, dude, sorry. Ryan and I have been decorating like beasts."

"It looks good in here. Nice curtains."

"You seriously like it?"

He nodded. "It's different. Not quite as 'you' as your old place."

I stared at him for a sec. "Yeah, well, how do you know this isn't, like, the new me?"

He snorted and shook his head.

"How is it not me?" I needed to know.

He laughed. "Chevron curtains? In teal and white? And what the hell is that?" He pointed to the ledge above the sink.

"A decorative vase."

"Did you just pronounce it *vah-z*?"

"Ryan says that's how you pronounce it."

He shook his head again. "Your old place looked like a garage sale at a frat house. I kind of miss it."

I figured it was subject-change time. "Did you find a place for the fair?"

He picked up the burger. "Maya and I looked at a community center the other day. It's pricey, but nice. And in a good location—lots of foot traffic." He took a bite. Chewed for a few seconds. "But the owners are like, 'Don't put anything too provocative on the sign out front.' Like, we can't call the event 'Night of a Thousand Butt Plugs' or anything."

"What *are* you gonna call this thing?"

"Miles wants something boring, like 'the Alternative Lifestyles Exposition.' Gould suggested 'Kinky Kollege' with a K, but that's already a thing somewhere—Chicago, maybe? So who knows?"

"I'll try to think of some stuff."

"Thanks, buddy."

Dave had been calling me "buddy" since high school. I'd loved it even then, because there was this little gay kid calling me buddy and slapping me on the back like he was one of the jocks. Dave and I had lost touch after graduation, then had reconnected after seeing each other in a BDSM club two years later. We were both in school at the time—at different nearby universities—but I came home most weekends, and Dave came with me, since his parents had moved to

Canada after he went to college. We'd met Miles and Gould and Hal through a munch, and we'd all become really good friends.

"Do you need me to do anything else to help with the fair? Gould told me you were gonna get people to do panels and stuff."

He shook his head. "Nah. All you need to do is stand there and look pretty. It's still a long time away, though, so I'll let you know if anything comes up."

"You guys doing good? I swear I'm coming to the next Subs Club meeting. And bringing all kinds of guac."

"Well, the next one's tomorrow."

Shit. Yeah, tomorrow was Sunday. And I'd promised Ryan we'd go to the indoor climbing wall downtown.

Oh well. I could go hang with the guys for an hour or so, then go to the rock wall. No problem. "Cool. I'll be there."

He leaned against the counter. "Anyway, we're good. Except Miles has become some cracked-out version of himself getting ready for Zac."

It still blew my mind that Miles was about to be a father. He was gonna be awesome, for sure. But he worried all the time anyway about things being perfect, so you had to kind of figure the stress of adopting a kid might kill him. I'd had to give him a reality check a few months ago, because he'd been going into an OCD nosedive about how he wasn't good enough to be anyone's friend or boyfriend or father. I didn't even know what he was so worried about, because he was ridonk smart and a really fun guy when he just *relaxed*.

Plus, total hard-core pain slut, which was hilarious.

I nodded. "I'll bet."

"You should talk to him." Dave glanced across the room. "He's always way calmer when he talks to you."

"Pfff. Because he thinks he needs to break everything he says down so that I understand it, and it distracts him from being nuts."

"Well, whatever it is, he listens better to you than the rest of us."

I reached past Dave and tried to smack a fly that had landed on the counter. I looked at my palm, which was clean, then glanced up and saw the fly buzzing around on the wall. "I want to meet this kid. Miles keeps saying he's indescribable, and I don't know what the hell that means."

"Right. Especially since Miles can describe pretty much anything. That man wants to hump the English language." He took a giant bite of burger.

I laughed. "So is hair school going good for you?" It was weird to be talking to my best friend like I hadn't seen him in years.

He bopped his head back and forth a little as he finished chewing. "Yep. About to finish the online classes." He wiped his mouth with the side of his fist. "So this winter I have to start commuting to and from campus. Bleehhhh."

"That's awesome, though. I keep telling Ryan he needs to get a haircut from you. He goes to this, like, stupid-expensive barber downtown."

"Tell him I'll hook him up. I'm doing D's hair regularly now. He still refuses to admit his sideburns were uneven when I met him."

"But we all know the truth."

He looked at me. "You noticed, right? The first time you saw him?"

"Oh, yeah," I lied. "Yeah, they were like . . . painful to look at. I gotta get you to do my hair sometime."

Sometime when I had three hours to spare. Dave was really good with hair. But he also took *forever* to get things the way he wanted. Plus he always felt the need to experiment with, like, feathering. But he'd be an awesome stylist once school trained him to be faster.

"Yup. Just say the word." Dave whacked my arm and wandered off to find Gould. I went to the kitchen to get another beer, and D came up to me, his burger dripping juice onto his plate.

He stared at me for a moment, his blue eyes glinting, his mustache twitching slightly. "Your burgers are the victual equivalent of silence."

D was Dave's dom. He was this really awesome mountain man who loved meat more than anything in the world except Dave. He was also a big fan of silence. And monster movies, so he and I were always trying to think of creatures that could be combined into supermonsters. Like Trisharkatopses and Squidodactyls and shit. I grinned. "Thanks. I think."

"You understand that beef *should* be pink on the inside."

I laughed. "Yeah. Well-done is like eating cardboard." I nodded to the stove. "There's plenty more."

He glanced at the skillet of burgers. Hesitated. "I am... attempting to cut back on meat in deference to David's concerns about my cholesterol. But thank you."

Awww. "So, what do you think of the place?"

He gazed around and nodded. "I admire your fortitude in attempting to live with another human being so soon after meeting him."

That, like, smacked me around a little, but I'd gotten used to D being blunt, and I was more than used to my friends thinking I'd rushed into my relationship with Ryan. So I just turned it on him. "When are you and Dave shacking up?"

He looked scared as *shit* for a second. Then he did his badass grunt-sigh thing that I really wanted to learn how to do. "I find this prospect intimidating. Though it would be easier to keep an eye on him if we were under the same roof."

"Has he been behaving himself lately?"

"Very well."

D and Dave had a relationship I didn't exactly get. Well, I got it more after Googling it. They did all this punishment role-play, which I understood, but then they also did domestic discipline. Which I guess was D spanking Dave for real-life stuff, like not getting his schoolwork done. And not just spanking him, but *caning* him. Which sounded fucking awful. But it had totally been Dave's idea.

I dropped my voice. "Can I ask you a question about caning him?"

This was probably way inappropriate, but I didn't think D would mind.

He nodded again.

"Do you feel bad when you do it?" I would feel like a giant shit-sword if I caned someone, period. Even if they loved it. So I could only imagine how it felt to do it when someone *didn't* like it.

D took another bite of burger and appeared to contemplate this. "I feel like I am giving him something that benefits him. But it does not make me happy to see him in pain."

"So why do you do it?"

"Because he asked me to."

"But, like, you have to get something out of it too, right?"

He chewed slowly. Swallowed and glanced down at the half-eaten burger. "David is a force of nature. If I can help him be that safely, it feels satisfying." He looked up. "Like installing a ceiling fan, or replacing the regulator on a camping stove."

"You think caning my best friend is like installing a ceiling fan?"

He picked the lettuce off his burger, used it to sop up the meat juice and mustard, licked the lettuce clean, then set it on the side of his plate. "In a way."

He patted my shoulder and lumbered off.

Someone had turned on music in the living room. Dave, since it was Enya. Dave was always saying bitches love Enya.

I enjoyed a few minutes of relative peace in the kitchen before my mom found me.

My mom was, like—I don't even know. Picture an aging Marilyn Monroe as a domme, and then imagine she thought of everyone in the world as her kid, even if they were thirty years older than she was. She had a voice like she'd swallowed flour, and she always smelled a little bit like blue raspberry slushie.

She hugged me even though she'd already squashed my guts out when she'd arrived. "Hi, hon." Possibly she was a little drunk.

"Hey. You having a good time?"

"Of course. I was just talking to Miles's boyfriend. The vampyre? He's lovely."

"Yeah, Drix is cool."

"He told me I carry a lot of tension in my sphincter."

I barfed in my mouth pretty much immediately. "I don't even want to know how he figured that out." Drix was seriously interested in bodies. He did some sort of yoga/massage therapy program for members of his vampyre coven and helped people figure out how to release their tension. One night last month, he'd made me breathe ten times in this special way before bed, and I'd slept for like sixteen hours straight. That dude was full of vampyre magic.

Mom reached for a bag of chips on the counter. "I think he's right. I rarely bottom, but when I do, I have the most trouble with anal play."

"*Mom*!"

"What?"

I clapped my hands over my ears. "*Don't talk about anal play.*"

I waited several long seconds, staring at her. When she didn't say anything, I slowly lowered my hands.

She immediately opened her mouth. "If you have any pointers, I—"

"Noooooo!" I put my hands back over my ears. "What is *wrong* with you?"

She shrugged, smirking, and placed a stack of tortilla chips in her cupped palm, then began picking them up and eating them one by one. That was how I ate chips too—the ol' stack-on-hand. I'd never realized I'd gotten it from her.

"I can't believe it took me this long to meet him." She glared at me kinda nastily, like I was personally responsible for her not learning about sphincter tension until tonight. "You boys haven't done a very good job of coming to see me these past few months. I already scolded Miles."

"We've all been ridick busy. Miles is, like— His head's gonna pop off with this whole adoption thing."

"Well, he's doing a good job hiding it. He just talked to me about it, and he sounded so happy."

"Oh, he's happy. He's just cracked out." I felt kinda guilty, like I was just borrowing what Dave had told me and making it sound like I knew what Miles was feeling. I really hoped he was doing all right. I mean, he'd called me a few months ago having some kind of spaz attack about cribs, and I'd had to, like, talk him down.

"He's going to be a wonderful father." She scratched the corner of her mouth with one long, rounded nail. "Did you hear Cobalt's closing?"

I stared at her a few seconds, stunned. Cobalt was one of two dungeons in the city. My friends and I were members of Riddle, the other one, because Cobalt was kind of gross. Dave said it was a place where dreams were carried to the Underworld on a river of tears, but I didn't think it was that bad. "I heard it might. I didn't think it seriously would."

"Well, it is. The owners are selling."

"Jesus. So now you're gonna be at Riddle all the time?"

"I won't have much choice."

I shrugged, trying to play it cool. "The guys and I hardly go to clubs anymore."

Which sucked, because I actually liked the clubs. Even Cobalt. But Riddle was where Hal had died, so my friends hardly ever wanted to go there anymore, and I'm pretty sure they thought I shouldn't want to either. Especially 'cause GK and Kel, Riddle's owners, had let Bill Henson be a member again. Which *was* kinda creepy—like, *Hey, you accidentally strangled someone at our club, but it's fine, you can still hang out here.* And I almost never went to Cobalt because it was where my mom played, and there was nothing more awkward in the world than running into your mom at a dungeon.

But I *missed* that scene. I'd had a whole bunch of friends at Riddle, before Hal died. I mean, they were probably still there even now that he was dead, but *I* wasn't. I'd had the same issues my friends did with going back: Yeah, it was weird to be in the same room where Hal had been killed. Yeah, it sucked that we might run into Bill or Cinnamon the ponygirl, who'd been the only person in the room with Hal when he'd died, and all of us were still trying to wrap our heads around how she hadn't noticed. But we had to move on at some point, right?

We didn't say much else for a few seconds. Then:

"Hon?" It was her fucking decepte-tron tone, like, *Oh, let me sound so casual when I'm about to say something that's gonna ruin your day.* You should have heard her when she told me she and Dad were separating. Or when she told me about Hal—that was the fucking worst. Because yeah, even though Dave was at Riddle when Hal died, I guess he was too freaked out to call the rest of us right away. So my mom heard about it from some of her scene friends and called me and was all, *"Kamen? Hon?"* like she was just gonna ask me how to take a screenshot on her phone.

Except I'd known better, because she always did that fake-casual thing, and because it was late at night, and—this'll sound weird—I'd been thinking about Hal all day. And sometimes when something big—good or bad—was about to happen to someone I knew, I thought about them a lot just before the thing happened. I wasn't saying I could predict the future, but I *was* obsessed with Stephen Hawking and very aware of the changeable nature of space and time, so we had to at least consider the possibility I was tapping into other dimensions where these things had already taken place.

"Yeah?" I said.

"Have you talked to your friend Ricky?"

I glanced toward the living room, where I'd last seen Ricky Chuy. Ricky was new to kink, and had been the Subs Club's MVP for a while—he'd helped us with our website, and he'd contributed lots of articles to the Sounding Board and had participated in pretty much every discussion. He was this skinny little guy who looked about twelve. Dave called him the Little Mermaid, 'cause he thought Ricky was super innocent and asked way too many questions. But I figured Ricky was way filthier than he looked. I mean, Miles dressed like Jimmy Carter but liked to be cut with knives, so . . .

"You mean tonight?"

"I mean recently."

A group of Ryan's friends came in looking for the brownies. "Hey, Mrs. Pell," Amanda said, stopping to hug my mom. They took the whole tray back to the living room, one holding each corner, like they were carrying a casket.

I turned to Mom again. "It's been a while since I've hung out with him. I think he's with some guy. I told him he could bring the dude with him tonight, but I guess he didn't want to."

She pushed her platinum-blond curls behind her ear. "Yes." Her expression was strange. She seemed like she wanted to say something more.

"What's wrong?"

She looked at me sort of pleading-like. "He seems very happy."

"Okay. That's good, right?"

"Just keep an eye on him. He's new, and it's easy to be . . . taken advantage of."

Ohhh. So that's what this was about. My mom's first serious play partner had pretty much tricked her into being his sugar mama, then made off with a bunch of her jewelry and credit cards. Now she had a real thing about warning newbies to be careful. "We look out for him."

"Good." Mom made another chip stack in her hand.

I decided to change the subject. "So what's Dad coming here for?"

She picked up a chip. "I think he's missing you."

"Yeah, but he never leaves Oregon. And I told him I'd fly out there as soon as I can get the time off."

"Well, I don't know." She glanced into the living room. "I haven't talked to Maya yet. I should go catch her before someone else takes her." She turned back to me. "Congratulations, sweetie. The place looks beautiful. I like your painting."

She headed off in search of Maya, leaving me alone in the kitchen once more.

Except I didn't even have time to put a burger on a plate before I heard commotion on the back balcony. I went over to check it out.

Gould was standing by the deck's wooden staircase, his arm around Dave, who was holding him up by the waist. He looked pretty drunk, for Gould, and he was glaring at Ryan. The only other people around were a couple of Ryan's friends out in the yard, who were staring up at the deck, watching. And Ryan was getting pretty loud in terms of, like, "I didn't *mean* it like that! It was just a joke."

Dave held his other hand up. "It's okay. It's fine." He saw me in the doorway and gave me a sheepish smile. He turned to Gould and jostled him. "You, my friend, have had enough to drink."

"What's going on?" I asked.

Ryan's face was all red. "I made a joke—"

Gould stumbled dangerously close to the stairs, jabbing a finger at Ryan. "It's bad taste. Bad *taste*, man."

Since Gould didn't usually say much of anything, let alone get openly pissed, I figured whatever'd set him off had to do with Hal. That was the only thing I could think of that would get Gould pistols-at-dawn mad.

I was right.

"I was making a joke about—" Ryan shook his head at me. "I don't know, we were doing BDSM puns. And I said something stupid, like, 'I already used all my best *gags*, but if I think of *smother* one, I'll *throat* out there.'" He gave me this look that was possibly defiant. "I wasn't even thinking about what happened to your friend. I was just thinking, like, gags, smother boxes, breath play, etcetera."

"It's fine." Dave tightened his hold around Gould's middle. "It just caught us off guard."

But I could tell from Dave's tone and the way he was eyeing Ryan that it wasn't fine. Normally I was all for puns. But, yeah, I could totally see how this had blown up. Gould *really* didn't do great with reminders about Hal dying. And since he hardly ever got drunk, probably the alcohol was making this ten times worse.

"How could you not've known what you were saying?" Gould demanded, still staring at Ryan. "You *know* about Hal."

"Yes," Ryan snapped. "I wasn't thinking. Take it *easy*."

Ryan's friends were still watching kinda wide-eyed from the yard, and I didn't see any of the people who would've been a real help in this situation: Mom, D, Miles, and Drix . . .

"Hey." I wasn't sure who to reassure first. "Why don't we all go back in? It's cool, Ry, they know it was a joke." I glanced at Gould. "Dude, he really didn't mean anything by it."

Gould was breathing hard. He looked into my eyes like maybe I'd betrayed him a little. The weirdest thing was that when I'd heard Ryan's joke, I'd gotten a little jolt of, *Whoa, too soon*. But it didn't *feel* too soon. Like, the joke didn't offend me personally. Maybe I should have been upset, but I mostly just felt like, yeah, the world was still allowed to make jokes, even jokes about stuff that wasn't funny to us anymore.

Dave helped Gould inside, and I held the door for Ryan, putting a hand on his back as he walked through. He turned to me once the door had swung shut behind us. "I'm sorry. It was stupid."

"It's cool, seriously. They're just—" I didn't want to imply my friends were making too big a deal of this, because their feelings were, like, their *feelings*. But I wanted to make Ryan feel better. "They know you weren't trying to be a dick. Let's get back to partying."

Around 2 a.m., Ryan and I lay on the couch in the dark, exhausted. The only light came from the streetlights outside and the glowing red switch on the power strip next to the TV. A veggie tray strewn with broccoli remains and random baby carrots sat on the coffee table next to a bunch of open dip containers, and the houseflies were having a field day pooping in our hummus and stuff. Empty beer cans were everywhere, and the empty brownie pan had a pile of plastic spoons in it.

I blew out a breath, making my lips flap. "That was crazy."

"Wild," he agreed.

"I didn't even know some of the people who were here at the end."

"Those were friends of my friends."

"Well, it was nice of them to bring us Fact or Crap." I glanced at the game cards littered across the floor.

Silence. I scratched my crotch. My balls smelled like sweaty bacon, which was a thing I wanted to change with some shower magic. But also I didn't feel like getting up.

Ryan had been in a shitty mood since the incident with Dave and Gould, and after a couple more beers he'd come up to me and been like, *"God, do they overreact much?"* I could tell he wasn't trying to be mean—just when Ryan felt guilty he got extra snappy. I hadn't known how to defend my friends without making Ryan feel worse. So I'd given him another beer because alcohol is like a grown-up pacifier.

Ryan's voice was quiet when he spoke again. "It feels like it's finally happening."

"What?"

He turned toward me. "Like we were saying the other night. We're a *couple*. We have a place, and we host parties, and it's cool."

"I know exactly what you mean!" I could barely contain my excitement. "This is all the stuff I never even thought about. Like, wall art and dishwashers, and now other people come over to *our* place to do their laundry . . ." I decided not to mention my sweaty bacon balls, 'cause that seemed like it might lose me some adult points. Also I didn't mention what Dave had said about this place not feeling like me. It *did* feel like me, just kind of a me I hadn't known was in there.

He snuggled against my shoulder. I seriously fucking *loved* when he snuggled, because he was small and warm like a bunny. Not a well-dressed hare, but like a die-from-cuteness *bunny*. I was about to give him a noogie when he said, "Amanda asked me if she left some underwear here."

I paused mid-noog. "No way. What'd you tell her?"

"I said no."

I snickered and let him go, flopping back against the cushions. "We're the worst."

"I blame you."

"Me?"

"You shouldn't look so hot in panties."

I yawned, bumping my head against his. "We should start having theme parties. I really l—" Another yawn. "I really like dressing up."

He shifted. "Would you dress like a woman for theme parties?"

Whoa. "Depends on the theme."

He was silent awhile. "That's what I love about you."

"The cross-dressing?"

"Just how imaginative you are. I always felt like maybe I had a decent, like— I was kind of creative. But my parents steered me toward noncreative, uh, pursuits. But you're good at sooo much things." He punched my chest a few times, lightly.

"So much things? Do you know English?"

"So. Much. Things. Kamen."

I grabbed his tiny doll hand. Held his arm back so he couldn't punch me again, and grinned at him through the darkness. He tried to swing with his other hand, but I could feel it coming and caught that one too. I held both his wrists. "Uh-ohhhh."

He struggled, laughing. "You're such a jerk."

"What happens when you try to punch Pelletor?"

He kicked my shin. "You become an asshole."

"Ohhh, nope, nope. You get tickled. And you know it."

He fell still and watched me, his eyes glinting. "Doooon't. Don't you *dare*."

I fake lunged, and he tried to jerk out of my grasp.

"Kamen. I order you. By the power of Gay-skull . . ."

Gay-skull was the power invoked by his gay dom alter ego, He-Manacles. And I was Pelletor, his submissive nemesis.

I pounced and tickled him.

"No! Noooo!" He brought his legs up onto the couch and braced his feet against my chest. I could only hold on to one wrist, because I was tickling him with the other hand. He was laughing so hard he couldn't breathe, which meant my work here was done.

I pushed his legs down and trapped his body under mine. Swooped to kiss him. "You have no power here, Gandalf Gay-hame." We also had Lord of the Rings gay alter egos. And Star Wars. And *Party of Five*, but we didn't tell anyone about that.

"Game, set, point, match," I declared.

He shook his head. "There's no point. It's just game, set, match."

"I like throwing a point in there."

He groaned, stretching underneath me. "Maybe I *don't* like your imagination."

"Yes, you do." I blew a raspberry on his cheek.

"Ewww." He pulled his hand up from between our bodies and wiped his face.

Most people saw the creative stuff I did as more reason not to take me seriously. Like my music was just part of my goofiness. Ryan was the only one who got how much it meant to me. And, like, maybe I should have told him how much I appreciated that, instead of summoning Pelletor. "Thanks. For what you said."

We shifted so we were lying side by side. I held on to him to keep him from falling off the edge of the couch.

I sighed. "I always thought I wanted to do music as a career, but honestly, I love being a cook. I don't *feel* good at so many things. But I'm okay with that."

He was silent another few minutes. "My job bores the crap out of me."

"Really?"

"Yeah."

"Lots of people hate their jobs. Drix? He quit being a private eye—a *private eye*—because he wanted to be some kind of vampyre yoga instructor."

"And is he happy now?"

"Yeah, dude. He just got promoted to vampyre king or something."

"It's just frustrating, because my height limits my job prospects."

"Wait, what?"

"I can't go in front of a courtroom." He gestured to himself. "Nobody would take me seriously. So I have to settle for being a paralegal."

"What are you *talking* about? There's a million short lawyers."

"Like who?"

"Theodore Boone."

"Did you just compare me to *Theodore Boone: Kid Lawyer*?"

"No," I said quickly. "But, like, you don't *actually* think you can't be a lawyer 'cause you're short, right?"

"I'm not making this stuff up. When I was sixteen, I applied for a job as a server, but they offered me a job as a dishwasher instead. It makes people uncomfortable to see a man so short."

I watched the shadows of the flies as they got down with the creamy ranch dip. "That's mostly in your head, I think. Short guys are everywhere."

"You comment on it all the time. My height."

I turned to him again, kinda surprised. "You know I'm just kidding when I say stuff like that, right? I mean, you *are* short. But I love it."

"I know."

"Did you get stuffed in a lot of lockers in school?"

"Nah. People actually really liked me. I think because I was scrappy."

"What'd you used to want to be when you were a kid?"

"An oncologist."

"What even is that?"

"Cancer doctor."

"Dude."

"My uncle was one, and I liked the word. Then I found out what it would involve, so I wanted to be an artist instead."

"An artist? For real?"

"Yeah, I used to draw a lot when I was little. Picked it up again in college."

"That's awesome. How have you never told me that?"

"I have some ancient, expensive painting program on my computer. But I never use it."

"Then use it. Make me a drawing."

He got quiet again. I tried to wrap my head around him feeling insecure about his shortness. He was amazing. I loved the way he moved and talked and yelled at the screen during baseball games and pretended not to watch *Elementary* when I had it on but knew key plot points when I quizzed him later. I loved his weird infatuation with megalodons. And the panty thing.

I gave this guy an eight hundred out of ten.

But clearly he had some confidence issues or something, because that law-school stuff didn't make sense. How could a dude who loved to argue about shit—and who, like, never let being short get in the way of arguing about shit—think he couldn't be a lawyer?

He shoved his elbow into my ribs as he sat up. "For you? I suppose I could."

We made a pot of coffee, and he got out his computer and opened the art program. I stood behind him, chugging my coffee like it was goddamn OJ.

"You can't watch me while I draw it." He glanced at me over his shoulder. "Shoo. Go on."

"Fine." I retreated across the room and picked up my guitar. Played softly and sang a little. Drank a lot of coffee. After about an hour, I looked up. "How's it coming?"

He shook his head. "It's shit." He glanced at me. "You can come look at it being shit, if you want."

I stood. "Yes. I want to see a giant, steaming pile of art shit."

I arrived behind him and folded myself basically in half to place my chin on his shoulder. "Oh my God."

It was definitely a drawing of a megalodon, but it was, like, abstract or something. He had the kind of style that would be— I mean, if he got famous, you would know that style anywhere.

He frowned at the screen, tapping the stylus against the counter. "I know, it sucks. I used to be better."

"No. That's fucking awesome."

"Can you tell what it is?"

"A megalodon jumping out of the ocean to eat a helicopter."

He nodded.

"Ryan. I don't think you understand. You have a *thing* going."

"A thing?"

"Like, surrealist, conceptual, abstract-y . . ."

"You're just saying words."

"You're just being a secret genius. How'd you learn to do this?"

He turned to me. "Do you really like it? Or are you just shitting me?"

"I frealz like it." *Frealz* was what I'd started saying sometimes in place of *for reals*. It drove Dave crazy, but I couldn't stop myself. "Can we print it and put it on the wall?"

"No!" He shielded the screen with his hands, like I might forcibly print-and-hang.

"Can you send it to me so I can look at it all the time?"

"You're a freak."

"You're a megalodon hog. Let me have more megalodons."

"I'm gonna hire a megalodon to eat you in a minute."

"Ummmm, extinct, one. Not for hire, two."

"Whatever."

"Can you write and illustrate a children's book about a megalodon that's a hitman?"

"Ooh."

"You can call it—wait for it . . . *Sharksassin*."

"Lame."

"*Megalodon Corleone*."

He snorted.

"You laughed. I'm funny."

He shook his head and went back to drawing. Added some shadows to the megalodon's fin. But he was smiling, which meant he *did* think I was funny, he just didn't want to admit it.

Which was fine. I didn't want to get an inflated ego or anything.

I pulled up a chair so I could watch him, and he didn't even shoo me away.

CHAPTER THREE

The guys applauded when I walked into Dave and Gould's kitchen the next day. "Well, look who finally showed up to a meeting." Dave grabbed a slice of deli turkey from a plate on the table and threw it at me. It stuck to the front of my shirt.

I looked down at it. "Did you just throw turkey at my shirt?"

He watched me peel the slab off and nodded. "In retrospect I should have used a chip or something. But life is too short for regrets."

Gould moaned a little and rested his head on his arms. "Applause was a bad idea."

Dave raised his eyebrows at me. "*Someone's* hungover."

"'M not," Gould muttered, sitting up.

Dave pinched the back of Gould's neck. "Grum-pyyyy."

Gould swatted at him. "Sto-o-op." He did like a bad Russian accent or something. "I kill you."

No one seemed to have any hard feelings about the party, so that was cool. I stuffed the turkey slice in my mouth, then took a seat at the giant kitchen table. Dave's dad had built the table, and it had been our hangout spot for years.

Years.

It was still crazy to think we'd all been friends for so long. I mean, it wasn't *that* long in the scheme of things. But considering high school still felt like yesterday to me, it kinda blew my mind that we were all in our late twenties now.

"What is this?" I nodded at the plate of deli meat, olives, and tiny pickles. "What about Mel's?"

In the past, we'd always ordered lunch from Mel's Sandwich Shop for Subs Club meetings, and it was meta because we were subs eating subs.

Dave grabbed a tiny pickle and crunched it. "The Subs Club is spending all of its budget on the kink fair. Not that we really have a budget. But, like, the money we got from giving the talk at Hymland College and the money I got from GK and Kel for being part of Riddle's advocacy program. It's all fair funds now."

"Does this mean no snacks?"

"Nah, we'll always have snacks. D gave me this whole tray the other night after a scene. He's a snack dom who gives *to-go* food. What a guy."

I fake pouted. "I don't get snacks after scenes."

"Ryan's not a snack dom?"

"I mean, he'd give me snacks if I asked. But we hardly ever do, like, *scene* scenes. Plus we live together now, so I can just get my own snacks."

"What *do* you do? If you don't do scenes."

In my head the eighties power ballad played again, and I was pulling on a pair of red lace panties.

I snapped back to reality. "Stuff."

Dave looked at Miles. "Is Drix a snack dom?"

Miles folded his hands. "I don't require snacks before a scene. Or after."

"Yes." Dave folded his hands in a parody of Miles's. "You run on intellectual fart juice."

"That means nothing to me."

Dave took another pickle. "D's more like a fucking *meal* dom. He'll stuff me full of sausage before we even start playing."

I glanced at the others, and we all laughed.

Dave rolled his eyes. "You know what I mean."

"Guys, settle down," Gould said mock-sternly to Miles and me. "David only means that D feeds him tube-shaped animal innards before a scene. Not that D has a giant *chhhmmk thhuuhh feee . . .*" He struggled, laughing, as Dave pressed his hand tighter over his mouth. Dave finally let go when Gould was quiet.

Dave stretched his arms across the table and plopped his head down between them. "Because I feel so sexy playing when my stomach is bloated with animal flesh and there's grease on my face."

Miles leaned over to stab some olives on a toothpick. "How very primal."

I freaking hated olives, so I started working on the deli meat. "I'm gonna tell Ryan he needs to be a snack dom. Even though he's already perfect. I could make him even more perfect."

"Awww." Dave lifted his head.

"He's *amazing*." I shook my head. "You know what I mean? How you fall in love with someone because they're awesome, but you don't even realize *how* awesome until later?"

Dave peered over his outstretched arm.

Miles gracefully slid an olive off the toothpick and into his mouth. "Yes, I actually am familiar with this."

Dave sat up. "Or you fall in love with someone and you know they're psychotic, but you don't realize how psychotic until they offer to teach you to hunt squirrels with a bow. Or casually let slip they own land north of the city but won't tell you what they plan to do with it, but you know it's for a future army of Friesian horses. Or expect you to calmly bend over to get caned when you do something wrong."

I leaned my chair back on two legs. "Pfff. You *asked* him to do that."

Dave slid his hands over the sides of his face, pulling the corners of his eyes downward. "I know. What was I thinking?"

Miles clucked. "But look at everything you've accomplished with his . . . encouragement. You got into school. You paid your parking tickets. Your vocabulary has matured."

Gould nodded. "You stopped calling my hair a Jewfro."

"Oh, I still do that," Dave said. "Just not to your face."

"Okay, that's worse."

Miles went on. "Didn't you even do your taxes on time this year?"

Dave nodded. "Truth. I'm growing up all over the place."

I wanted to keep talking about Ryan. "Ryan did these drawings last night. I knew he could draw, but not like this. He's really good."

"That's cool." Dave didn't seem to be listening. "So, anyway—"

"And then the other night, he was doing this impression of the news guy with the fake teeth, and—"

"Buddy," Dave interrupted. "Can we talk about something else?"

I stared at him.

He opened his mouth and inhaled like he was getting ready to speak, but he hesitated a few seconds. "I just . . . We hardly ever get to see you these days. And when we do, you're always talking about Ryan."

I glanced at Miles, who looked sympathetic, but didn't rush to my defense. "Is this about what happened at the party?"

Gould turned away like he was embarrassed.

Dave shook his head. "No, it's— Forget it."

I didn't usually get grumbly, but I kinda grumbled then. "Well, I'm sorry I'm finally *happy*."

"You were happy before too," Dave said.

"Not this happy."

"You totally were."

"I think I'd know how happy I was."

"Oh my God, you guys." Gould flicked an olive across the table at us. "Don't be idiots. I'm sorry about the party, and, Kamen, it's awesome that you're happy."

I swatted the olive away, 'cause olives were basically the devil's eyeballs.

We talked about some other stuff for a while, but I couldn't quit feeling annoyed. My friends were beyond the best. Except . . . we'd been friends almost our entire adult lives. And now I was twenty-seven, and I was getting a chance to see what life was like when I was my own person instead of part of a group. But people still didn't see me as an individual. Even my mom, when we went over to her place for dinner sometimes, would count us as we entered the house, like chickens.

"There's Kamen and Miles and Gould and Dave . . . one, two, three, four."

And if someone couldn't make it, she'd be like, *"Oh, I miss Miles. I miss my boy."* Even though he wasn't her boy. Most of the time I thought it was great that we were this posse—that she expected us to hang together. But sometimes I wanted to be like, "*I'm* your kid. Just me."

"So what's the deal with the fair?" I asked. "Like, what kind of stuff are you gonna have there?"

"Well." Dave rubbed his chin. "Some games. A silent auction. We're gonna try to raise money to cover costs and donate whatever's left over to the Regional Leather Society. We also want to have vendors and demos. Right now we're trying to find people to do the demos."

Miles delicately spat an olive pit into his hand. "No luck?"

"Maya and I put out a call on the Sounding Board for people who can contribute unique skills. We've had some doozies." Dave paused. "I never know if that word means something positive or negative."

"Doozy?" Miles asked.

"Yeah."

"It can be good or bad. It's just something big and unusual."

"Pfff, I'll show you something big and unusual."

Miles stared straight ahead like he was contemplating something in the distance. "I don't know why I bother."

Dave took out his phone. "Okay, cool. Then yeah, some doozies. But only a couple Maya and I are pumped about."

Maya was a recent addition to the Subs Club. We'd met her while giving a talk to Hymland College's Kinky Students Society in the spring. She was only like nineteen or something, but she knew her shit. She'd been a total newbie when we'd met her, but according to Dave, she was learning about kink at a scary rate. Apparently Miles was transferring his whole BDSM mind-cyclopedia into her brain.

"So . . ." Dave glanced around. "We need to up our game. Oh, and you guys will love this. *Cinnamon* messaged me on Fetmatch. About the kink fair."

Miles frowned. "Does she want to do a demo?"

"No. She wanted to tell me this." He typed on the phone for a moment, then read, in a high-pitched, whiny voice: "'Dave. How cute that you and your friends are striking out on your own. Did Riddle get too crowded for you? Kind of ironic that you want to be ambassadors to the public after you alienated pretty much everyone in the scene with your review blog. But good luck with your little fair. Horse chips, Cinnamon.' Swear to God, she's been sending me bitchy messages at least once a week since I gave up my membership at Riddle."

"Aw," Gould said quietly. "She misses you."

Dave rolled his eyes. "The only reason she wants me—or any of us—at Riddle is to torment us. She's an asshole who did fuck all to stop Hal dying, defended Bill at the trial, and then couldn't be bothered to show up to the memorial service. And now has the nerve to treat all of *us* like shit."

"You know," Miles said, "I'm always afraid if I go to Riddle I'll see Bill. But I think I'd almost rather encounter Bill than Cinnamon. She's *so* unpleasant."

I kept an eye on Gould, because sometimes when we talked about Bill in front of Gould, he got weird. But his voice was totally normal when he said, "I wonder if she thinks we have, like, a friendly rivalry, but she just takes the joking too far."

Miles shook his head. "I think she's a genuinely wretched human being."

I kinda agreed with Miles. I know I said I was moving on okay from Hal, but running into Cinnamon at Riddle was still rough. Like, the room where Hal died was not a big room. If you were in it, you'd have noticed a guy strangling to death, unless you were a complete fucking dingus. So the fact that Hal had died basically right beside her made me kind of want to microwave her head.

I turned the food tray so the meat was facing me. "Ryan says people like that are just insecure."

They all looked at me. "Yes, Kamen," Dave said. "That's not exactly groundbreaking psychology."

I reached for the olive I'd flicked earlier and chucked it at him. He dodged it. Dude's a pretty good olive dodger.

"*Anyway.*" Dave focused back on the screen. "Just wanted to share that. Our favorite ponybitch is still going strong. GK and Kel really will let *anyone* into Riddle." He glanced at Gould. "Sorry. They have some good qualities. But even you have to admit they could be more discerning."

Dave had never gotten along great with GK and Kel. They'd clashed *a lot* during the whole review-blog incident, and things had gotten weirder last year when Gould had started playing with them. At first it was just a couple of scenes, but now Gould played with them pretty frequently. I didn't know how that worked, since Gould had been, like, the most traumatized of any of us by Hal's death, because he and Hal used to date. So it was kind of: Um, yeah, start a relationship with the people who totally forgave your boyfriend's killer. That makes sense.

But now Dave was trying to be more supportive of Gould's thing with GK and Kel, because he was obsessed with Gould in a way that kinda seemed less like friendship and more like a Nicholas Sparks separated-by-circumstances-but-destined-for-eternity deal.

Awkward as fuck.

Gould changed the subject. "So what were some of the doozies?"

Dave raised his brows as he stared at the screen. "Well, for starters, a dear friend of ours contributed—not a demo offer, but more of a life update."

"Who?" Gould asked.

"Someone who's eight shades of f—"

Miles tugged his slipping cardigan up over his shoulder. "Is it Fucktopus?"

Oh God. Fucktopus scared the crap out of me, but was also *the best.* He'd posted a personal ad on the Subs Club blog when we were just starting out, describing how he was a tentacle furry with a bunch of robotic arms he'd built himself, and he was looking for someone to do Moby Dick–themed role-play with him.

Dave grinned. "The one and only. Gather 'round children, and you shall hear the whole sordid tale."

We were already gathered 'round, so we just ate some more pickles and waited.

Dave read: "'Greetings. It is I, the tentacle harbinger of delight. This summer, I found the sea captain of my dreams. For many weeks, my captain chased me through briny waters, and when I was at last caught, I was punished harshly. But soon the tables were turned when I seduced the fair captain and claimed my master using one tentacle at a time.'"

Gould nodded. "Considerate."

"'Alas, the captain has returned to Baton Rouge, leaving me to wander the endless dark seas alone. Unless someone out there is willing to fill the captain's shoes.'"

Gould whistled softly. "After Fucktopus has already filled the captain's everything else?"

Dave leaned back. "Who do you think this guy is? Seriously? Old? Young?"

"Early thirties," Miles said. "Lives in his parents' basement. Sleeps on a mattress with no bed frame."

Dave swept his hand toward Miles. "Ladies and gentleman, Miles Loucks, the Will Graham of pervert profiling. He empathizes so deeply with these deviants that he—"

Miles cut him off. "You think he's good at fucking?"

Dave shook his head. "He's never actually done anything with those tentacles. I'm not even sure they exist. If they do, he's definitely compensating for something."

I grabbed the last turkey slice. "Hey. It's not what you have between your legs; it's what you do with it."

Gould looked at me. "That's profound. Especially since I've always assumed your dick is scary-big."

I bit a hole in the center of the turkey slice. "Mine? No, it's really small."

"Yeah, right."

Miles sighed. "This is *not* a suitable conversation."

Dave jumped in. "It's true, though. Kamen and I had gym together in high school, and he's not as big as you'd think."

I finished the turkey. "My dick's small, but my balls are huge. My junk looks like a legless salamander between two avocados."

Dave cracked up, and Gould smiled a little too. Miles rolled his eyes toward the ceiling and looked like he was mentally crossing himself. "Oh my *God*."

"What?" Dave held his hands up, palms out.

"I can't believe I'm here listening to this when I have a *child* arriving in less than two days. I could be home remopping the floors." He started to get up.

"No!" Dave said. "We have to keep Miles here."

"I'll play him a song," I volunteered, leaping up to get my guitar from its usual corner.

It wasn't there. 'Cause I'd taken it to my place a few weeks ago.

I owned two guitars, one that stayed with me, and one I'd kept here so I could play while we were all hanging out. But since I wasn't hanging out here as much anymore, I'd brought that one home.

For a second, that empty corner made me so fucking sad.

"Ha-ha!" Miles smirked. "You don't have your secret weapon here any longer."

I grinned. "I can still block the door."

"Staaayyy, Miles," Gould begged.

Miles shook his head. "I really do have things to take care of."

I went back to the table and sat. "Ryan and I were talking the other night about, like, stress levels. And he says the more you try to prepare for a big life event or whatever, the more you—"

"Is there *anything* Ryan doesn't know?" Dave was maybe trying to say it like he was teasing, but it didn't work.

I stared at him for a moment.

Something was going on here that I was not down with. When I'd first met Ryan, he'd hung out with our entire group, and everyone seemed to get along with him. We'd even made him an associate member of the Subs Club, because he had pointed out that we should have a dom's perspective in our discussions. Except he pretty much never came to meetings or hung out with all of us. And the others never begged me to invite him to do shit with us the way Miles and Gould and me always wanted to see D, and Gould and Dave and me loved chilling with Drix.

"Probably not." I shrugged. "I really like my boyfriend. What's wrong with that? I love Drix and D, why can't you guys respect Ryan?"

Dave looked kinda guilty. "Ryan's just a little—"

Gould hit Dave's shoulder. "Shut up."

"Ryan's a little what?" I demanded.

Dave opened his mouth again, but Gould glared at him.

Since Gould was pretty much the only one of us Dave listened to, Dave backed down. "Sorry. Sorry, sorry. I didn't mean to make this a thing. I was just observing that we've got a couple of crazy lovebirds on our hands. Which is cute. I'm glad for you, buddy."

But he looked unhappy, and now I felt uncomfortable—not angry, exactly, just . . . deflated or something. "A little *what*?" I repeated.

"A little blunt," Dave said before Gould could stop him. "He barges into conversations and doesn't think before he speaks, and . . ." He looked at Miles, like maybe he wanted backup.

Well, that's ironic, coming from you. I didn't say it, though.

"I gotta go." I stood. "I'm supposed to go to the rock wall in like an hour. With *Ryan*." I punched Dave playfully on the shoulder, but it was definitely a little too hard, and he definitely looked like he wanted to punch me back.

"See you," he said, all snippy.

I normally would have grabbed him and hugged him and broken the tension. I didn't like any bad feelings between me and the guys, but in this case, my feelings were pretty hurt.

So I just went to the friggin' rock wall.

With Ryan.

That night, I lay on my stomach on the bed while Ryan straddled me and rubbed my shoulders. I closed my eyes and sighed.

He slid his hand up the back of my neck. "You're real tense."

"I'm sore from the rock wall," I mumbled.

"Mmm. You've been quiet all evening. You tired?"

"Eh." I rolled my shoulder as he dug the heels of his hands into the knotted muscle. "Just had kind of a weird day with the guys."

"Wanna tell me?" He rubbed lower, and I moaned.

"I want . . . I want this forever."

"I'll give you this forever."

I panted slightly as he worked under my shoulder blade. "Really?"

"Or until I get tired."

I smooshed my face deep into the pillow and kept groaning. "Oh my God, you make me want to give you millions of dollars."

"Oh, good."

"Live in an enchanted forest with you."

"Sounds pleasant."

"Eat buffalo wings off your face . . ."

He dragged his fingertips down my back in squiggly patterns, and I felt it in my dick. Then he pinched my ass.

"Ow."

He made circles around my tailbone. Laughed.

"Mmm, fuck." I wriggled against the bed, enjoying the heat and sting from the pinch. "Do it again."

He pinched harder. I rubbed against the bed.

"Look at you." Ryan clucked his tongue. "Ya big whore."

I wiggled my ass a little.

He slapped it. "You like that?"

Smiling, I lifted my head and hooked my chin over the top of the pillow. Kept my eyes closed. "No."

"I think you do."

A swat on the top of my right thigh. I hissed exaggeratedly. Hugged the pillow to my chest. "Noooo . . ."

I wiggled again, waiting for the next one.

Nothing.

"Beg me," Ryan said softly. "Tell me what you'll give me."

I closed my eyes even tighter, trying to keep a straight face. Whispered, "Don't make me say it."

I knew exactly what he was fishing for. And I really hoped he'd get that I, like, unbe-fucking-lievably wanted him to make me say it.

"Oh, I'm gonna make you." He ran his hand down my back, and I tensed my legs to keep from coming, because I seriously could go off like a rocket.

The first dom I ever played with was all like, *"Don't come until I say you can,"* and I was like, *Dude, I don't know when it's gonna happen. It's like nuclear war. There are protests for peace, and higher-ups negotiating to try to stop it. But someday, suddenly and without warning, it's gonna occur.*

"You know how it works. You want something, you have to earn it."

I spread my legs, and he slid his fingers—not through my crack, exactly, but right along the edge of it, stopping at my inner thigh. I held my breath.

"Do you want to come?"

I nodded, my face buried deep in the pillow.

He traced my balls with one fingernail, and my whole body trembled. "So tell me what you'll give me." I heard the grin in his voice. "What you'll *promise* me."

I didn't answer.

He put a hand on the back of my head and pushed my face into the pillow, and didn't even really slap my butt as much as skim his hand across it, like really sharp. He let go of my head, and I lifted it and sucked in a breath.

I squirmed against the bed. "Please . . .?"

He started squeezing my ass—pinching and kneading, bringing a warmth to my skin that made me crazy. I panted, gulped, and tried to hold still as the heat built.

He moved his other hand between my legs to play with my balls.

I jerked my head up. "Oh my God. No— *Fuck*! Am I allowed to come?"

"Let me think . . ." He ran his finger quickly back and forth along the skin behind my balls while I clamped my teeth around the pillow and shook with the effort of holding back. "Only once I hear what I'm going to get from you."

I lifted my head again and took a deep breath. Then I sang, running the words together: "Myfirstbornchildandallmypants, ahighendescortplusacastleinFrance. EverycakeintheUSA, adifferentponyeverysingleday. Threemoreseasonsof*VeronicaMars*, twentythousandrealnicecars. A swimmingpoolwithawaterfall andawaterslidebuiltintoyourbedroomwall. I'llgiveyoumylove, I'llgiveyoumysoul. I'llgiveyoumyheartandI'llgiveyoumyh—" I cleared my throat exaggeratedly "—*whole* . . . life. If you please just leeeeet meeee cooooommmme."

He laughed, then trailed off in a sigh. "I love the 'Promises Song.'"

I'd actually written it for Gould and Hal, years ago when I'd been trying to get them to blow off work and road trip to New Orleans for Mardi Gras. Obviously it had ended with "please go to Mardi Gras," not "please let me come." I hadn't told Ryan that. The first time I'd sung it for him he'd liked it so much that I'd wanted to pretend I'd made it up just for him.

"Ryan?" I braced the balls of my feet against the mattress and raised my hips. "Please?"

He reached around and grabbed my dick, stroking it lightly.

I pushed my face back into the pillow to stifle a moan.

"Good?"

I nodded. "Mhh-hmm."

He pumped harder and slapped my ass again. I arched my neck and came with a strangled grunt. Collapsed as soon as I was done.

He tugged some hair on the back of my thigh. "Hall of Fame?"

I turned my head to the side. "Almost. I think I need to be more choosy. 'Cause I keep putting all the hand-j's you give me in the Hall of Fame."

He stroked my shoulders. "It's a big hall."

I flexed my ass and felt a slight soreness where he'd done all the pinching and slapping. "Question."

"Yes?"

"Do all doms like spanking?"

He laughed. "Probably not. I'm not, like, nuts about it. But if a guy's got a great ass, I definitely wanna smack it."

"Why?"

"*Why*?"

"Yeah." I rolled over. "I've been trying to learn more lately about what this stuff is like from a dom's perspective."

"Well . . . because it jiggles."

"The ass?"

"Yes. You spank it, and it kind of quivers a little. And some guys, if it stings enough, they clench, and they get these great . . . dimples—I guess?—along the sides of the cheeks." He traced the area on my ass.

My breath caught for a few seconds, then I let it out. "What else?"

"They make noises. Like you did. Either because they're excited, or they're having trouble taking the pain."

"Do you like noise?"

He laughed again. "Ummm, I like quiet noises mostly. Like . . ." He demonstrated a little whimpery-panting sound. "But there was one guy who cried every time I spanked him. Full-blown sobs, even if it was a light spanking."

"Did you like that?"

"I thought he was bullshitting. But maybe he wasn't. I dunno."

"Oh."

"I'm more into breathing."

"Breathing?"

"Yeah. If I hear a guy's breathing get fast and heavy, that's my favorite. Or if it hitches a little, like—" He demonstrated again. "That's the best."

"Am I a good breather?"

"One of the best."

"Seriously?"

"Yes."

"You're not just shitting me?"

"Top notch."

"I didn't think I liked spanking much. But when you do it like that, where it doesn't really hurt . . ."

He stretched out beside me. "The first time we met, I made it really hurt."

Ohhh *fuck*, it had hurt. But it had been so good. I could still remember the ache of my stomach hitting his thigh when he'd pulled me over his knee. How awkward I'd felt, with my limbs hangin' down everywhere and the blood rushing to my head.

"In front of my friends," I whispered, my face getting a little hot at the memory.

He stared at me through the darkishness. "Do you like that? Being watched?"

"Uhhh. I never really thought about it. I always played in the clubs, so I don't have a problem with it. But it's not usually a super turn-on."

"Did I embarrass you that night?"

"Nah. It was my friends. So I wasn't too embarrassed. And I was kinda drunk."

He grinned. "You and your friends are . . ."

"What?" I propped up so I could see him better.

"I've never seen anything like it. You guys are so close."

I felt a moment of mega-pride, and then I got sort of bummed, thinking about what had gone on earlier today. "They think I'm too obsessed with this."

"What's 'this'?"

I couldn't tell him they thought I was too into him. Or that Dave thought he was *a little* who-knows-what. "They think I don't spend enough time with them anymore."

He kissed my jaw. "They might just be jealous that you're really getting your life in order."

"Yeah. This is a weird time for me. So many changes."

"Miles is making big changes too. Are they giving him trouble?"

I put my head on his chest. "No, but Miles gets treated different. Because 'I have more important stuff to do than hang out' has always been his thing. So no one minds if he misses a Subs Club meeting or can't watch a movie or whatever."

"I can see that. He's very aloof."

"Yeah! He's all 'Never share your feelings,' and people are like, 'Oh, that's just Miles.' He's such a . . ." I felt Ryan's heartbeat against my cheek. "An emotional puritan." I meant for it to come off as a joke, but it was kind of like earlier at Dave's house—I could hear that little edge in my voice.

"I did kind of think when I first met him that he needed, like, a joint."

I snorted. "And you met him when he was *drinking*. And you *still* thought that."

"Poor guy. Let's bake him some pot brownies or something."

"I've tried." I paused. "We're so weird. Like, we've always ragged on each other and stuff, but over the last couple of years we've been . . . It's like we're married, man, the way we *bicker*. Miles can get really condescending. And Dave's just . . . *so* enthusiastic and wants everything to be a certain way. Gould's kind of an emo Jew, but—"

Ryan burst out laughing. "*Emo Jew*?"

"Am I not allowed to say that? Can I call Jews 'Jews'?"

"Why wouldn't you?"

"I just never know what words are okay."

He laughed again and nudged me with his foot. "You guys'll get things sorted out. It's just like you said: a lot of changes right now."

"Yeah." I hugged the pillow to me.

My two guitars were propped in the corner of the room. I had another vision of my group a couple of years ago. Pot smoke filling Dave's kitchen, me playing the guitar. The table covered with junk food, and everybody laughing.

Ryan's hand trailed down my side. "Well, you guys are still kinda . . . Hal only died a couple of years ago, right?"

"Little over two years." Sometimes it felt like yesterday, sometimes it felt like ten years. "He was one of those guys who didn't care about—whatever. If you were too busy to hang out or flaked on plans or whatever. He showed up whenever the hell he wanted to and would just leave randomly. Like, we'd all be hanging out and then look around and be like, 'Where's Hal?' You didn't really 'make plans' with him, you just did stuff in the moment."

"That would drive me crazy."

I grinned. "Uhhh, you're not huge on plans either. I mean, how many times are we in the middle of something, and then you're like, 'Let's go do this other thing *right now*'?"

"I'm not like that!" he protested, laughing. "I need structure."

I gazed at the wall. At the crown molding he and I had spent hours sponging the cobwebs off when we'd moved in. Thought about the well-dressed hare in our front hall. "Hal didn't drive me crazy," I said at last. "Not really. The others got annoyed with him sometimes, I think, but I didn't."

Another silence. He was breathing so slow I thought maybe he'd fallen asleep. Then he said, "Just don't ever let them make you feel like you're the one who needs to change."

"No. Of course not. They never make me feel that way."

I kind of didn't want to talk about this anymore. I felt guilty for complaining about my friends to Ryan, but also still pretty pissed at Dave. I remembered that look Gould had given him, and it made me wonder what they said when I wasn't around. I'd never been very sensitive about stuff like that, but tonight it kind of bothered me.

I pulled on the corner of my pillowcase. "I think I'm moving on faster than they are."

"Yeah?"

"Yeah. I miss Hal a lot. But Gould's still *so* pissed at Bill, and Dave's still, like, everything reminds him of Hal. And I just feel kind of . . . He's gone. There's nothing we can do about it."

Ryan nodded. "Well, people grieve for different lengths of time. There's no rules."

"I know. I'm not blaming them."

"Oh, I didn't think you were. I just meant you shouldn't feel bad if you think you're moving on faster."

"I don't." I paused. "*Should* I feel bad?"

"No. I just said that."

"Okay." I shifted. Everything inside me felt kind of sour and sloshy, like I'd swallowed ocean water. "Can we not talk about it anymore?"

"Sure. What do you want to talk about?"

"Can we go get our juicer tomorrow?"

"Yeah, if you want. Our gift card's not gonna cover that, though."

"Credit card."

He tipped his head to look at me. "We should be a little careful. We've been putting a lot on the card."

"Does this mean we can't get the Geegs salad bar when we go?"

"Geegs? Is that what we're calling Giant Eagle now?"

"Yuss."

"Well, we could get salad ingredients for, like, five bucks. Instead of the bar for eight million dollars."

"I guess." I tightened my arms around him until he grunted. Shook him a little. "I want to make carrot juice. And experiment with kale."

"Patience. Patience."

I kissed his shoulder, right on top of my favorite mole. "Tell me a story."

"About what?" He licked my neck, so I murdered him a little bit, very gently, by rolling on top of him.

"Megalodons."

"What do you want the megalodons to do?" His voice was muffled underneath me.

"Eat some people and fuck some shit up."

"All right." He pushed on my chest. "Stop smothering me."

I rolled off him and onto my back, looking up at the ceiling. Then his, like, really fucking pleasant cartoon voice filled the darkness.

"Thousands of years ago, megalodons roamed the seas. These massive predators would—"

"How massive?"

"Sixty feet. Longer than a semitruck, with a head the size of a garage."

"Ermahgerd."

"I know. And although some scientists believe it to be an ancestor of the great white, the fine serrations of the megalodon's teeth suggest it's more closely related to the modern mako shark. But, at any rate, it was king of the seas, feeding on whales and other megalodons, until the changing climate and dwindling food sources trapped it in the ocean's deepest trenches, beneath miles of frigid water."

I yawned, trying to imagine the darkness of the room was the darkness of the ocean's deepest trenches.

He bumped me. "You sleepy?"

I yawned again, my voice going high. "Nooo, I waa-aa hear bowww the . . . deeh trenshizz." I closed my mouth with a hum and nestled closer to him.

"Okay, well, the megalodons were lurking in the deepest trenches. Until one day . . ."

I half listened as he told a story about a megalodon named Devil's Tooth that escaped the trenches and rose to the surface to eat an evil surfer named Bodhi.

"Wait," I mumbled, almost asleep. "She ate Patrick Swayze from *Point Break*?"

"Yep." Ryan stroked my hair. "Her cruelty knew no bounds."

"*Your* cruelty knows no bounds," I murmured.

And then I must have fallen asleep, because I woke up in the night with him snoring softly beside me and yellowish streetlight coming in through the slats of the blinds.

I got up, pissed, then got back into bed and pulled him close to me. Lay there for a few minutes. Sometimes I had trouble sleeping in this apartment. And there were still mornings I woke expecting to see my old bedroom and feeling confused for a second about where I was. What was *really* weird was that sometimes this place made me feel homesick—not for my old apartment, but for my mom's house. Which, don't even ask me how that worked. I guess I'd felt so totally comfortable in my frat-house garage-sale pad and so glad to be living on my own for the first time that homesickness had never come up. But here, in this house full of adulting, I sometimes missed *not* being an adult.

Weird. I glanced over at Ryan, wondering if he ever felt that way.

I reached out and poked his jaw to see if I could get him to make an annoyed *I'm sleeping* noise. But he didn't make a sound.

I'd never had a serious relationship before. I'd dated in high school and college, but I dunno . . . high school was high school, and in college guys maybe thought I was too immature for long-term stuff. What was happening right now was a *big* deal to me. I kinda wished I could talk to Ryan about that. I mean, I *could*. I could talk to him about anything. But sometimes with deep stuff, it was harder to start the conversation.

It was way easier to talk about megalodons and juicers and even panties.

I closed my eyes and imagined the room smelled kinda like dirty clothes and toast crusts instead of like new curtains.

And eventually I fell asleep.

CHAPTER FOUR

My dad arrived in town Tuesday, and he asked if I'd go with him to get ice cream. Like I was seriously six.

So of course I said yes.

I was quiet as we headed out of the city in his rental car. We were going to this drive-in he'd been obsessed with years ago, out in the suburbs. He'd asked me if Mom and I still went there much, and I'd been kinda like, *No, dude. Mom and I don't really drive forty minutes to get ice cream together.*

I still felt sort of shitty about making fun of my friends with Ryan. I mean, I hadn't really made *fun* of them, but . . . The whole thing seemed stupid now. I got it: People in love were obnoxious. So I was driving the guys crazy right now by hanging all over Ryan, and everyone would get over it eventch.

Gould called during Dad's and my attempt at small talk to ask if I was still friends with the woman who ran a bondage group called Rock 'Em Sock 'Em Rope-bots, and if I could put him in touch with her. I glanced over at my dad and said into the phone, "Yeah. I'll text you the info." I felt crappy enough about yesterday and desperate enough for distraction to try to engage Gould in a conversation, but he sounded like he was in a hurry.

"Hey," I said finally. "I'm really sorry I haven't been around lately. I seriously do miss you guys."

"No worries."

I'd been hoping for something like, *Dave's crazy, and we all love Ryan, and everything's awesome.* "We cool?"

"Yup. I gotta run. Love you."

"Love you too."

I hung up.

Dad glanced at me. "Was that your boyfriend?"

"Nah. Gould."

Dad didn't say anything for a moment. "He doing well?"

"Yeah. He's had a rough time since Hal—like, worse than the rest of us, maybe. But he's better now."

I still didn't think anyone knew this but me, but two weeks after Bill Henson's trial ended, I'd gotten a call from Gould to come pick him up at the hospital. I'd gone to get him, freaked out as all fuck that he'd been in an accident or found out he had cancer or something. Except it hadn't been an accident. He'd taken a whole bottle of pills, and then called 911, and he'd been in the hospital for two days under observation.

"You can't tell the others. Please. It was a mistake." Over and over. I'd been too shocked to focus on anything beyond the fact that he'd *tried to fucking kill himself.* And the fact that he'd called *me.*

That was usually how it worked. People acted like I couldn't be trusted with serious issues, and yet when they had a real problem—or something they wanted to keep secret—a lot of times they came to me.

If you're a good listener, people tell you shit.

If you pretend you're dumber than you are, they tell you lots of shit.

I guess I believed him about it being a mistake, since he'd called his own ambulance. Plus the hospital should've kept him for a week at least, but they let him go after two days because the psychiatrist basically concluded he wasn't at risk for another attempt. I'd made him swear on Hal's memory he wouldn't try it again. He kept going on about how I couldn't tell the others—especially Dave. I'd refused to take him back to his place. Made him stay at my apartment for a week. Gave him my bed, and I took the couch. He mostly didn't argue, and we actually had a pretty good week together, talking and shit. He'd said he hadn't really wanted to die, he was just tired of missing Hal and feeling angry at Bill every single day, and he couldn't think of a big enough way to let out all those feelings. When I finally let him go, I made him promise he'd call me if he ever needed me. But he didn't call.

Like, where was the balance? If you had a group of friends, and you were used to being up each other's butts all the time—not literally, although Dave and Gould, who knows?—and then you started to realize that even though you wanted to be there for them, you also wanted to have a life where maybe *all* their problems weren't also your problems, what did you do? And I didn't mean that as, like, I resented being there for Gould when he needed someone, because I would have done that a thousand times over. I just meant . . .

I didn't know what I meant.

I tried to focus on Dad, who was talking about how some plaza we were passing had changed in the years since he'd lived here. He always reminded me a little of someone whose job it was to lure people into the circus back in the day. Everything he said kinda sounded like you were being told to step right up and see the bearded lady. "What an Old Navy! Three stories high. Tallest Old Navy I've ever seen!"

And he'd bark away about dumb stuff like that, but the second he tried to talk about anything remotely serious, he'd stammer and trail off every couple of words. If the bearded lady had come to him and been like, *I have the clap; I need a few nights off*, he'd have been all, *Oh . . . um. I see. If you could just . . . Can you finish your shift, or . . . No? Well, of course . . .*

He'd cheated on Mom when I was a kid, and I'd always felt bad because, like, I still loved him, but I was on *her* side, so I treated him pretty shitty. He was really supportive of me, though. He worked as a financial advisor and was plenty loaded, but he didn't care that I loved being a cook at the Green Kitchen, or that my goals weren't super lofty. He liked that I wanted to be a musician, and every year for Christmas, he got me something music-related, so that was cool. He said "follow your dreams" a lot, which was pretty cheesy, but it made me feel good.

I had a lot of dreams. For instance, I wanted to launch a fake review trend for an Amazon product. Like that hundred-thousand-dollar watch that everyone started sarcastically reviewing and saying it had saved a bus of school children and raving about the fifty-eight-thousand-dollar discount you got when you bought it on Amazon. Or the book *How to Avoid Huge Ships*, which had a whole bunch of reviews from people pretending they'd been smacking into huge ships for years before this book came along.

Also, I liked writing, even though I wasn't great at it. I once wrote a comic called "Snow Wanderer," about a homeless kid who wanders around during winter, surviving on the carrots from snowman noses. He finds some that have eyes made of zucchini slices too. I'd done the illustrations, which basically looked like that guy with the splattery paintings except with crayons, but hey.

I didn't know if I was really stupid or not. My mom said I just saw the world differently, but that sounded like the kind of thing moms said when their kids were basically dimwads. I definitely cared more about my own life than world issues. Which was probably why I always kind of sucked at the Subs Club. Because I used it more as hanging-out time than a way to talk about Important Shit.

But I wasn't, like, *not interested* in things besides me. For instance, I loved Stephen Hawking's books. I didn't understand everything in them, but I really was fascinated by his ideas. I'd watched like eight documentaries about him, and *The Theory of Everything* was pretty much my favorite movie. Except watching it for the first time was suspenseful, because I knew he was gonna come down with that disease, I just didn't know when. It was like *Ghost Dad*, where you know Bill Cosby's going to die, but they have all those red-herring almost-deaths to keep you on your toes.

"So the move went okay?" Dad asked.

"Yeah. Ryan and I love the place. We've been decorating like fiends." I paused. "What's chevron?"

"An oil company."

"No, but, like, Dave called my new curtains chevron."

Dad sped up to keep someone from passing us. "Uh . . . I don't know. A color, maybe? Why didn't you ask Dave?"

I shrugged. "I dunno."

"So you like this guy?" he asked. "Ryan, I mean?"

I shot him a pretty world-class *duh* look. "I wouldn't have moved in with him if I didn't. He's the best thing that ever happened to me. Literally."

Dad moved his jaw back and forth for a second and glanced out his window. "And you're still doing the—the stuff your mom does? At the clubs?"

"God! Don't put it like that. We don't do the same stuff. But, yeah, I still do BDSM."

He nodded and didn't say anything for a while.

Then he adjusted the AC and said, "I actually wanted to talk to you about that."

I got really freaked then. A few months ago, Miles tried telling his mom he was into kink, and she didn't approve at all. My mom'd had to give her a talking to, which had been supes awkward. What if my dad was about to tell me he thought I was fucked up or something?

Which would be weird, since he'd known since I was twenty-two. I'd told Mom, and she'd told him, and then she'd told me she'd told him, and said he was "coming to terms with it."

He cleared his throat. "As you know, your mother and I separated for several reasons. One of them being her . . . needs, which at the time I didn't understand very well."

I'd been eight when they'd split up. When I was sixteen, I'd found Mom's BDSM stuff in her closet when I was looking for a hat to borrow for a school project. We'd had a talk, and she'd explained what BDSM was and how it was totally normal but that a lot of people didn't get it. I'd been too shocked to tell her I watched leather porn all the time. Then she'd told me about my grandma starting a leather group for women in San Francisco in the 1970s, which was awesome but crazy. And then I hadn't been able to watch BDSM porn for like two months after that, because gross, my mom.

Anyway, she'd explained that Dad hadn't shared her interests, and that was part of the reason for the separation. I'd gotten sort of pissed, because I thought that was a stupid reason to split. Then she'd reminded me cheating was the *big* reason, and I was like, *Oh yeah.*

"We, uh . . ." Dad trailed off awkwardly. "She tried to introduce me to some of the—the lifestyle . . . aspects . . . but . . ."

Oh man. This was stuff I didn't need to hear.

"I just couldn't wrap my head around it. At the *time*." He glanced at me, then turned back to the road. "You okay with all this?"

The government should probably give free cyanide capsules to everyone, just in case we ever get captured by terrorists or our parents start talking about sex in front of us. "Yeah. For sure."

We passed a billboard for *Abortion Is Murder*.

"Over the past couple of years," he went on, "I've realized that I do have a certain amount of the interest in me. I've done some experimenting. With Kim. You remember Kim?"

Kim had been the HR director at Dad's firm. She'd left the company a few years ago to get back into horses. I knocked my head gently against the window. "Yeah."

"I've also acquired a considerable amount of equipment." He bobbed his head as road signs flashed by us.

Gross.

I sat up and checked the speedometer. "You're going, like, eighty."

He also had the wheel in a death grip. He slowed down. "Sorry. I just rarely talk about this out loud. Guess I'm nervous."

I seriously had no idea what to say.

"I've been updating my living will. And I'd like you to be in charge of—when I . . . pass away—going to the house and . . ." He took a breath. "Clearing out all equipment of that nature."

"*What*?" Fucking for real? I already had a mom who stepped on guys' balls in high heels, and now I had a dad who was gonna make me throw away all his butt plugs when he died?

He shot me a glance. "I need someone to do it. And I'd rather it be someone who understands and is compassionate than . . . You can donate it, throw it out, keep it . . ."

"Why would I *keep* it?" This just kept getting worse.

"Well, throw it away, then." He sounded vaguely annoyed. Which was unfair, given that he was the one crapbliterating all the standards of decent father-son conversation.

"Did you come all the way out here to tell me this?"

He sighed. "I came back in part to apologize in person to your mom for some of the things I said to her years ago. About her lifestyle. Particularly things I said when she told me you had come out about being . . . having the interest."

Now I was curious. "What did you say to her?"

My dad took his hand off the wheel to rub the black fuzz around his bald spot. "At the time, I was worried about you. And I thought—I implied that maybe she'd encouraged you to believe you were like her."

"You think she made me kinky?"

"I don't think that anymore." His voice was kind of clangy and jarring, like when you try to put a pen between the bars of a fan. "Anyway, I figured while I was out here—"

"That's our exit."

"Shit." He swerved into the exit lane. "While I was out here, I thought I'd talk to you about the will. I wanted to visit you anyway, and this way I get a chance to talk to each of you face-to-face."

He slowed as we came off the ramp. Got in the left lane at the light.

I watched the turn signal blink on the car in front of us. "Mom has a friend who's doing that for her. Clearing the weird stuff out of her house. Don't you have friends?"

He laughed uncomfortably. "None I can talk to about this."

I always forgot that other people didn't have friends they could talk to about BDSM. I was lucky as shit.

We were silent until we reached the drive-in. We sat for a moment in the parking lot.

"So what do you think?" he asked.

A server was coming toward our car. I nodded. "All right. But you owe me."

"Anything."

Anything? Well, then . . . "When we go back to town, stop in the Twin Oaks Plaza. At the Bed Bath & Beyond. There's something there I've been waiting for."

I walked into the kitchen two hours later with our new juicer. "You'd better buy some carrots and kale, mothafucka," I called to Ryan, setting the box on the counter. "'Cause we're having fresh juice every goddamn morning."

"What the hell?" Ryan padded in from the bedroom, wearing a flannel shirt and boxers. He touched the box. "Did you put it on a card?"

"Give your regards to Jimmy Willman."

"Who?"

"My dad." I slit the tape on the box with a steak knife. "He wanted to buy us something."

"Why does he have a different last name than you?"

I ripped the box open. "I told you this. He wanted to keep his name. My mom wanted to keep hers. She gave me her last name."

"I don't think you told me that."

"Pretty sure I did." I pulled the juicer out and set it beside the box. "Hallelujah. How the . . . frizzles does this thing work?" I picked up the plastic-wrapped parts.

"But he's your real dad?"

I tore open the plastic. "Of course."

"That's cool." He came over and helped me unwrap the pieces. "Did you have a good time with him?"

I summed up my convo with Dad. Ryan's eyes got wide. "So do you think kink really is genetic?"

"Well, I apparently got it from all freaking sides, so yeah."

We made pasta for dinner using the Pasta Boat, and then Ryan had some files to look over for work, so I promised I'd sit with him on the couch and not bother him.

It worked for like half an hour. I played QuizUp on my phone, and he scowled at some documents on his tablet, and then I got bored and asked, "What are your files about?"

"They're about how Erica can't type up a brief to save her life so I have to redo it." He looked up. "You know how I feel about Erica."

"You wanna put her in a hamster ball full of turds and roll her down a hill."

"I do. Kind of. Yeah. She really just *bothers* me."

He didn't say anything else, so I changed the subject. "Do you wanna meet my dad on Thursday? Tomorrow he has a thing with an old coworker, but he wants to hang out again Thursday."

"Uhhh . . . sure." He swiped through some pages on the tablet, frowning. "I was gonna work late that evening. But we could do lunch break."

"That'd be cool. Lunch is good because we've got an out if we need one."

"I want to thank the man who bought us a juicer."

"Who knows what else he might buy us if he feels guilty enough."

"I think we should get a bagless vacuum. With hose attachments."

"Okay."

"But the one I was looking at was three nineteen."

"Holy cat balls."

He looked up. "You know what, though? We spent two hundred dollars on that sex sling when we were drunk last month. And we never even use it because we're too lazy to put hooks in the ceiling."

"We'll do the hooks. This weekend."

"We could send it back, though, since we never used it. And use the money for a vacuum."

"I'd rather have the sex sling."

"Then figure out how to mount it."

There were so many "mount it" jokes I could have made in that moment that I just sat there hyperventilating until my brain exploded.

He focused on his tablet again and was quiet for a while. I beat Captain Wizzerbam from Romania in a name-that-celebrity round of QuizUp.

Eventually Ryan sighed. "I should live in Seattle."

I lifted my head. "Huh?"

"It's one of the best cities for paralegals. They pay a lot."

"But you don't want to live in Seattle." I paused, because something had just occurred to me. "*Do* you?"

"Why not?"

"Doesn't it rain a lot?"

He put the tablet on the coffee table and leaned back, hands laced behind his head. "I'd get used to it."

"It's freaking far away."

"From what? If we lived there, it would be our home. Everything else would be far away."

I hesitated, not sure how serious he was. Laughed. "Um, Mr. I-don't-get-to-see-my-family-enough. You'd be like a million miles from them."

He put his feet up on the coffee table. "You're right. Maybe a cool city closer to here. That pays paralegals a lot."

"What's wrong with here?" I slung my arms over the back of the sofa. "Just not enough money, or what?"

"No, it's fine here. I just like to try new places."

Uhhh . . . "Well, bad news. We have a year lease, so we're stuck here for a while."

He didn't say anything for a moment. "Maybe someday, though."

I gazed up at the ceiling. I thought about Mom telling me I liked to take risks and try new things, and how it wasn't really true, but I wished it was. "It must be cool. I mean, you've lived all over, and I've just lived here."

"Only San Fran. And Annapolis, for school. There's a lot I haven't seen."

"Maybe you should sell your art and make millions of dollars, and then we could travel all the time but still live here."

"Pfffff." He grinned, shaking his head.

"Why's that so funny?"

"Because I'm not an artist."

"Shut your tiny face."

He turned toward me. "You're sweet."

I didn't push. But it kinda bugged me that I suggested a real thing he could do to be happier, and he was like, *Oh, how cute.* But the thing was, I could tell he liked the idea. That it was more than just flattery to him. That somewhere, deep down, he believed he had talent and that it should be recognized. I'm not that great with words. But I know what people's faces mean.

After a while I said, "I guess I'd like to see other places. But everything I need is here in this city, so I've been too lazy to, you know. Explore or whatever."

He nodded, leaning forward to play with his tablet again. "Bet this was a fun place to grow up."

"Oh yeah. I got into all kinds of trouble."

He laughed without looking up. "You?"

"Yeahhhh."

"I'll bet it was pretty adorable trouble, though."

"How do you know I wasn't a total gangster?"

He snorted. "Uh-huh."

I shifted, leaning closer to him. "I did a lot of bad stuff when I was younger."

"Like?" He was typing a message to Amanda.

I pulled some lint off his shoulder. "Me and some guys from high school, we were friends with Dumb Josh. Dumb Josh wasn't dumb—he was the only one of us in honors classes. So we thought it was hilarious to call him Dumb Josh. But he was, like, he really did sound— There was something wrong with his voice. So there was this bingo hall in town, and we'd always go and play—"

"What were you, seventy-five and desperate for a free lava lamp?"

"Shut up. Pelletor needs your kindness now, not your censure."

"What does that even—"

"Bingo is a game of skill."

"It's a game of luck."

"It's a game of looking. And listening."

"Fair enough."

"We'd go and play, and we'd make Josh pretend to be mentally . . . disabled? Is that okay to say?"

"Developmentally disabled, legally speaking."

"Okay, yeah, so Josh would pretend to be that, and they'd always give him free games or count his bingo when he called it, even if the numbers were wrong."

"You're a bad person."

"No. Josh is a bad person."

"Guilty by association."

I eventually curled up and dozed while he edited the brief. But I kept getting pulled awake again, thinking about Seattle. Or, not Seattle specifically, but just the idea that Ryan and I still had years stretching ahead of us. Were we really gonna spend them here? Watching the same movies and hanging with the same people and talking about the same stuff? That had been enough for me my whole life so far.

But maybe there was more we needed to do, more we needed to try. I mean, look how we kept surprising ourselves. Moving in together and realizing we loved one another and drawing and music and, like . . . panties.

The thought made me really nonsexually excited, but also pretty nervous. I hated change. When Hal had died, I'd just kept thinking, *Everything's gonna be different now.* And it had bothered me that my brain didn't seem as upset about Hal being dead as how this was gonna change the group. And maybe that's why I was a little better at moving on than everyone else. I wanted everything to go back to normal.

I looked over at Ryan, who was cursing Erica under his breath. How did you get someone to understand your history if they hadn't been there for it? With my friends, it had happened really naturally. It was like we'd understood one another right off the bat, and the things each of us didn't know about the others' pasts and personalities and whatever, we'd osmosed by hanging out together.

It had been sort of the same with Ryan, but now that I was older, it was a little harder to get other people caught up on my story. And harder for me to catch up on theirs. But maybe that was the point of this relationship. It was a new phase in my life, so I had to kind of step away from my old stories and get ready to make new ones. Yeah? Maybe with the right person rocking it with you, change wasn't so bad.

Maybe panties and kale juice were just the beginning.

CHAPTER FIVE

Dad came to see me perform at Pitch the next night. Ryan had a coworker's retirement dinner and couldn't make it. And I wasn't sure if my friends even knew I was playing. I'd thought about texting them earlier in the day, but figured they'd already come to my gigs lots of times, and it wasn't like I had anything particularly exciting in store that night.

I played at Pitch once a month. Used to be more often, but then I got busy with work and stuff, and started to suspect I might not ever actually become a famous singer. I was twenty minutes late tonight because I'd freaking forgotten how far away Pitch was from my new place. Used to be I could just roll out the door ten minutes before my set and be fine. The usual crowd was there, plus some new faces. I wasn't nervous, but I guess I did feel this extra need to be *on*, with my dad watching. I played a few covers—"Fast Car," "Telephone Line," "Bye Bye Symphony." I tried some original stuff, including a song I'd written about a bottle of Lysol Multi-Purpose Cleaner that comes to life and kills a guy, called "Everyday Tough Messes." The audience laughed pretty hard. Probably because they were drunk.

Afterward, I found Dad at the bar with a beer. He grinned at me. His bald spot was sweaty. "Well done, Kamen. You just get better and better."

I couldn't tell if he meant it or not. When I was younger, my parents used to compliment me on everything, and I never questioned it. I thought I really was the best player on every team, or the most creative person in each class or whatever. And honestly, it didn't go to my head. 'Cause I had teachers telling me I needed improvement in pretty much every area except attitude. But I developed this inner confidence that didn't really get shaken until I was an adult and started to realize that not everyone thought I was as awesome as my parents did.

"Thanks." I noticed Gould and Miles at a table a few feet away. They waved at me. I grinned and waved back.

Dad looked where I was looking. "Oh—wow. Is that Miles and . . .?"

"Gould."

"*That's* Gould?"

"Yes. That's always been Gould."

"I haven't seen them in years."

"I know," I said, a little sharply. For real, it didn't bother me that Dad had his own life in Oregon. I'd always been closer with Mom anyway, and I didn't feel, like, abandoned or whatever. But sometimes it just dug at me a little that he didn't know what was going on with me. I wouldn't have had a clue how to start telling him about all the stuff I'd been dealing with lately—growing up and having a laundry room and thinking about Seattle and all that.

Mom thought I should have invited him to Hal's funeral. But I'd been like, why ask him to come all the way out here for the funeral of someone he'd only met a couple of times?

This memory hit me all at once of Mom at the funeral. Crying like she was going for an Oscar or something. And I was so weirded out by how hard she was crying that I didn't even cry at all. Not until way later.

Dad and I went over to say hi to my friends. It was awkward, because my dad tried to hug Miles, and Miles was always, like, rigid with general life terror. You had to give that dude about five minutes warning before you hugged him, so he could mentally prepare for affection.

Dad just shook Gould's hand, but I wasn't sure if that was because hugging Miles had gone so lousy, or because Dad still suspected I wasn't telling him the truth about this being Gould.

"What do you think?" Dad asked them, slinging an arm around me. "Isn't he talented?"

I tried to grin, shrugging away. "Dad. You don't have to *present* me to my friends."

"That was really nice," Gould said. "I liked the Lysol song."

Really nice.

If I actually had the talent to make it big in the music industry, people would say much better things than that, right? They'd be, like, pressuring me to send my demo to record labels or sharing my YouTube channel with everyone they knew. They wouldn't be like, *That was nice.*

Suddenly I just wanted to be home with Ryan. Or I at least wanted a beer.

Dad said he was gonna head back to his hotel, and Gould had to get home because he went to bed at Old Man O'Clock. But Miles said he'd stay and have a drink with me.

I collapsed in Gould's vacated seat and tipped my head back with a sigh.

Miles took a sip of beer. "Everything okay?"

"Yeah. Just tired."

"Your dad's a lot balder than the last time I saw him."

I straightened, scooting back in the chair. "Does this ever happen to you, since your dad's away a lot? Like, he comes back, and you feel kinda weird, like, 'Who is this guy?'"

Miles's dad was a truck driver. Miles's mom lived about half an hour away, so Miles saw her a decent amount, but he only saw his dad a few times a year.

Miles nodded slowly. "I suppose."

"I'm not mad at him for leaving. I mean, I was when I was a kid, but I'm fine now."

Miles grinned. "Are you?"

"Uuuuughhh, yes. Yes. I don't know why. I just get impatient with him for not being up-to-date on my life. He couldn't even remember Gould."

"You want a drink? I'll buy."

"No, dude. I'm sorry. I need to shut up about myself and hear all about Zac. I got your pictures from his first day at the house. He looked, like, psychotically joyous."

Miles's grin broadened. "He's incredible. I won't pretend it hasn't been stressful. But I'm trying to roll with the punches, I suppose."

"But you got to sneak away to do some drinking tonight?"

"Zac loves Drix. He was ecstatic at the idea of getting to hang out with Drix for an evening."

I squinted at him suspiciously. "Does Drix live with you?"

Miles shook his head. "No. Absolutely not." Then he took the kind of nervous beer sip only a liar would take.

"It seems like he lives with you."

"He stays over four nights a week. Sometimes five."

"Miiiiiles."

"Go get a drink, and I'll tell you more."

I headed up to the bar and ordered a beer. After a few seconds, I sensed someone behind me.

"Hello, Kamen," said a smooth, icy female voice.

I turned. "Cinnamon."

Cinnamon flashed me a smile. She was in her early thirties, with long legs and red hair. Wide lips and dark-brown, kinda root beer–colored eyes. She was a big deal in the pony play world, and a regular at Riddle—she and her partner Stan were always doing grooming stuff next to the bondage furniture. So, I mean, try getting blown on a bench when a woman in stiletto boots and with a bit in her mouth is, like, having her ass currycombed a few inches away. I thought what she did was cool. She just wasn't a very cool person.

She tossed her head. "Interesting set."

I was wary. "Thanks."

"You ought to record yourself singing that Lysol song and put it on YouTube. Be one of those so-bad-he's-good YouTube stars."

My jaw tensed, and I thought about pointing out that I *did* have a YouTube channel, and I actually had followers who really dug me. But I stayed quiet hoping she'd take the hint and go away. The bartender brought my beer.

She moved closer. "Was that your dad here a minute ago?"

"Yeah."

"He's handsome. In an old-guy way."

I handed my card to the bartender, then turned back to her. "That's kind of a weird thing to say."

"He and your mom are separated, right?"

"How would you know that?"

"I've talked to your mom before. At Riddle."

Small world. I signed the slip and picked up my beer. “If you’ll excuse me.”

“Kamen,” she called as I walked toward my table.

I turned. She was smiling. And it was not a pleasant smile. “I know a secret. Something that might interest you.”

Part of me was instantly curious. Except it was totally a trap. What secret could Cinnamon know that I’d care about? Dave claimed I was nice to everybody, but it wasn’t true. There were definitely people whose heads I wanted to throw bricks at, and I didn’t always make an effort to hide it. I ignored Cinnamon and walked to my table.

“Cinnamon’s here,” I told Miles as I sat.

He turned to look. “Oh my. I’ve never seen her outside of Riddle.”

“She said my dad was hot.”

“She’s an odd one.”

“Why *does* she hate us so much?”

He sipped his drink. “She’s insecure. And hey, maybe we make her jealous. If the shit people say about her at Riddle is any indication, she doesn’t have many friends.”

That actually was sad. Not sad enough for me to feel sorry for her, though.

I swigged my beer. “So you were gonna tell me about Zac?”

“Yeah. It’s been crazy. But not as crazy as I thought. He was spending weekends with me for the last month, so he knows me, knows Drix, knows the house. Knows my mom and sister and even some of the neighbors. But it’s just . . . now he’s there *all the time*.”

“And it’s great.”

“It’s great,” he agreed. “But . . .”

“But crazy.”

“Exactly.”

“When can I meet him?”

“Well, I actually wanted to ask you,” Miles said. “Would you be able to come over Saturday afternoon? Dave and Gould are coming, and I’d like the three of you to meet him all at once. I was thinking around two?”

“Awesome! Yeah, I’ll check with Ryan because he was maybe gonna have coffee with Amanda, but I’m sure he can schedule it around this.”

Miles hesitated, looking guilty. "Actually, I—and this has nothing to do with anything that was said Sunday. Ryan's great, and I think it's . . . it's very bold of you to have moved in with him. But I'd prefer to just keep it us, for now. So we don't overwhelm Zac." He met my gaze and added quickly, "It's not just Ryan. I asked Dave not to bring D yet either."

I tried to hide my disappointment. What he was saying made sense—a little bit. I mean, what was the difference between introducing Zac to four people or introducing him to three? I guess I'd just kinda figured once I moved in with Ryan, people would treat us like a couple. If you invited one of us somewhere, you invited the other too, by default. And the whole "bold that you moved in with him"—WTF? I *loved* him. Why was that so hard for the guys to understand?

But I nodded. Smiled. "No problem. I know Ryan really wants to meet him, though."

Thing was, I didn't even know if that was true. This was so weird. My friends were awesome. Ryan was awesome. So why the hell weren't they gelling? How could I care so much about all of them and still not know how to make this work?

"Oh, certainly," Miles said. "I'm really looking forward to Ryan meeting the whole family."

Whole family. We *were* a family. Ryan was part of that family. My friends loved me. I loved them. Except I couldn't pretend anymore that this Ryan-versus-my-friends thing didn't exist. Dave thought Ryan was blunt, and Gould thought he was insensitive, and Miles didn't want him to meet Zac yet, and all of them thought I'd rushed into this relationship without giving it any thought.

I didn't. I'm not stupid. I'm just not afraid of what I want.

I mean, how long had Miles spent being all, *Oh, I'm not good enough for Drix*, or *Oh, he has some miniscule flaw, so maybe I should break up with him*?

And that had been a waste of time, right? Because now his kid and Drix were BFF and Drix basically lived at Miles's house, and they were in love as shit.

So I don't waste time trying to talk myself out of good things. That kinda makes me the smartest guy in this group.

And if I wasn't afraid of what I wanted, then I'd find a way to work through this. Because I *wanted* my friends and Ryan to get along. They'd liked each other before, and I was confident they could fall in love all over again if I just helped each party see the awesomeness of the other.

So that was what was gonna happen.

Even if I had to *Parent Trap* this shit.

Friday, the clothes arrived while Ryan was at work. I tried really hard to ignore the packages. I wanted us to open them together.

It was my day off, so I picked up my guitar and worked on my music. Stopped to text Ryan that I loved him more than the eleven-dimension multiverse. My plan was to gross my friends out less with my lovey-dovey shit, which meant I deserved to be extra nauseating when it was just me and Ryan.

God, even my dad yesterday, when he and Ryan and I were having lunch, was like, *"Didn't waste any time, did you?"* when we told him about moving in together.

And Ryan was great, just like, *"Why would I want to waste a single moment I could spend with Kamen?"* Then he and my dad had started talking about lawn mower parts, and everything was cool. When Dad had left for the airport yesterday, he'd said, *"You hang on to him."* Dad hadn't told me anything about how his talk with Mom went.

Ryan texted back: *I LOVE YOU MORE THAN THAT. ALSO ERICA IS LISTENING TO NICKELBACK. O_o*

I grinned and messed around on the guitar some more.

But it was like those boxes were fucking taunting me.

It wouldn't hurt to try the stuff on, would it? Just make sure it looked okay?

I put the guitar aside and went over to the boxes, which I'd left by the door. Poked them with my toe.

I picked up the first one and ripped it open. I pulled out a plastic-wrapped floral dress. Stared at it for a moment, then tore off the plastic and held up the dress, letting the folded skirt fall.

It looked kinda, I don't know, big in the boob area.

I checked the invoice. *Floral Swing Dress, 16.*

A swing dress. I didn't know what made a swing dress a swing dress, but I was glad as fuck to have one because it was beautiful as a friggin' spring day. The fabric was a little stiff, and it had some wrinkles where it had been folded. The waist had a bow on it, and the skirt was froofy, and the whole thing smelled like cardboard box.

I set it down and opened the next package.

Holy shit.

It was like looking in a goddamn treasure chest. Four pairs of lace panties in various colors. A red lace bra. The garter belt was bright, like, teal—I guess?—with a tiny satin bow at the front. Satin ribbons dangled from it, little silver clips attached to the ends. The stockings were, according to the packing slip, sheer thigh highs with lace stay-up silicone tops. Whatever that meant. I stretched one over my hand. Then I made it be a puppet for a minute. It talked to the well-dressed hare in a high-pitched voice, and I stopped to make a note on my phone that Stockie & Hare could be a children's crime-fighting duo.

Then I went to my room and got naked.

I tried on the garter belt in front of the mirror. It looked really nice. I mean, you could see my pubes all around the sides, and also through the lace, plus, like, my dick and balls were making it bulge. But I liked that. I put on the stockings, but I ripped the first one because I kinda fell over while I was standing on one leg trying to stuff my foot in. So that one was pretty bedraggled once it was on. But the second one I got the idea to scrunch it up first and then put my foot in, and that worked a lot better. Except my big toe poked a hole in the end of it.

It took me a solid twenty minutes to hook all the little dangle-ribbons to the stockings, but once I did, I looked in the mirror again and started getting pretty turned on. Like, who invented this shit? Who was like, *You know what's gonna make people want to get nasty? Some lacy underwear attached with ribbons to what are basically tall flimsy socks?*

I would shake that fucker's hand.

Swing dress next. It fit a little weird, since there was a ton of space for boobs and I didn't have boobs. But it looked amazing at the waist.

Maybe I should have put the bra on. I turned to the side, rocking my hips back and forth to watch the skirt sway. Then I started twisting from side to side to make it billow. I tried to make it fly up enough to get a glimpse of the garter belt, but then I got dizzy, so I stopped.

I needed heels. Did they make heels big enough for me? They had to, because drag queens. And I still wasn't sure about makeup, because I for shizzballs did not have the face for it. Dave? Yes. Ricky? He'd look like a goddess. Me? It might be the stuff of nightmares, on account of I could shave and have basically a full beard fifteen minutes later. But it was worth a try.

And a wig? I studied my reflection. Eh. There was something kind of exciting about my short hair and stubble and the gun show you couldn't even get tickets to because that shit was sold out—and then a floral swing dress and stockings.

I unzipped the dress and pulled the top part down. Put the bra straps over my shoulders, then reached around to the back to hook the bra.

It did not go well. Finally, it occurred to me I could leave the straps off my shoulders, hook the bra at my chest, then slide it around so the boobs part was up front. *Then* put the straps on.

The bra actually looked fucking fantastic, because it was padded, so it wasn't, like, sagging empty cups. And I had enough definition between my pecs that it almost looked like cleavage.

"I'm fucking hot," I said to the mirror. I pulled the top of the dress back up and zipped it. Way better in the chest area. I grabbed my fake boobs and honked them a little. Awesome.

I walked out to the living room. Walking in the dress was amazing because of how the skirt swished. And how I felt, like, weirdly naked between my legs. And the stockings were great too, because each step I took pulled on the belt, and the lace rubbed my dick, and all was pretty much right with the world.

I wasn't sure what to do now. Ryan wouldn't be home for another two hours, but I really wanted him to see this. I could text him pics, but he needed to see it in person. I was definitely working my way up to a boner, and I tried reaching under my dress to feel myself up, which was awesome, except that I needed Ryan to be the first one to make me come in this outfit.

I looked around the room. Lifted my skirt and flashed the well-dressed hare. Then I picked up my guitar.

I took a deep breath. "Pretend I'm an actress. In, like, the 1930s. And I'm auditioning for you."

I was standing in the living room, shifting giddily. Ryan was sitting on the couch, just staring at me, chewing a nail. His pupils were gigantoid, and he kept kind of ducking his head like he was trying to see under my skirt. I wished I had heels.

I slung my guitar over my shoulder. "Got it?"

"I'm a director?"

"Yeah. And I really want this part. And you, like, call me doll and stuff. Don't call me dirty things. Not at first."

He nodded, looking stunned and a little nervous. I'd basically accosted him when he'd gotten home from work. I'd tried a lot of different positions before he'd arrived—draped on the couch with my legs open, sitting on the arm of the couch with my legs crossed. Posing in the doorway with an arm over my head. I couldn't find anything that felt sexy enough, so I'd been standing all deer-in-the-headlights in the middle of the room when he'd come in.

He scooted back slightly. "Whatever's about to happen, I'm looking forward to it."

My heart pounded. "Me too. First we need to do some dialogue. So pretend I just came into your audition room." I backed up to the doorway and entered the room, trying to swing my hips.

"What do I say?"

"Whatever. Director stuff."

I turned and walked back to the door, then entered again.

He cleared his throat into his fist. Crossed his legs. "Hey there, uh . . . doll."

"Hello!" My voice was so high-pitched it sounded ridiculous. "Wait, wait," I said in my normal tone. "That voice is stupid. Let me try again."

"Okay. Hey there, doll."

"Hello." I said it in my own voice, but a little softer.

"What's your name?"

I hadn't even thought about that. "Um . . . Tracy?"

He grinned. "You don't sound too sure, babe."

The "babe" was good.

I looked at my feet in their ripped stockings and sighed exaggeratedly. "My real name's Kate. I just thought Tracy might be a good stage name."

"It's gorgeous. Just like you."

I actually fucking blushed. "Thank you, Mr. Wheeler."

"You been onstage before, Tracy?"

"Once. I was a backup dancer. In a Broadway show."

"Oh yeah? Which show?"

"Uh . . . *Wicked*?"

He laughed. "This is 1936."

I made a face at him and switched to my normal voice. "I don't *know* any Broadway shows from 1936."

"Okay, okay, Tracy. You've got an impressive résumé. And you look like a star. Now I just need to see what you can do."

"Thank you." My hands were sweating so bad I didn't even know if I could play the guitar. Why was a fake audition for my boyfriend making me so nervous?

Ryan clasped his knee. "What've you got for me today?"

I shifted, the lace of my garter belt rubbing my balls, straining as my dick hardened. "I'm gonna sing. And dance."

He was checking out my skirt again. Pervert. "Okay."

I smiled. "I think you're really gonna like it."

I cocked my hips and started strumming. Hit one bad chord, but hey, I'd only written this song like two hours ago. I went back and gave it another go. Nodded, satisfied, when I got it right. I looked straight into Ryan's eyes and started singing.

"I . . . want . . . this part.

"I want this part." I looked at his crotch.

"I need this part,

"Need it real bad, honey.

"Don't care about the fame

"Or the fans or the money,

"I just want a chance

"To show off for you.
"This is the part
"I was born to do."

I walked up to him, swinging my hips and banging out the chords pretty aggressively now. He was trying real hard not to laugh. I hiked one leg up onto the couch.

"So put your part in my mouth.
"Yeah put your part up my ass.
"I dunno how to act,
"Need a ma-aster class.
"No other part's gonna do,
"I need to get this from you.
"Let me sit on your part,
"Yeah let me sit on your paaart . . ."

I stopped. "Quick, flip the lights on and off real fast!"

"What?"

"Please, just do it for a minute. It's important."

He got up, went to the light switch, and flipped it up and down rapidly.

I strummed furiously.

"You put a guitar solo in a striptease?"

I nodded. "Keep flipping the lights."

I fucked up the end of the solo a little, but whatever. He went back to the couch.

"Key change!" I shouted, and shifted up a half step.

"So rub your part on my face,
"Put your part up my butt,
"I'm your sweet little girl,
"I'm your big sexy slut.
"Stick your part down my throat,
"Yeah, I'm ready for you,
"Now give me this part that
"I was boooo-oooorn to do!"

I tossed the guitar aside and straddled his lap. My bra strap slid down my shoulders and my skirt rucked up around my hips. He grabbed my waist and kissed me, and I scooted back so his knee was all jammed against my lace-covered dick and balls.

"I am so gonna give you this part," he whispered, still kissing me.

I laughed and yanked his hand under my skirt. I couldn't believe how easy it was to grope someone in a skirt. Like, why the fuck did dudes not wear dresses? If I had a dime for every time some guy tried to grab my crotch and ended up with just a handful of jeans, I could probably buy another freaking juicer.

He unclipped one of the garters, and I forgot how to breathe for a sec. He slapped the other side of my thigh, then undid another clip, then another. The stockings strained at the last connected points. I wanted to stay *right fucking there*. In that moment where my stockings were only connected by one ribbon each, and I could feel the pull on the fabric and the heat in my groin and his hand against my leg.

He undid the last clip on one side, and the stocking slipped down to my knee. He left the other one connected, and he stuck his hand down the back of my garter belt, his warm palm sliding in circles over my ass.

I started rocking against his hand, my dick straining the lace. He smiled at me, and I laughed, grinding harder on his hand. "We should get the clappy lights so I can clap them on and off when I need strobes."

"You think we should get clap lights just so you can do your stripper routine?" He traced a light line with his fingertip down one ass cheek.

"It's an *audition*." I kicked at his leg with my stockinged foot. "I'm not that kind of girl."

"Really? What kind of girl are you?"

I laughed. "Mmm."

"What kind?" He played with the last clip.

I closed my eyes with a soft gasp as he moved his hand back to my balls. "Your kind."

"Then why don't you get on all fours so we can finish your audition?"

I groaned, still trying to rub against his hand, but he let me go.

"Come on."

I slid off his lap and got on my hands and knees on the couch.

"Stay right there." He stood and went to the bedroom. Came back a moment later and jumped on the couch behind me.

I looked over my shoulder at him and grinned. "I thought I already had the part."

He stroked my ass through the skirt. "I need to make *sure* you're right for it."

I faced forward and bowed my head as he ran his palms up the backs of my thighs, teasing the skirt higher. I shivered. He let it fall and leaned farther down to kiss the back of my bare thigh. My breathing roughened as he trailed his tongue upward, his head pushing my skirt up again. His stubble scratched the base of my ass cheek, and I got goose bumps all over. I arched my shoulders and dipped my head lower, my mouth falling open.

I wasn't sure what I wanted him to say or do. I hardly even felt like we were playing anymore. I got my nose as close as I could to the front of the dress and inhaled. Got the cardboard smell, plus a hint of sweat and deodorant and balls.

He kissed the edge of the garter belt. Bit it and tugged with his teeth. I tucked my hips under me, then released, pushing my ass up and out. He licked under the belt. Let go.

Next thing I knew, his fingers were sliding along the waistband, pulling the belt slowly down. When he finally let it drop to my knees, one stocking stayed up, stuck around my thigh by sweat or me having huge thighs or something. He had to roll it down, and swear to God, I almost came from that.

My dick and balls were just hanging there under my skirt, and I would have given him pretty much a million dollars to touch them, but he came up with better stuff. He reached around and grabbed handfuls of the front of the dress and the padded bra cups and squeezed, pulling me back against him so I could feel his boner through my skirt. I jerked my head up and gasped, and had this sudden vision of myself with soft, curly blond hair and a feminine face, and makeup. Breasts nearly spilling out of my bra, shaved legs. Another second and the image was gone. He ran his hands down the front of the dress. Slowly raised the bra strap that had slid down my left shoulder, and put it back in its place. Then he lifted my skirt and tossed it up over my shoulders.

I was seriously convinced dresses were magic. How could a piece of clothing feel so beautiful and classy and dirty at the same time? Like it was fucking made for . . . access?

He kissed my hip. Made a trail of kisses down to my thigh and across the underside of my cheek, and then started lapping the skin behind my balls. Over and over, pushing at it with his tongue, making circles, sliding up almost to my hole. Just that area, until it started to lose sensitivity, until I was going wild wanting him to touch me somewhere else. Then he stopped and straightened. I listened to him open the condom, then the lube. It took a minute, but he got his dick stuffed all up in dat ass. I was in some sort of haze, my head drooping, my breath harsh and backed by these little high-pitched moans.

He didn't fuck me that hard, but it was fast, and he didn't let up. Even when I kind of thought he'd already come, he was still gripping my hips and fucking me, until one of my knees slipped into the crack between cushions and jolted me out of my, like, fugue state.

He pulled out, and my legs shook a little as I tried to hold myself up. My dick was still rigid, and I realized a few seconds later when he pressed against me that his was too.

"Can you blow me?" he whispered. "Please?"

They say there's no such thing as a stupid question, but dude. Come on.

He sat back, and I climbed off the couch and knelt on the hardwood. My knees hurt, and I didn't give a fuck. He scooted to the very edge of the couch and stripped the condom off. I got on my knees between his legs and, you know. Put his part in my mouth. As I sucked, he ran his fingers through my hair. I pulled up slowly, releasing his dick for a second to breathe before plunging down again.

He put his hands on my shoulders and slid the bra straps down. He leaned forward, groaning softly in my ear as I continued sucking, and unzipped the dress. His fingers grazed the bumps of my spine as he unhooked the bra. He eased the top of the dress off and stroked my bare shoulders. I hummed around his dick, pulling up with my lips and then touching the head as lightly as I could with the tip of my tongue.

He rubbed his palms in broad circles over my shoulders, then down the front of my dress to rub my pecs. I arched away from the couch so he could reach better, trying to keep my lips on his dick. He leaned back, moaning, and pumped his hips gently until he grabbed fistfuls of the couch cushion and tipped his head up and closed his eyes. As he came, I switched from sucking to licking—long, broad swipes of my tongue until he was done. He lay sprawled like that while I swallowed and wiped my mouth. Cracked his eyes open to look at me. Smiled. "You," was all he said.

I propped my elbows on the couch and grinned. "Hall of Fame?"

"Yes. For the fucking dress and bra alone. But also . . ." He panted for a few seconds. "Your skill." He reached out and ran a hand over my head. "And in a minute, I'm gonna return the favor."

He did. Me on my back with my legs spread and my skirt around my hips. It took about two seconds.

And he did eventually decide I'd gotten the part.

CHAPTER SIX

"What *is* this thing?" Dave picked up Miles's remote. It had six separate sections to control the TV, cable box, streaming channels, and, like, three different players. "You could brain someone with this." He looked up. "Miles, you don't even watch TV because you think it only engages the mind on the most basic of levels."

Miles shook his head. "Ask Drix. Apparently vampyres require forty-six different sports channels." He went to the stairs and called, "Drix! Zac! We have company."

I heard pounding in the upstairs hall: Drix's heavy footsteps plus a lighter set. Then laughter and a loud double-descent down the steps. And then a six-foot-seven vampyre dressed in black jeans and a black T-shirt was standing in the living room next to the world's most freaking adorable five-year-old, who looked . . . weirdly like Miles. Maybe it was just the outfit.

"Are you seriously dressing him in tiny Mr. Moseby sweaters?" Gould whispered.

Miles swatted his arm and addressed Zac. "Zac. These are your uncles Dave, Kamen, and Gould."

Thanks, Miles. Way to destroy me emotionally. I had an actual friggin' lump in my throat.

"Hi," we chorused.

Zac looked back and forth between us, sort of laughing behind closed lips like he was plotting extreme mischief. Then he peered up at Drix and smiled.

"You should probably say hi, huh?" Drix suggested.

Zac faced the three of us again, twisting with his hands behind his back and a huge grin on his face. Then he shook his head.

"Don't let him fool you," Miles told us, holding out a hand for Zac to high-five. "He's not shy at all."

Drix put a hand on Zac's shoulder, and the height difference was just . . . even better than Ryan and me. "We were just upstairs wondering whether werewolves enjoy being werewolves."

Zac glanced up at him again. "They're monsters," he said seriously. "And monsters . . . maybe wanna be . . . um . . ."

Dave tilted his head. "What do they want to be?"

Zac turned to him. "Humans."

Dave nodded. "Maybe so."

Gould spoke up. "Hey, Zac? We've heard a lot about you from your dad. He says you're really, really cool. We've been excited to meet you for a long time."

This time Zac looked at Miles. Miles nodded. "I do think you're really cool. And your uncles are also cool. So it's all gonna be pretty cool-cool around here today."

"Cool-cool," Zac repeated.

Then he ran to go get a balloon to show us.

Dave started humming the *Fresh Prince* theme.

Miles glared at him. "He *likes* cardigans."

"But there's still time to save him," Dave insisted. "And you are enabling."

Zac brought the balloon back and started running his hands all over it to make it staticky.

"That's an awesome balloon." I crouched in front of him. "Think we could play baseball with it?" I ignored Miles's groan. "You like baseball?"

Zac nodded. "Yes."

"Favorite team?"

No answer except that adorable, closed-lipped smile.

"We've been watching the Indians," Miles said.

"Awesome!" I stood and picked up his giant remote. Took an exaggerated batter's stance next to the TV.

"Pitch it to me! This is Pell, batting for the Win-dians."

"Wait, I have to get my cap!" Zac raced from the room.

Miles stepped closer to me. "The Indians most certainly do not win with any kind of regularity."

I smirked. "You don't have a bowel movement with any kind of regularity."

Miles rolled his eyes. "So mature."

"Actually," Gould said, "if any one of us is super regular, it's probably Miles."

Dave nodded. "Yeah. Miles's shits are probably tied to the waxing and waning of the moon."

Zac loped back into the room. "You said 'shit.'" He reached out and patted Dave's hip as he passed. He slowed to a stop in front of Miles, wearing a blue ball cap and shaking the balloon by its tie.

Miles turned to Dave. "Thanks a lot."

Dave shrugged sheepishly. "He's five. I didn't think he—"

"Had ears?"

Dave sighed and faced Zac. "Hey, Zac. I'm sorry. The word I used is a bad word, and you should never use it."

"I know 'shit.'" Zac flipped the balloon back and forth by the tie.

"Could we step away from the TV, maybe?" Miles asked.

I took a step forward and to the side. The others backed up. "I'm ready!" I told Zac.

He wound up and pitched to me.

The balloon sailed a couple of inches before dropping to the carpet, but I took a mighty swing anyway, letting the momentum spin me all the way around. "Whoaaaa!"

Zac laughed.

"Strike!" he yelled, at the same time I yelled, "Ball!"

"*Stri-ike*," Zac insisted.

I put on a really bad New York accent. "Whaddis this joker tawkin' abahht?" I turned to the other guys. "Ump?"

"Definitely a strike." Dave gave Zac a thumbs-up.

I sagged my shoulders in mock defeat while Zac did a victory dance. I picked up the balloon and tossed it back to Zac.

Zac moved his hands all over the surface of the balloon, making squeegee sounds. Out of the corner of my eye I could see Miles wincing. Zac squeezed the balloon. "I wanna bat now."

We switched places, and the baseball game continued for some time. I convinced Dave and Gould and eventually even Miles to participate. At one point I was pitching, and Miles, crouched in the catcher position behind our throw-cushion home plate, started doing all these weird gestures. Pinching his nose, pulling his ear, holding up two fingers, then three, then four. Puffing his cheeks out.

"What are you *doing*?" I asked.

Zac turned to look at Miles.

It was so rare to see Miles do anything silly that the rest of us didn't know what the hell to do. We all burst out laughing at the same time. Miles looked embarrassed but was smiling. "What? I'm just communicating with you."

Zac put down the "bat" and placed his hands on Miles's head. Dragged them along Miles's face until Miles's cheeks were squished. "You're weird."

"I know," Miles said through fish lips.

"Your dad has *always* been weird, Zac," Dave informed him.

That cracked Zac up, and man, I freaking loved it. Little kids were the shit.

We played ball awhile longer, until we were all tired and had had one too many close calls with some decorative glass thingie on the bookshelf. Then Drix took Zac out to the backyard to water the garden, and the rest of us sat down.

I plopped onto the couch next to Miles and let my hand flop so it smacked his stomach. "Look at you, all being a dad."

He ducked his head, smiling.

Dave whistled innocently. "I guess having Drix around doesn't hurt either."

"Oh, it hurts," Miles said. "Believe me."

It took us all a second. Then I laughed. "Miles made a sex joke."

He lifted his chin. "I'm not unversed in double entendres."

Dave was scoping out the bookshelf, which had about eight million parenting books. "Zac's a *really* cool kid."

Miles seemed like he could have exploded with pride. "He's incredible. Though—" he glanced around as though Zac might be listening "—he is one of *those* children."

Dave turned. "One of *what* children? The Goldshire six?"

Miles sighed. "The ones who say creepy things, and then you submit their eeriest lines to BuzzFeed for some asinine article."

Dave and I exchanged a glance. I turned back to Miles. "Um, more info, dude?"

"Like the other evening he dropped his truck down the basement stairs, because someone—and I won't mention names, but it was Drix—left the basement door open. Now, Zac knows he's not supposed to go into the basement, but instead of calling for me, he stood at the top of the stairs until I noticed. And when I approached, I heard him say, 'tomorrow.' Not to me, but to the blackness at the bottom of the steps. 'Who are you talking to?' I asked. And he goes, 'The white lady.' I wasn't sure who he meant. He calls Ms. Brennan, his teacher, the white lady, because she's one of about two white teachers at the whole school. But I knew Ms. Brennan wasn't in the basement."

Dave laughed. "So who was he talking to?"

Miles shook his head. "Who knows? But now I'm terrified my basement plays host to some disheveled Victorian ghost with a bruised neck and unfinished business here on earth. Drix loves it, of course. He bought a ghost-hunting kit."

I got up to get a drink. Saw a note on the refrigerator whiteboard. *Love you through all the ages. – Diaemus.* Which I was pretty sure was Drix's vampyre name. I grinned. So I wasn't the only one who was gross and mushy. I wondered briefly if D ever said stuff like that to Dave. I couldn't really imagine D saying "I love you" to anything except maybe a plate of steak tartare.

All Miles had in his fridge was prune juice, milk, and water, so I grabbed a bottled water and headed back to the living room. Sat in the armchair this time.

Drix and Zac came in a few minutes later. Zac took his sandals off at the door, but Drix just headed for the kitchen. "Shoes off!" Miles called, without even looking up.

"Sorry," Drix called back. He shuffled back to the door and removed his shoes.

Miles smiled and rolled his eyes at the rest of us. "It's *him* I have to worry about."

Drix entered and sat beside Miles. Took his hand and then bent his ridick-tall body to rest his head on Miles's shoulder. "What are you saying?"

Miles gripped his arm and shook it gently. "I'm asking for tips on how to train my vampyre."

Drix laughed, looking a little embarrassed. Drix had probably the best embarrassed laugh of anyone I'd ever met. Hard to believe the dude was a frealz sadist. He lifted his head and kissed Miles's cheek. "Sorry. I'll learn."

Zac climbed onto the couch on Miles's other side, braced his hands on Miles's shoulder, and kissed his other cheek. "Is, um . . . is . . ." Zac scrubbed Miles's scalp with his tiny palm and almost whispered: "Is Drix staying here tonight?"

Miles glanced at Drix. "*Is* Drix staying here tonight?"

Drix nodded. "Drix could definitely stay here tonight."

So . . . probs the cutest family of all time.

We talked some more about werewolves and about Monroe Elementary and a computer game called *Thinking Up* that taught reading and story structure.

I didn't miss the way Drix occasionally dug his nails into Miles's arm, or the way Miles straightened just a little when he did.

Like, holy actual shit. We *were* a family. And our family kept growing. This wasn't even something I could have envisioned a few years ago: sitting here in Miles's house with Miles's *son*.

I got a flash of pain, of *something's missing*, but it was gone quick. Hal would have loved this. He would've ragged on Miles for settling down and becoming a dad, but he would have, like, been *thrilled*. Hal had loved kids. For the general safety of all involved, it was probably for the best he'd never had any of his own. But he'd been good with them.

I watched Miles lean against Drix with a long sigh. I caught his eye and smiled. He smiled back. I got these moments sometimes where I, like, *knew* one of my friends was thinking the same thing I was. Made me feel good to have that connection. It seemed like something that would always be there, no matter what else changed.

That evening, Ryan was in bed early, reading *Meg: Primal Waters*, so I spent some time writing a fake review for a sprinkler system on

Amazon, hoping it would catch on and encourage others to start fake reviewing it. Then I broke out my guitar and worked on "Fast Car."

I still wasn't tired, and I thought maybe Ryan was more interested in megalodons right now than sex, so I went into the back room we were using for storage and stood among the boxes and piles of junk.

There was a box of my old school stuff somewhere, which, yeah, it's not like I ever did anything that impressive in school, but my mom had saved everything. And I'd kept the box with me because I guess I'd figured at some point it would be fun to go back and read my fifth-grade essay about the trip to the turkey farm or whatever. I found the box buried under lots of other boxes of, like, Ryan's and my board games and extra dishware and stuff we hadn't found a place for yet.

There was a lot of random crap inside, including an essay I'd written for freshman English about how I wanted to be a museum curator. Did *not* remember that dream, so there was a small chance I'd plagiarized it from someone on the baseball team. I didn't see what I was looking for, and I was about to give up when I spotted the corner of a crayon drawing underneath a college tennis plaque.

I uncovered the drawing, and sure enough—it was "Snow Wanderer." Four pages of glory. The date was twenty years ago. The drawings were even scribblier than I'd remembered, and the story was a little weak on spelling, syntax, and punctuation.

Once there was a boy who hated lima beans and I want a dog.

Then the boy was exaped into the SNOW!

He wonderd all winter with NO COAT and his mom was at home.

He ~~new~~ knew he was going to starve and cryed help me but no one heard. Him.

Then he found a snoman and the snoman had ~~ka~~ carrots nose and the boy ate the nose.

The next page just said. *HA HA HA.*

Zukinis for eyes in the snoman and the boy ~~eat~~ ate zukinis.

He did not starve.

His moms bought him a coat.

THE END.

I took "Snow Wanderer" out to the kitchen with me and made a sandwich. Then I grabbed my guitar again and started fooling around. It took me a while to come up with a tune. And then I started tackling lyrics, trying to write a song about the Snow Wanderer. I didn't want to make it a literal adaptation of my comic—no zukinis—but I wanted something kind of sad and weird and creepy and funny.

Ryan came out after a while to ask what I was working on. I showed him the comic.

"Oh my God." He grinned at the pages. "This is *hilarious.*" He cracked up suddenly. "What the hell is up with his mom depriving him of coats? Sorry, *moms*. Wow, you were progressive."

"He had a tough life, okay? That's the whole point."

He flipped through again. "Did you, by any chance, hate lima beans at the time? And want a dog?"

"Still true. Anyway, I'm writing a song about him."

"Ooh. A 'Snow Wanderer' song?"

I nodded and played a few chords. Looked up at Ryan. "Don't laugh. I actually want this to be kind of good. But you can hear what I have so far, if you want."

He didn't laugh. He just sat down to listen.

CHAPTER SEVEN

The Subs Club meeting on Sunday was crowded. Maya was there, plus I'd convinced Ryan to come, since he hadn't been to a meeting in ages. I was rocking some lace panties under my jeans, and I kept reaching back to make sure my shirt was totally pulled down and covering my waist.

Maya gave me a high five when I sat down. "What up, K-snoot?"

"Nothin', M-skillet. I like your bag." She had a messenger bag with a real cute kraken on it.

Lots of our online members were women, but Miles and Gould and Dave and me were the ones who met in person and made decisions about the club. So now Dave had basically merged the Subs Club with Finger Bang, and Maya reported back and forth between the two groups.

Maya was a freaking trip—a good trip, I mean. She had this giant cloud of black hair and moles like polka dots on her neck. She sniffed a lot because she had allergies, but it wasn't the long wet sniffs you usually heard from people with allergies—it was these short little cokehead sniffs.

Dave kicked off the meeting with, "So Cobalt's closing."

"Don't remind me." I folded my arms on the table. "Now my mom's always gonna be at Riddle, so I'll never be able to go there again."

Miles shuddered. "I say good riddance."

"Why's it closing?" Gould asked.

Dave played with a Bobby's Discount Dentist pen, clicking it over and over. "Cobalt is closing because it's the moldering diaper on the Unabomber's rashed behind."

Gould snatched the pen from Dave and tossed it aside. "Yeah, but they have free snacks. Like, old-school stuff—Nutter Butters. Fun Dip."

Miles looked at him sharply. "We all need to stop being so snack-motivated. The phalluses of every man in that club have taken a 'fun dip' in innumerable orifices."

I nudged Ryan and spoke in a low voice. "Write this down for a concept: dirty picture book called *Isabelle's Innumerable Orifices*."

He snorted. He'd been texting with Amanda since we got here, and I kept catching the others giving him looks of disapproval. Which was frustrating, because come on, it wasn't like they never played on their phones during meetings. But I kinda wished Ryan would try to make a good impression.

Dave leaned back. "Cobalt's status as the Bates Motel of BDSM clubs aside, I don't know if you guys caught the story going around about the woman who was raped there last year? Gould, I know you heard. Kamen?"

I shook my head.

Dave continued. "Okay. Well, she sent us a message specifically asking if we could use the Sounding Board to open a discussion on the 'two DMs must agree to intervene' rule that some clubs have in place."

Gould nodded. "That's Cobalt's policy?"

"Yep," Maya said. "Some clubs, including Cobalt, have a rule that *two* dungeon monitors have to agree to intervene if a scene looks unsafe or nonconsensual. In the case of the woman at Cobalt, her dom had her tied down and was fingering her, even though they'd negotiated no sex. I guess one DM saw the scene and thought at first she was, like, in ecstasy rather than having a panic attack. Once the DM got suspicious, she had to go seek out another DM. And by the time both DMs agreed to stop the scene and see if the woman was okay, the rape had been going on for a while."

Gould shifted. "So what'd they do to the dom once they figured it out?"

"Nothing." Dave sounded pissed. "She didn't feel comfortable calling it rape in front of the dom, and she told the DMs she was okay, just a little overwhelmed."

"The house safeword there is red," I pointed out. "Couldn't she have said that, and no one would've been confused?"

Dave glared at me, so I knew I'd said the wrong thing. "Bottoms aren't always in a headspace to be able to safeword. And if something traumatic was happening to her, it's easy to understand why she didn't say red."

"Okay, sorry."

Most of the time I just let other people tell me what was okay to say and what wasn't. One time I was commenting on the fact that Miles, despite being a total nerd, is, like, a chocolate motherfucking stallion, whose skin makes his teeth look amazafreaktron white. Dave explained to me why I'm not supposed to think Miles is hot based on his skin, because it's objectifying or whatever. But I never quite got that. Because Miles's skin is, like, the *best*, so why can't we talk about it? Also, Miles told me it wasn't a big deal—he was glad he was hot and black, and he loved his teeth.

It's just messed up is all, because you're allowed to say you like blonds, or you think big lips are the best kind of lips, but you're not allowed to say brown skin is hot? I wouldn't care if someone was like, *Pale skin gives me a huge boner*. But Dave said that was because I'd never been oppressed.

"So," Miles prompted. "This is going to be a discussion topic?"

Dave refocused. "Yes. The woman's not looking to press charges. She just—"

"You know what the dungeons ought to do," Ryan interrupted loudly. "Ban penetration from public play spaces. Lots of states do it."

"Dude." I nudged him and whispered, "You're talking in shouty caps."

Dave was staring at Ryan with his mouth slightly open. "*As* I was saying. She wants us to talk about the two-DM rule on the Sounding Board. Because, as her experience shows, waiting until two DMs agree means an assault might go on longer than it has to." He paused. "And if a scene is, like, life-threateningly unsafe, a few seconds can make all the difference."

Silence.

"With Hal," Gould said slowly, "we saw how long it can take *one* DM to notice something's wrong." He glanced at Ryan. "And that violations can occur without penetration."

Ryan set his phone down. "I just think if bottoms can't take more responsibility for who they play with and how, then the rule makers need to take a more active role."

I seriously thought Dave was gonna explode. But Gould was the one who spoke up. "If that's a way of saying Hal—"

"It's not about Hal. That's the thing, you guys. If we want this group to have a wider reach, then it can't just be about this one experience you all had. We've got to be ready to talk about the issues objectively, without letting emotions rule us."

I tried to step on his foot or something, but it was too late.

"I like how you include yourself in 'us,'" Dave said. "Because you obviously feel *so* much emotion about Hal's de—"

Ryan just talked right over him. "Even the tough issues. Even the stuff that makes *us* uncomfortable. We need to be able to consider all sides, and to disagree."

Dave nodded, shrugging. "You know what, I'll give you that. Good point."

I closed my eyes for a second, relieved. Ryan loved to debate—I'd seen him take sides he didn't even agree with just to keep an argument going. And Dave was a wild card—sometimes when he fought with someone, it was like those dogs that snap at each other for a minute, then a second later are wagging their tails and licking each other's butts. And other times it was ugly and went on and on.

"*Anyway*," Miles stepped in. "Back to our topic. And yes, we are going to use our experience as an example. *If* Riddle had a two-DM rule, and *if* Michael had noticed Hal that night, I presume he would have had the sense to realize that the rule doesn't apply when someone's life is in danger. Because the minute Bill left Hal alone, that ceased to be a 'scene,' and became instead gross negligence."

Maya and Dave were having a conversation with their eyebrows. Gould was staring blankly at the table, which I kind of imagined was what he did when he was fantasizing about chainsawing someone in half. But when no one else spoke, he looked up. "So what's the argument *for* the two-DM rule? Just privacy?"

Maya sniffed and rubbed her nose. "Uhh. Yeah, I think. I'm not sure why there's a debate. Isn't it waaayyy worth the risk of briefly interrupting someone's headspace to make sure someone isn't getting assaulted?"

Miles raised his eyebrows. "A lot of people wouldn't agree. In an intense scene, fucking up your headspace can ruin the whole thing."

Dave shrugged. "Who cares? If you're gonna play in a public place, you've got to be prepared for the possibility of headspace invasion."

Maya nodded. "And in a space where most pairings are male/female, it's better safe than sorry. Which is why I kind of agree with Ryan about rule makers maybe needing to get more involved, but—"

"God," Dave muttered, "have you *seen* Riddle's new entry contract? They couldn't *get* more involved unless the DMs stood there and personally rolled the condoms on you."

"—but I don't agree that banning penetration's the answer," Maya finished.

Miles leaned back. "Probably most boundary disputes don't even involve penetration."

"Why male/female pairings specifically?" Ryan asked Maya.

"Because in general guys have more trouble respecting boundaries than women do."

"Uh, not to sound like a total douche, but: hashtag NotAllMen."

"Dude, don't be that guy." I knew from a bunch of Sounding Board discussions why it was shitty to use "NotAllMen," and I kinda couldn't believe Ryan would go there.

Maya gave him a *you dipshit* look. "I said 'in general.' Finger Bang has been running events for over a year now, and their event committee says they've had zero reports of sexual assault at all-female kink events. In fact, their biggest complaint is that nobody can get any action at the play parties because the women are all politely nibbling snacks in the corner instead of going up to one another and being like, 'Please pound me into next week.'"

Dave whistled. "Sounds like a blast."

Maya laughed. "I've heard it's better than it used to be. But my first play party with them a few months ago, oh my God. Zero playing until, like, an hour in. No fucking until two hours in. There really are differences in the way men and women play. And there really are differences in the way queer people and straight people play."

"Uhhh, no kidding," Dave said.

Maya rubbed her nose again, more vigorously. "But, yeah, that's why I thought it was so great when you suggested hooking the two groups up in the first place. Because the Subs Club is doing an awesome thing, talking about rape and abuse in the kink world. But you're a bunch of guys. And it feels a little like you're taking over an issue that mostly affects women."

Ryan looked right at Maya. "Guys can also be raped. And we understand why this is an important issue. Nobody owns rape."

I elbowed him. "She's just saying we need more perspectives. You felt the same way. You liked our club, but you thought we needed to consider the dom's perspective, or whatever. Because we were all subs."

"True."

Maya stank-eyed Ryan a little. "There've been women's groups talking about these issues for decades, but we don't get as much traction because it's easy for people to dismiss us as hairy-armpitted Feminazis who cry rape every time someone brushes against us in a public space. Like, honestly? It kind of infuriates me how people are willing to listen to you guys when you talk about it."

"Not totally." Gould was almost too quiet to hear. "When we started, we got a lot of backlash."

"That was your review blog," Ryan pointed out.

Dave shook his head. "The review blog was just a springboard that let people express the, uh, like, broader sentiment that we didn't have any right to be complaining about abuse in the first place. Or that we were creating injustices where none existed."

"All right," Maya said. "Genderalizations aside, we should definitely open the two-DM topic up for conversation. I'm happy to kick it off."

"So it would behoove us to find a DM to participate in the discussion," Miles suggested. "And tops as well. We can ask the tops about whether they've ever done a dubious-looking scene in a public play space, and if so, how did spectators and/or DMs react? And we could ask the DM to share stories of scenarios that were tricky to gauge."

I scratched some gunk off the surface of the table. "That sounds awesome possum."

Dave cleared his throat. "Do you think Michael would participate as the DM?"

Michael was the DM who'd been on duty the night Hal had died. Dave almost never talked about him. Dave blamed Bill, he blamed GK and Kel, and he blamed Cinnamon. But he never shit on Michael for not noticing Hal was in trouble, and I could never figure out why. I mean, I wasn't pissed at Michael either, just because I kept thinking how awful it would be to be him. Like, you've got this whole club to keep an eye on, and you're in the wrong place at the wrong time and miss the *one* serious thing that happens all night. Fuuuuck.

Miles looked at Dave. "I don't know how we could ask him the question I just posited without seeming vindictive."

"I'm not being vindictive," Dave insisted. "I just figure he of all DMs has an important story to tell. I mean, when I first heard about DMs, I pictured, like, the Buckingham Palace guards. These people whose only job it was to stand at the periphery of a scene and listen for a safeword and not move even if you kicked them in the nuts. Then I started going to Riddle and realized they were just volunteers who like hanging out and talking to people." He paused. "So maybe Michael tells the Sounding Board about, just, a night in the life of a DM, or whatever. Help us figure out what the challenges would be and how it's possible to fuck up."

"He would get crucified on the Sounding Board," Gould said. "Let's ask Regina."

Dave gave in, kinda grumbly, and then said, "So this segues nicely into our next topic: the kink fair."

Maya perked up. "Working title: Kinkstravaganzapalooza."

Dave high-fived her, then faced the rest of us. "So we're shooting for maybe June of next year to make this thing happen. And Maya and I were trying to think of ways we can address safety as part of the event without it sounding like . . . you know."

"Do we know?" Miles asked.

Maya jumped in. "Like, we don't want to have some trifold board with construction paper letters that's all, 'Step One: Be Aware of Your Surroundings.' We want something fun, but accurate."

Dave nodded. "We talked about putting on skits, but we'd want serious actors. Actors who would move the audience to fucking tears.

Meryl Streep and Daniel Day-Lewis star in *Why Pre-Scene Negotiation Matters*."

Maya nodded too. "Maybe some interpretive dance."

"Or juggling."

"But we couldn't get DDL or Meryl. And we can't dance or juggle." Maya gave a *what can you do?* shrug.

"Soooo, we're back to square one," Dave admitted.

I glanced up from a game Ryan and I were playing where we rubbed the sides of our thighs together under the table. "I could write a song. People would just think it was funny or whatever, a song listing off all these BDSM safety rules. And then at the end one of you could be like, 'But seriously, this shit is real.'"

"I support the safety song." Ryan put an arm around my shoulders.

I put my arm around his shoulders too. "Yeah. This is Team Safety Song right here. We're on this like guac on ribs."

Gould gave a single nod. "Team Safety Song *is* pretty damn adorable."

Dave sighed. "You two are so cute it's gross." He didn't sound like he meant it, though. "I'll bet you do all kinds of weird shit that would totally ruin my impression of you."

I got kinda freaked for a second, like maybe I'd leaned over too far at some point and the guys had seen that I was wearing lady underwear. "We're just doing the regular stuff."

"Yep," Ryan confirmed.

Miles looked all sly-like. "What's 'the regular stuff'?"

I cleared my throat. "Uhhh . . . flogging. Bondage."

"Hand—" Ryan glanced at me "—cuffs."

"—jobs," I said at the same time.

"Handcuffs, handjobs." I nodded. "Lots of hands."

Dave tilted his head and narrowed his eyes. "You guys are into something really weird, aren't you?"

Ryan and I shook our heads.

"Nope," I said innocently. "We're just a normal couple, doing laundry in a legit laundry room and arguing about what to get at Geegs."

Dave frowned. "Jigs?"

"Geegs."

"What the fuck is Geegs?"

"It's what we call Giant Eagle."

"Oh my God, you two are such nerds."

"*Are* we? Or are we masters of adulting?" I leaned forward. "Here's a little herb hack for you. You know the cashier with the orangish-blond hair, Cary? Well, she's super proud of herself for finally figuring out what cilantro is. So when she sees it, she doesn't check the PLU number to see if you got the organic kind or the regular. She just enters the PLU for the regular. So you can get the organic stuff for sixty-nine cents instead of ninety-nine." I turned to Ryan, high-fived him, and sang, "Then you're not eatin' pesticiiiiiiiiiides!"

Dave stared, trying not to laugh. "Herb hacks? Who *are* you?"

We talked a while longer, and then when things were winding down, Dave looked right at Ryan and said, "I'm really glad you made it to a meeting, man."

That made me so incredibly freaking happy.

Ryan grinned. "Me too. I always forget how fun you all are together."

Dave nodded. "We're super fun, and the best of friends. Like the Baby-Sitters Club."

"I had to watch that movie eight hundred times with my little sister when I was younger. Which one of you is Dawn?"

"Is she the blond one?" Dave glanced around the table. "I think we all want to be Dawn."

Maya raised her hand. "I do *not* want to be Dawn."

"Though Stacey's blond too. And she's the smart one, so I guess that's Miles. And Gould's totally the shy one—Mary Anne? So I'm Dawn. And Maya, you're the one who gets added later—Abby?"

Ryan grinned at me. "And Kamen's Claudia. Because he's creative." He ruffled my hair and looked back at the group. "So who's Kristy?"

Dave made a face. "Nobody wants to be Kristy. She's too controlling."

We all stared at him. "You sure you're Dawn?" Gould asked, grinning.

Dave mock-sighed. "I'm *not* controlling. I'm just a born leader."

"It's okay," Maya said. "Kristy is actually an astute and assertive businesswoman who doesn't take shit."

"Well that's me all over. Not the astute and assertive part, but businesswoman, for sure. You should see my collection of professional blouses."

That made me press my legs together for a second. Which was *weird*, because I'd gone my whole life seeing women's clothes or hearing about them without getting boners. Why all of a sudden was a blouse the world's most exciting thing to me?

Maya reached for her glass of water. "Nobody uses the term 'blouse' anymore. Except old people."

Dave ignored her. "Let's all put our hands in and do a one-two-three Subs Club."

We all groaned.

"Come on, come on," Dave urged us. "I feel like we have to. I mean, we don't have a theme song because Kamen promised to write one and never did. So the least we can do is a hands-in."

We all leaned forward and put our hands on top of one another. Then we one-two-three-ed, and everyone yelled something different, from "bacon" to "enema buckets."

It was a pretty beautiful moment.

"Do *you* think Bill should be forgiven?" I asked Ryan later. We were in our room, sitting on the edge of the bed, dicking around on our phones.

He glanced at me. "I don't know him. At all."

"But based on what I've told you?"

Ryan frowned at his screen for a second. "Based on what you've told me, he's a shitty dom. But maybe it's better that they're teaching him how not to be a shitty dom, rather than just letting him serve some time and then releasing him back into the wild."

"If you were counseling him, what kind of stuff would you say to him?"

Ryan had worked briefly as an advocate in San Francisco for doms who'd been accused of overstepping boundaries and, I dunno, needed help processing their guilt or something.

"I'd try to get his perspective on what happened. Find out if he's remorseful. If he blames Hal or himself."

I wanted to know that too. "And if he blames himself, are you supposed to, like, reassure him?"

He went back to his phone. "Not exactly. But we'd talk about how he could move forward and have healthier partnerships in the future."

"But he, like, *killed* someone. By breaking a really basic rule."

He shrugged. "I never had to be an advocate for anyone who'd killed someone. Honestly, you know what the most common scenario was? Doms would come in because their partner had safeworded, and they'd stopped."

"What do you mean?"

He set his phone aside. "I mean they were just really shaken up that they'd been on a different page than their partner. Like, there'd be these guys—mostly, but sometimes women—who'd been topping and having a great time and thinking their partner was having an equally awesome time—and then suddenly the partner safeworded, and they were like, 'Holy shit, how did I not realize she was reaching that point?' or whatever."

I thought about this for a moment. "It would probably be awesome if all sexual partnerships had a magic word that was a polite way of saying, 'Cool it. This isn't going as good as you think.'"

"Have you ever safeworded?" he asked.

"Yeah. When I was twenty. I thought flogging looked cool, because all my friends were doing it. So this guy starts whipping me, and I'm kinda like, 'Okay . . . yeah . . . ow . . . This isn't . . .'" I laughed. "And I kept waiting for it to get better, but it didn't. So finally I just straightened up and was like, 'Nope, nope . . .' And he stopped at the first nope. So I didn't actually have to safeword."

He nodded. "I guess it's just hard for me to imagine all this predator stuff your friends talk about, because it's never happened to me. Like, all these shitty doms you apparently have around here . . . In San Francisco there were one or two I was warned about, but I never felt like there was an abuse epidemic."

"Dude, you worked with shitty doms."

"No. I just told you, I worked with people who made mistakes and were willing to admit it." He yawned, holding the back of his hand over his mouth for a moment. "Whatever. I'm not a great fit for activism. I learned that a long time ago. I've always wanted a relationship more than I've wanted a community."

I climbed up onto my knees on the bed. "That's always kind of how I've been too. I mean, I like going to Riddle and seeing people I know." I flopped on my back, setting my phone on my chest. "But I'm just as happy here with you."

"Well." He stretched out on his stomach beside me. "When I have someone who's willing to do *anything* . . ."

I turned my head toward him. "Do you think we should try more stuff besides panties?"

He bumped his head against my shoulder. "Like what?"

"I'm thinking costumes. In general."

"What kind of costumes?"

"Is there anything you wanna see me in?"

"Like, girl clothes?"

"Any kind of clothes. Uniforms, maybe?"

Ryan was silent for a second, and I was a little freaked that maybe he wasn't into this. But then he said, firmly, "Military."

I grinned. "Yeah?"

He leaned closer to me and whispered. "A suit."

"Huh?"

"You'd look so fucking hot in a suit."

I think maybe I blushed. "You should talk. I get so hot when you dress formal."

He laughed. "I know. We should try, like, dirty-altar-boy stuff too."

"Let's just make a deal to try anything we can think of that doesn't hurt. Except pooping. If you ever poop on me, I'll leave you."

"What about pissing?"

"Ewww!" I pulled my head back to look at him, and my phone slid onto the bed. "Are you into that?"

"Not *into* it. But what if I wanted to?"

"*Do* you want to?"

"Not particularly. But, like, I don't know. Maybe it would be fun."

I thought for a moment. "I guess it's not off the table. I don't even understand how it *works*, though. Like, what's the thrill?"

"Everyone I know who does it, it's like a human-toilet kind of thing."

It took me a few seconds. "Oh, *hell* no! I wouldn't let you do it in my mouth. But my body, I guess it wouldn't be a huge deal."

"But would it turn you on?"

"I don't know." I rubbed his back. "A lot of stuff turns me on. You?"

"I did it once when I first started domming, and it was pretty good."

I pinched him. "Oh, so you've *done* it before, and you were just gonna pretend you'd never really thought about it—"

He jerked away, laughing. "I just haven't really thought about it with *you*."

"Because I'm so pure and innocent?"

He stopped laughing. Gazed at me real seriously. "Because this stuff is totally different for me with someone I love."

I didn't answer right away. I knew from past conversations I was the only guy Ryan had ever been in love with, aside from some boy when he was eighteen that he thought, looking back, probably wasn't really love.

I also knew from Subs Club discussions that it was insulting to say that if you were a dom and really loved someone, you shouldn't want to hurt or humiliate them, even as a game. I agreed with calling bullshit on that, but wasn't it different for everyone? Like, it made total sense to me that it would be easier for some doms to hurt or humiliate partners they didn't love. I remember Kel talking once at the roundtables about lending GK out to other women so she could watch him get topped, because she knew other women would be harder on her husband than she was.

"Different how?"

"I don't want to, like, degrade you."

"Why?" I asked softly.

"Because it's not what you're into."

"How do you know?"

He ran a hand down my chest and lifted the hem of my T-shirt. Put his cold, tiny hand under there and made me jump. "I just assumed. You don't like being punished. And you . . . you really like . . ."

"What do I like?"

"Umm . . . you like to feel good."

"Well, duh."

"I mean mentally, I guess. And I don't think being pissed on would make you feel great about yourself. Right?"

"I guess." I wasn't *surprised*, exactly, that he'd thought about what I liked or needed as a sub. But I was kind of embarrassed to realize I didn't know what he wanted as a dom. So he'd enjoyed punishing and humiliating guys in the past, but he didn't need to do that stuff with me? Then what *did* he want from me? "But everything we do is fun. So I don't think I *would* feel bad about myself. You know? Even if you pissed on me."

He drew circles around my belly button. I had an outie belly button that he always pretended he wasn't creeped out by. I grabbed his hand and tried to make him touch it.

"Ahh!" He attempted to pull back.

"Touch it."

"No."

"Touch the weird belly nub."

"Oh my God . . ." He yanked his hand free of mine and then poked my belly button with one finger. "There. Happy?"

I nodded, grinning.

He drummed my stomach with the flat of his hand. "You're so weird."

We were quiet a minute. I was thinking about what he'd said about what I was into. On one hand, I was sometimes better than my friends at knowing what I wanted. Because I didn't overthink. On the other hand, I saw how deep they were able to go psychologically in their D/s relationships because they *did* think so much, and they *were* articulate about what they wanted. What if I couldn't have that with anybody because I never thought about what submission meant, or how to get better at it?

"I would let you pee on me," I said finally.

He glanced over at me. "Oh, come on. You would not."

"Yes-huh! I said I want to try everything."

"If I volunteered to pee on you right now, you'd freak out."

"Try me."

He stared at me. My heart pounded, and my dick stirred. I wasn't really hot for the idea of watersports so much as I liked the idea of a challenge.

He stared back. "Okay. I'm gonna piss on you, then."

He lay there like he was waiting for me to back down.

"Fine," I said nonchalantly.

"Come *on*. You would so not let me."

I stood. "Where do we do it?"

He laughed like he couldn't fucking believe me. "Uhhh, in the bathtub, I guess. For easy cleaning."

I pulled him up, and we headed into the bathroom. "So I just . . . get in the tub?"

"Yep. And if you don't tell me right now that you're kidding, I'm gonna do it. I'm gonna pee all over you."

"Good." I stripped. "Because that's what I want."

I climbed into the tub.

"Welcome to the Watersports Event of the Year," I said in a semisatanic pro wrestling announcer voice.

Ryan unzipped his fly. "This is gonna be one for the ages."

"What position?" I leaned against the wall and threw an arm up over my head. "Gently reclining? Kneeling?"

"Um, how about kneeling?"

I knelt, facing him. The texturing of the tub floor hurt my knees a little. I grabbed the bar above the soap dish. Opened my mouth to make another joke, then stopped.

Tried to think about submission.

Gould always said submission was about knowing what you could give to your dom. So what could I give to Ryan? Like, was letting him humiliate me enough?

Except I never felt humiliated by him. And even though I liked doing what he said, I didn't look to him as a leader—at least, not all the time. He was my best friend, and I loved him. But he didn't feel like an authority figure. Was that okay?

Miles had said something a while back about how he wasn't really submissive—he was a bottom who liked telling guys how to hurt him. Which made sense for Miles, since he was terrible at relaxing and letting other people handle shit. But I wasn't like that. 'Cause I'd always liked guys telling me what to do at clubs. But then I didn't have to *live* with them. They were just dudes I played games with sometimes.

I made a mental note to ask Miles if I was a real sub or not.

Ryan stepped up to the edge of the tub. "You look like you're concentrating really hard on something."

"I'm trying to feel submissive."

He laughed. "Oh. That's so cute."

"Shut up! Be full of darkness and cruelty."

"Okay. Uh . . ." He took his dick out and aimed it at me. Gave me a look that was actually pretty dark and cruel. "Are you ready for me to own you?"

I got shivers. "Ooh, yeah."

That seemed to give him more confidence. "Are you ready to take all of my piss?"

"Oh my God," I whispered. "That's good. You're good."

"Don't move," he ordered, and I got a little hard.

He started to pee. It hit my chest first, then slid down. It was warm and smelled not so great, and really, I didn't know what I'd been expecting, but it was, like, gross as fuck. "Ew! Okay, no, stop. This is awful. Stop!"

"I can't just—" He stopped for a couple of seconds, but then it started trickling again.

"Quit!"

"I'm trying!" He aimed down so it hit the tub, but it still kept splattering me.

I pressed against the wall, holding my hands out like I was gonna fend off the piss stream. "Ewww! Safeword! Safeword!"

"There's a lot in there, and it really wants to come out. Also, your safeword is not safeword!"

"I can't remember what my safeword is because I'm covered in urine!"

"It's not even on you anymore! I'm angling away."

"I'm still sharing a bathtub with it!"

"Well, stand up or something! Get away from the drain."

I hunched as far from the piss stream as possible until it stopped. "Gro-o-oss," I moaned, knocking my head lightly against the wall.

"Oh my God. You are *such* a baby."

"You *peed* on me."

"Are you actually upset, or are you just being a drama queen?"

I tried not to snicker.

"You little . . ." He leaned forward, laughing. Gave my shoulder a super dainty slap.

"Wash me now," I ordered.

He turned on the water. On cold.

"Owww! Abuse!"

He grabbed my hair and tugged it gently. "You want me to show you abuse?"

I splashed him with pee water, so then he had to strip and get in the tub with me. We stood and pulled up the shower thingie.

The water warmed up, and he rinsed the bottom of the tub before putting the showerhead back. He started lathering me up. I crouched so he could reach.

"Will you be nice to me all night now?" I asked.

"You were the one who told me to piss on you." He rubbed shampoo vigorously into my scalp.

"I know, but now I'm traumatized. Can we order wings?"

He shook his head, clearly trying not to smile. He scrubbed my shoulders with his fingernails. "Yes. We can order wings because I peed on you."

Game. Set. Point. Match.

EIGHT

"His *head*," I repeated for about the seventh time. "It's so big he keeps falling forw— Look at this. Ry. *Look* at this!"

Collingsworth had started walking toward me, his massive head dragging closer and closer to the floor, until finally he basically face-planted on the hardwood and lay there with his legs sticking out, rasping away in a puddle of his own drool.

Ryan, who was making dinner, glanced over. "They should stop breeding bulldogs. And all brachycephalic breeds. It's cruel."

"But then Collingsworth wouldn't *exist*."

"He can't breathe. And he can barely move."

"But he's a freaking dog butler."

"Yes, as long as you go to the fridge yourself, take out a beer, and set it on the floor, then go back to wherever you were sitting, he will bring it to you in his disgusting mouth."

I gasped softly, rubbing Collingsworth's wrinkled head. "Your mouth's not disgusting. No. No, it's not. You're a good boy. They should keep making brachiosaurus breeds so there will be more dogs like you."

"You and he are startlingly similar."

I stood and walked over to him. "Hey. Just because I drool and bring you beer . . ."

"And snore, and would probably make friends with a serial killer if he came into our hou—"

I shut him up by grabbing him and slobbering all over his mouth.

For the next three days, Collingsworth and I chilled together whenever I wasn't at work. We watched TV, ate sandwiches, and went for walks—except we couldn't make it more than like a block before his head weight became too much and he face-planted. Which was fine, because it was freaking hot. I took him over to Miles's house one day to meet Zac, and that kid and that dog were seriously calendar material. Collingsworth even listened to me work on "Snow Wanderer" each day after sandwich time.

I ended up thinking about Hal a lot. Like, where he'd be right now in life, I guess. Would he have a dog? A boyfriend? An apartment that wasn't a total shithole?

Probably not a dog, because he'd sucked at being responsible. He'd spend days crashing on someone's couch for no apparent reason, just saying he "didn't feel like" going home. So a dog, not so much.

And maybe not a new apartment, because whenever anyone had suggested he try living somewhere that wasn't, like, horror movie levels of cockroach-infested, he'd said he loved his place. So, I mean, kinda not making a lot of sense. Loved his place but never felt like going home?

Now I wondered why I hadn't questioned that more. He was one of my best friends. I should have been like, *Dude, what's wrong? Why don't you like going home?*

Sometimes it might have seemed like my friends and I used to be closer, more supportive of one another when we were younger. Because everything was new to all of us back then, and because now we bickered like idiots and assumed we knew better than one another. But actually, for all our dumb spats now, we were way closer than we ever were. We knew each other so freaking well.

I kept that in mind while I worked on "Snow Wanderer." Like, tried to imagine this boy who *didn't* have friends, and how fucked up and lonely that would be. I played what I had for Ryan each night, and honestly, I was proud of how it was going. He really seemed to like it too.

"It's dark," he said. "Weird and dark. You're using awesome images."

He'd been spending a lot of time over the past few days with his laptop and the digital sketchpad for his art program. He got on another kick about Seattle. Then about Austin, because he said the music scene there was perfect for me, and plus it was dog-friendly, so if we got our own dog, we'd be able to take it everywhere. Except now he was thinking we should get a cat instead, because they were less work. I just kinda tried to nod along when he said stuff like that. I really hated to think about moving. I tried to make myself interested in it. But the truth was, moving sounded like the getting-pissed-on of vanilla life.

"What do you think about that?" I asked Collingsworth one morning after Ryan had left for work. "Would *you* ever want to leave this city?"

He just panted and drooled on the floor.

I gave him my toast crusts and stood to get the guitar.

Got restless as soon as I started playing.

So I put the guitar down and practiced kneeling instead. Practiced spreading my legs and pretended I was waiting for Ryan to give me orders. Then I started thinking it was weird to practice *feeling* submissive, so I stood up and cleaned the kitchen and tried to figure out what the fuck was wrong with me. Even at work that evening, I felt weird. Like it suddenly occurred to me how many years I'd been doing the same exact thing at the Green Kitchen: Chop vegetables. Chop meat. Break down displays. Talk to Hannah about where to set up stations. Joke around with everyone—same jokes we'd been making forever.

Why *was* I so content with ordinary shit unless I was with Ryan? That night, when I got up for some midnight Fruit Roll-Ups, I looked across the kitchen and into the front hall at the well-dressed hare painting. Imagined it hanging in a different house, someday. In Seattle or Austin. Or else in a storage unit while Ryan and I went off and, like, Peace Corps-ed or something.

I thought about how my dad had lived in this city his whole life before his separation from Mom, and then he went to Oregon and made a new home. People changed—houses, careers, friends...

Changing from jeans to a dress for a few hours felt amazing. Moving from my little studio into an apartment with Ryan had been awesome. Getting a dog would be the shit. Everything else was hard for me.

"Fuck it," I whispered to the well-dressed hare. "If I have all these things, and they're the things I want, then why do I feel weird?"

The hare didn't answer. Probs because he was never gonna change. He was always gonna be well dressed and smug as fuck about it.

I punched out a piece of Fruit Roll-Up and fed it to Collingsworth. Ate the rest and reached into the box for a new one, but it was empty.

Weird wasn't bad. *Different* wasn't bad. Not always.

I made up my mind that the next opportunity I got to do something totally crazy, something that didn't seem "like me" at all, I was gonna do it. Like if I saw a brochure for skydiving, or that kind of paintball that's based on the Hunger Games, or even for fucking knitting, I was gonna be all over that shit.

"Get ready for the new me," I told the hare. I tried to dramatically spike the Fruit Roll-Up box into the trash can, but it hit the edge and fell on the floor. So I picked it up and put it in nicely, and then Collingsworth and I went back to bed.

"Let's go to Riddle," I said to Ryan Friday night while we were making out on the bed. I only had a halfway boner, which was surprising, since normally I got hard if Ryan so much as fist-bumped me. I figured we could break out any of our costumes and props and get a party raging, but I was in the mood to go out.

He wrinkled his nose. "Now?"

I kissed his disgusted wrinkles. "Yeah."

"Bleh."

"Why? You loved it when we went a few months ago."

"I mean, it was fine. I just don't like clubs much."

"Why?"

"Because they're loud and crowded. And guys don't play with dudes who look like me. Or they assume I'm a sub."

"Aww. Then carry, like, a quiver of crops and canes on your back, and if anyone thinks you're a sub, pull out a crop and beat them."

His phone buzzed on the nightstand. He glanced over at it.

I grabbed his wrists, laughing. "Uh-uh. You love me more than texts. Say you love me more than texts!"

He grinned at me. "It's not a text. It's this real estate alert thing I signed up for."

"Real estate?"

"Yeah, it just lets me know when there's new apartment listings in certain cities."

"Dude." I let go of his wrists. "You do realize we have almost a year before we can go anywhere. *If* we even go anywhere."

"I know." He was still breathing hard from the making out. He arched his back. "Relax. I'm not signing any leases. I just like to look. My dad looks at cars online all the time, and it's not like he buys them."

I still felt a little strange about the whole thing, but I took his wrists again, trying to smile. "So, Riddle?"

"If you really want to go, I'll go."

"We could try the sex sling," I reminded him. "That'd be fun, right?"

Really, I was kinda lonely, which made no sense because I had Ryan and my friends and my coworkers. But sometimes I needed *different* people. People were just . . . I got why they sucked, but they were so fucking awesome too. You had to figure, when you chilled with someone you barely knew, you learned about their life, you both told stories or talked about some TV show or whatever, and you *connected*. And, like, that was fucking *cool* that you could go from being just two people out of seven billion to having changed each other's lives for a hot minute. I kissed Ryan again and humped him a tiny bit.

He gazed up at me, breathing hard. "Will you wear panties?"

"Uhhh, are people gonna see them?"

He squirmed under me. "Uh-huh."

Heat rushed to my dick. "I'll wear panties." I braced my hands on either side of his shoulders and stared down at him. "Which ones?"

"Surprise me."

I got up. He went to the bathroom, and I went to the underwear drawer. Rummaged under all the boxers and briefs and boxer briefs until I got to the panties—a small stack of them, folded neatly. We had quite a collection now.

I decided on a pair of light-pink cotton hipster briefs we'd bought at the mall the other day. I didn't just choose them because they were less conspicuous— Though, okay, maybe I was kinda nervous about openly wearing women's underwear in public. But I liked that they gave me a different feeling than the lace. Lace was sexy. Lace was for when I was a slut, a bitch. Cotton was cute. Cotton was like, *How crazy would it be if Ryan and I went to this dungeon full of torture stuff and just ended up doing kind of a sweet scene?*

One time, I was in Riddle and this woman wanted to watch her husband give me a handjob. He was this straight dude, and he was trying to be all butch about it—you know, like, *Oh I just do it because it's what the wife likes*. But she was so cool and fun that I wanted to help her out. So I sat on the padded table in one of Riddle's playrooms, and this guy started jerking me off. I expected him to be really awkward and terrible at it, but I mean, he was gentle as a fucking *fawn*, if fawns gave handjobs, which—gross. And he wasn't bad looking either, so here was this hot straight dude giving me pretty much the pleasantest hand-j of my pre-Ryan life, and whispering things like, "*That's it. Let go for me. Let me see you come . . .*" like we were lovers.

And my eyes were about bugging out of my head, because I hadn't expected dirty talk, and it wasn't even *dirty* talk anyway, it was sweet talk. He petted my hair and drew patterns on my chest, and she was watching and saying stuff to her husband like, "Be good to him. Make sure he likes it." And she was saying stuff to me like, "Tell him if it's not good enough. Tell him what you want." But it was totally good enough, and I got off *hard*. And he just wiped me up and went back to being that obnoxious type of guy who butts into every conversation and, like, probably Dutch ovens his wife on their anniversary morning. But he also gave me this big hug that made me kinda tingly.

I'm just gonna throw it out there that he probably wasn't that straight, but I didn't care. If he said he was a straight guy who just really liked making his wife feel good by making other guys feel good, I believed him.

My friend Girltoy, who'd been watching, came up to me later and said she'd never seen me do anything that "lovely." Said anytime she saw me in a scene, I was either doing something goofy or else having loud sex.

I guess the whole point of that story was that maybe I wanted to do something a little lovely again.

I pulled on the pink underwear. Arranged my dick so it was tucked down and to the right. Faced our bedroom mirror and then turned to see my ass. The cotton stretched over my ass, just barely covering the whole thing. I could see the shadow of my crack. I glanced down at my front again. The material was thin enough that if I started pre-splooging, you'd be able to see the wet spot, and—

"Have you seen my gold tie?" Ryan called from the bathroom. "With the anchors?"

"I used it to tie the screen door open the other day while I was groceries-ing. So it's probably still out on the deck. I'll get it in a sec."

I hurried up and put my jeans on, so he wouldn't see what underwear I'd picked.

He stepped out of the bathroom wearing a light-blue dress shirt and khakis that were almost just a little too tight over his butt. His hair was combed and the shirt was, like, flawlessly ironed. I immediately wanted to jump him.

"You used my tie for that?"

I was still staring. "Are you dressing like a lawyer for me?"

He smiled, finger-combing his hair. "You said you like me when I'm formal."

I put on my T-shirt. "People are gonna stare at you."

"Mmm." He stepped up behind me and dragged his fingers down my back. I shivered. "Not as bad as they're gonna stare at you when you take your pants off."

I hopped the bullet train to Bonertown.

We kissed again, then drove to Riddle. I debated texting Mom to make sure she wouldn't be there tonight, but since Cobalt wasn't closed yet, I figured I'd take my chances rather than, like, have my mom be aware of my sex plans for the evening.

Regina was at the front desk, and her hair was like a giant volcano—this pointy-ish stack of black with red streaks running down the sides. "Kamen!" She came around to give me a hug. "Long time no see."

"Heeeyyy." I squeezed her and lifted her up for a few seconds.

She stepped back when I put her down, and looked at Ryan. "And I've seen you a couple of times before, but I can't remember . . ."

"MonsterMeg," he said.

"MonsterMeg. Welcome. Are you a member, or . . .?"

"He's my guest." I got out a ten and slapped it on the counter. She gave Ryan the guest contract to fill out and took his photo ID.

She turned back to me while Ryan was initialing. "I heard Dave dropped his membership."

"Oh, uh, yeah. He decided to take a break from the clubs for a while." It wasn't really a lie. I just didn't want to mention that he'd decided to take a break because he hated GK and Kel.

"Well, we miss him."

"Yeah, he's . . . Maybe he'll be back someday."

"I hope so. I love him—he's so funny." She took Ryan's form. "Thanks!"

We walked away from the desk into the lounge. "You go by your Fet name here?" I asked him. I hadn't remembered that.

"Yeah. For public stuff. You don't?"

"Nah. Dave and Miles tried to at first, but now we all go by our real names. It's too weird when people are talking to me and calling me, like, Jocksub36."

He nodded. "I'm still . . . Confidentiality, man. I'm kinda paranoid."

I grinned. "So, MonsterMeg. Where to?"

He nodded at the largest room. "Let's check Chaos."

Chaos was loud—tons of people, and the music was always overkill in here.

I saw Gang Spank in the middle of the room. Gang Spank had started coming to the club a couple of months ago. He was this skinny—I mean supermodel thin—twink kid with dark hair that fell over his eyes and legs that were like rails. He'd find a group of people who wanted to spank him, and then he'd just let them pass him from lap to lap while his ass got redder and redder. And he was like a friggin' *eel*. Sometimes even strong guys couldn't hold him down. He made all these noises I'd thought were fake at first, but he made so many of them that maybe they were a legit expression of what he was feeling.

Dave had seen him one night and had gotten pretty eye-rollish about it, but I think he was jealous. He only played with D now, but I'll bet before that, he would've died for the chance to get gang-spanked.

Tonight, Gang Spank was wearing *tight* briefs, the kind of shamrock green you'd expect from, like, bridesmaids' dresses. And the woman whose lap he was on kept yanking the briefs down and spanking him eight million times super fast and then yanking the briefs up again. Then she'd do it again. And Gang Spank was moaning like he was getting drilled. I could hear him over the music.

We crossed the space and went into Refinement, the second room. It was quieter, but still pretty crowded. So we moved on to Tranquility, the room where Hal had died. BellaSade stood at the door—after Hal, GK and Kel had started stationing DMs at every playroom, instead of just having one or two walk around the club. I said hi to her, but friendliness wasn't really BellaSade's jam, so she just nodded.

The room was empty, so we put up the guard rope and sign. The rule with Tranquility was two scenes at a time, quiet scenes only, and you didn't come in if there were already two couples or groups doing scenes. Dave was always saying how they ought to get rid of the bench Hal died on because it was creepy. But I liked the bench. I think it would have made me feel weirder if they'd just, like, tried to erase all traces of what had happened.

Ryan glanced at the bench and seemed about to say something. He knew how Hal had died, but he hadn't known Hal personally. And he wasn't very involved in the *scene* scene around here, so he didn't care that much about the politics of Bill coming back and all that. Which was kind of nice in a way, because this was the first time I'd been to Riddle in a while where I hadn't had to listen to a rant from one of my friends.

I got to work clipping our sling to a frame that looked like a giant spider.

I took my shirt off. Then, really slowly, facing away from Ryan, I took off my pants.

"*Nice. Choice*," he said behind me.

I stood there for a moment. Let him come up behind me and feel my ass through the cotton panties. "You like?"

He slid his hand around and ran it over the front, stopping to squeeze my balls lightly through the fabric. He stepped even closer, so I could feel his dress pants against my thighs, and his shirt and tie against my back. "I *really* like." He kissed my left shoulder blade, and I relaxed back against him, letting my eyes close.

A moment later, they flew open when a voice said, "Well, someone went to a sale at Forever 21."

We turned. Cinnamon stood in the doorway, staring at my underwear. She wore a brown spandex bodysuit, dark-brown leather harness, and another harness-y thing around her head. Brown high-heeled boots and brown gloves. Her red hair was braided, and when she turned slightly, I could see a long red tail attached to the seat of her unitard.

I glared at her. "You're interrupting us."

She looked at my panties again. "Interrupting what, exactly? A gay *Nanny Diaries* reenactment?" She unclipped the rope and walked in. "I just came to see if the room was free. Looks like there's space for one more scene. So once Stan gets back, he and I will get started."

I glanced around for BellaSade, but didn't see her. What was the point of multiple DMs if they weren't gonna stay put? I turned back to Cinnamon. "Why do you even play in here? Don't horses live outside?"

"Ha-ha."

Ryan, who'd had the misfortune to meet Cinnamon when we came to Riddle a few months ago, joined in. "Yeah, what happens if you have to shit? Do you just do it wherever, like a real pony?"

She arched an eyebrow at him. "I don't know. Better watch where you step." She glanced at the bench. "I'm surprised you can still play in here, Kamen. Isn't it kind of morbid?"

I was so shocked for a second that I couldn't answer. Had she *seriously* just gone there? I thought about pushing her. I wouldn't even have to do it hard—just enough to knock her off-balance in those heels. And then I could pretend to the DM it had been an accident.

"I can play here," I said coldly.

She made a pouty face. "It was sad the other day when you ignored me at the bar. I was going to tell you something important."

"If you have something to say, say it."

She shook her head. "No. Now that I think about it, it's probably none of my business. Or yours." She tapped her foot and sighed, glancing around. "Where's Stan? We've got a lot of practicing to do."

"For what, one of your horse shows?"

"As a matter of fact, yes."

"So what, your rider dude puts all that stuff on you, and then you just walk around the club?"

She gazed at me coolly. "Stan is my handler, not my 'rider dude.' And being in the pony headspace takes lots of effort. What I do here is only a fraction of what I do in the wider pony world."

"You compete with other weirdos?" I didn't think it was cool to make fun of other people's kinks, but in that moment I really wanted to hurt her feelings.

She smiled and slid her gaze down to my panties again. "Takes one to know one." She tossed her braid. "I've got PetPlayFest coming up at the end of the month. I've been best in show two years running now, so I hope the competition's a little stiffer this year. I like to feel challenged."

I snorted. "Trotting around in circles must be tricky."

"There's quite a bit more to it than that." She rubbed her gloved hand against her side. "I compete in grooming, dressage, and cart racing. Dressage takes years of practice for ponies, just as it does for bio horses." She looked me over. "You wouldn't stand a chance."

For some reason, that pissed me off. I'd probably be a great fucking pony. "Pfff. Why would I even want to try?"

"You're right." She glanced at Ryan. "Though, PetPlayFest is open to all types of animals. Your friend here would make a great little lapdog."

Ryan stepped forward, and I actually grabbed his arm to make sure he didn't punch her. "Let me tell you something." His voice was, like, Boots the Monkey gone all Harvey Dent. "We could enter that competition and kick your ass."

"Yeah!" I wasn't actually sure we could, but I was pissed enough to bullshit.

She tucked her lower lip under her upper and laughed. "You seriously think you could compete in PetPlayFest?"

"Why the hell not?" I demanded.

She held up her gloved hands. "All right, all right. That would be hilarious. Please, just for the entertainment value, do it."

"Maybe we *will*," Ryan snapped.

She grinned. "Uh-huh."

"We *definitely* will," I said. Ryan and I looked at each other. Probably neither of us was thinking too clearly. But, like, all I wanted to do was prove Cinnamon wrong.

Cinnamon's mouth fell open in this kind of pretending-she-couldn't-believe-it smile. "Do you guys have *any* experience with pet play?"

"I guess you'll see what kind of experience we have at PetPlayFest." Ryan straightened his tie.

"Yeah," I said. "We're gonna beat you so bad, you're gonna w—"

Stan came in then. He was a wiry bald guy with half-moon glasses, and he was carrying a tarp, a bucket of water, and a sponge. "Hello there," he said to Ryan and me.

None of us spoke for a moment. Then Ryan said, "Hey."

"You being good?" Stan asked Cinnamon.

She just snorted and whinnied.

I raised my eyebrows at her. Tried to convey to her without words just how hard we were gonna destroy her in this PetFest thingie.

Cinnamon stared at me blankly. But as Stan led her to the far side of the room, she turned and smirked at us over her shoulder.

CHAPTER NINE

As soon as Ryan and I got home, we pulled up the PetPlayFest website.

"Holy shit." Ryan stared at the pictures on the home page. Guys in puppy hoods. Women with curly tails like pigs. People pulling carts or carrying riders on their backs. "People really do this stuff?"

"Yeah, man. It's serious."

"I know, but I've never . . . What is *that*?" He pointed at a picture of a woman in black latex with cat ears.

"She's a kitten."

"I get dogs and ponies. Everything else—"

"Oh my God." I leaned back. "You would die if— Okay, first of all, have I told you about Dave's thing with furries?"

"No."

"So, he's super freaked out by furries."

"What's a furry?"

"Like, when people dress up like animals. But it's not like this."

He knelt by the computer chair, looking up at the screen. "What do you mean?"

I tried to remember what Miles had told me. "It's . . . I don't know, dude. I can't remember. But furries are different. No, wait, I remember what it is. Furries want to be animals with human characteristics. But the people who do pet play are pretending to have *animal* characteristics." *Thanks, Miles.* "Anyway, Dave's scared of them for mysterious reasons, and there's this guy who posts on our discussion forum once in a while, named Fucktopus."

"Fucktopus?"

"Yeah. He's an octopus furry. And all he wants is for someone to act out the book *Moby Dick* with him."

Ryan turned to me. "But he's not a whale."

"No. He just wants something *like* that. He wants someone to harpoon him."

"I'll bet he does."

"Like, I just picture this lonely nerd dude in his mom's basement, building robot tentacles."

"He has robot tentacles?"

"Oh, hell yeah, he does. And he just posted the other day about how he found some guy to do ocean role-play with him over the summer, but now the guy's gone and he's lonely again."

Ryan frowned. "This sounds almost too weird."

"Dude, what we do is super weird."

"I know. I shouldn't judge." He looked back at the screen. "But maybe we shouldn't have agreed to this."

"No, we absolutely should have. Can you imagine anything that would shut Cinnamon up faster than us beating her at her own game?"

"Pushing her off a bridge?"

"Yeah, but murder charges. This is the perfect way to show her that all the stuff she's into that she thinks is sooo important is actually so easy anyone can do it."

"What if we can't win?"

I stared at him. "Are you doubting us already?"

He shook his head slowly. "In the moment it seemed like a good idea, but—"

"It *is*. You don't even know all this represents, because you haven't been dealing with Cinnamon for years like my friends and I have. If I put Cinnamon in her place, it'll be like the Eye has fallen, the fire's out on Pride Rock, fuckin' . . . I don't even know, but it'll feel so good."

He kind of smiled at me. "You really want to do this?"

"Dude. She was in that room with Hal."

This expression sometimes happened on his face when I talked about Hal or Bill or the whole incident, like when someone tells you they have cancer and you don't know what to say and you want to seem sympathetic but not like you're being condescending so you just sort of stand there awkwardly and don't say anything. "You're right. We can totally do this."

"Damn right we can. We wanted to try all the different kinks, right? Well, here's a way to kill two birds with one stone."

I'd promised the hare I was gonna try something new. And this fit the bill.

He fist-bumped me. "All right. Let's figure out what this thing is."

We read the overview together. PetPlayFest was held on the last Saturday in September, at a Girl Scout campground outside the city. It was in its third year and open to pets of all types. Last year there had been over seventy entrants. Competitors picked five events, and their combined score from all those events determined their eligibility for best in show.

"Okay, let's look at what competitions there are." I clicked the link. "Oh my God, there's eighty thousand options."

Ryan stood again so he could see the screen better.

"Dude, you want the chair? I can kneel." I stood, and he took the chair. I knelt on his right side and leaned against him. "Cinnamon said she's doing dressage. And the grooming thing."

"But you don't have to compete against her directly." He scrolled. "You just have to pick the events you're most likely to win. So we can skip dressage."

"Oh no. I want to compete against her directly." I paused. "What the hell *is* dressage?"

"It's like a . . . French fancy riding." We looked it up.

"So it's basically horse ballet," Ryan summed up when we were done reading the Wikipedia page.

"I can do it. I'm graceful as fuck." I reached up and grabbed a sticky note and a pen and started writing. "Dressage. Grooming. She said she's doing the cart race, right?"

"Yeah."

"Cart . . . race." I looked up. "So that leaves two more things she's doing that we don't know about. I wonder how we find out."

"Maybe just pick two things you know you'll be good at."

"I'll be good at everything."

He leaned down and slipped his hand into the back of my jeans. Snapped the waistband of my panties. "Cocky."

I wiggled closer to him as I read over the list. "Bobbing for apples! I haven't done that since I was, like, ten. My town had this Halloween at the Farm thing every year, and I was a bobbing for apples maniac."

"Well, sign up for that, then."

"And a balloon pop! Look: 'Pets will be set loose in an arena full of balloons and will have ten minutes to pop as many balloons as possible. Contestants must remain on all fours.' Okay, those are gonna be my last two." I wrote it down.

We looked at pictures from past events. Everyone seemed to be having a lot of fun. There was a picture of a pup with a tennis ball in its leather hood jaws. A cat doing a blindfolded obstacle course. A pony tied up in a stall while its rider dude brushed it.

Ryan scrolled down. "Where are we gonna get all this gear? Look at all the stuff the ponies are wearing."

I rested my chin on his thigh. "Let's go to a horse store."

"A horse store?"

"What are they called where they have horse supplies?"

"Uh . . ."

"Google it. Google 'horse store.'"

He Googled it. "Uh, feed and supply? No, wait. A tack shop."

"We'll go to one of those. Where's the nearest one?"

He checked. "It's, like, thirty minutes away."

"And I'm off work tomorrow."

"This'll be good," he agreed. "We can get a sense of what real horses need, and then we can look online to see how it stacks up with what human ponies use."

"And if we don't get a bagless vacuum, we can use our money for this. Because the entry fee's like a hundred dollars."

"Are you fucking kidding?"

"It said it on the home page. Plus gear."

He placed a hand on the top of my head. I held my breath for a second, leaning on his thigh.

"Love you," I murmured.

"Love you too." He petted my face.

"We only have four weeks. You know what that means?"

He looked down at me, and our eyes met. "It means we need a montage."

I laughed, pressing my face against his pants. I looked up again. "Yeah, we need a fucking montage."

"You know what?" He rubbed my scalp with his fingertips. "I'm not even worried. You'll be an awesome pony."

The weird thing was, I felt like he was right. Because even though it made us sound like a walking motivational poster, honest to God: if he believed I could do something, I could do it.

Except getting pissed on.

But everyone's got their Achilles' heel.

The next day, we drove out to Horseman's Needs, the tack shop. It was a small, white wooden building, and inside it smelled ridick amazing. Like leather and new clothes and Murphy's Oil Soap. The walls were mostly pegboard, and there was all kinds of stuff hanging from them—leather harnesses and colorful ropes and helmets and what have you.

The woman behind the counter had curly hair and kind of a big, flat face, like Collingsworth.

I smiled at her. "Hi, we're here for, just, um, some horse equipment. Do you have, like, the things that go over their heads?"

"Bridles," Ryan supplied.

She narrowed her eyes at us a little. "Yes, we have bridles."

I nodded. "And do you have any really light saddles? Like the kind they use for racing? Our niece is a jockey. I mean, she's getting there. You won't, like, see her in the Kentucky Derby or anything. Yet. But some day, man . . . Triple Axel."

"Crown," Ryan corrected. "Triple Crown."

"Trip-le Crowwwnnn," I agreed.

The cashier wiped her hands on her pants. "We don't have racing saddles."

"Let's just look around," Ryan suggested.

We wandered for a while. I found gloves with little bumps all over the palms. "Hey, what are these for?" I called to the cashier, holding them up.

She gave me that narrow-eyed look again. "Those are pebble-grip gloves. They help you grip the reins."

"Cool." I nodded and put them back. Wandered over to some bottles of liniment gel. I opened one and smelled it. It smelled like Icy Hot. "Ry, c'mere."

He came over. "What's that?"

"Smell." I offered it to him. "It's like Icy Hot." I sniffed it again. "I didn't know they put that on horses."

"Well, their legs probably get sore."

"You know one time Dave let D put Vicks VapoRub up his ass?"

Ryan glanced over at the cashier.

"Oops." I lowered my voice. "But, seriously, he did."

"Do you and your friends talk about the sex stuff you do?"

"Duh. Remember when Dave was, like, interrogating us about what we were into?"

"I thought that was a joke. That's kind of weird."

"You're kind of weird." *Was* it kind of weird?

"So you're gonna tell them you're doing pony play?"

"Uh, yeah, if it goes well." Except maybe not Dave, because furries.

I put the liniment gel back, and we headed into the back room, away from the cashier.

Ryan went over to a giant metal, like, arrow quiver or something. "Ooh, look. Here are the whips."

"Ryaaannn," I whispered, propping my arm on his shoulder. "You're not gonna whip me, right?"

"The whips are to give cues. You don't really whip a horse unless you're a dick. Aw, look." He picked up a crop that had a leather thingy on the end shaped like a little hand. He pointed it at me. "Bend over. I need to test it."

I glanced around to see where the cashier was. Looked back at him. "Don't hit me with the tiny hand! I already have to deal with that all the time with your tiny doll ha— Ow!" I backed away, laughing, as he started smacking any part of me he could reach with the crop.

"My tiny what?"

I squeaked, putting my arms up to shield myself. "Abuse!"

"My tiny what?" He smacked the top of my thigh. It didn't hurt at all through the denim, but I made a dying dinosaur noise and pulled my hips back, trying to get away.

"Doll hands. Your t— Stop! I'm just being real!" I was laughing so hard that it startled the crap out of me when I backed into a row of leather strappy things hanging on the wall. I turned to look.

Bridles.

Ryan stopped assaulting me and stared too. He set the crop down, and we looked through the bridles together.

"This is nice." I touched a black one. It was so . . . new. The straps were smooth and stiff and shiny. "But it wouldn't fit on a human, right? Pony people need ones designed for human heads?"

"Probably," Ryan agreed.

I checked the price tag. "Holy shiboles." I showed him.

"Oh my God. I hope human ones are cheaper."

"Are you finding everything you need?" asked a voice behind us.

We both turned to face the cashier.

"Yeah," I said. "We're good. Do you have anything more moderately priced? Bridle-wise, I mean?"

She nodded toward the end of the line. "Cheapest bridles are down there."

Even the cheapest bridles were kinda pricey. We moved on to saddles. Ryan picked up the smallest one and made me bend forward. He tried to sling it over my back, but it slid off. "I mean, how would we even get this to stay on you?"

"Yeah, it's too bulky. We might need one for miniature horses. But I'm doing the cart race, remember? I'm gonna be a driving pony, not a riding pony." We'd spent last night reading up on the different types of ponies. We'd also found a website with information for pony newcomers, and it had like a horse character sheet you filled out. So we were gonna do that tonight.

We put the saddle back and found a third room full of brushes.

"Hell yes. Look at this." I held up a red rubber mitt with little spikes on it. "You tell me horse riding isn't already kinky as fuck."

Ryan put his palm against the rubber spikes, making them flex. "I'll bet that feels really good. For horses."

"Are you gonna groom me?"

"Well, we are in the grooming competition. So, I mean, yeah. I guess I have to, like, brush you all over and braid your hair with ribbons and shit."

"Okay, get this thing." I threw the mitt against his chest. It fell to the floor.

"Jerk." He reached down to get it.

I grinned and picked up a brush. The bristles were stiff and left little red lines when I ran it down my arm. I got a strange feeling then, but I wasn't sure what it was.

I dragged the brush down my arm again.

If we did this pony stuff right, Ryan was gonna be touching me a lot. I know, *duh*, and he already touched me a lot anyway. But he'd do the kind of stuff that everyone knows feels really good, but you never hear anyone talk about. Like, it was amazing as fuck if someone else brushed your hair or washed you or whatever. Or if they petted you and it wasn't the kind of petting where they were just foreplaying their way to your dick. But sometimes it was tough to ask for that, because once shit got all hot and heavy, then you were just like, *Okay, yep, never mind petting, let's do the dick grabbing.*

And I loved sex. Seriously loved it. But I was also a total slut for just—touching. Backrubs, holding hands, all that shit. And the idea of being tied up while Ryan brushed me, like in those pictures, was doing a lot for me at the moment.

"Feel this one." He held out a brush with white bristles. I extended my arm and let him use it on me. It was like the feathers of a goddamn downy baby eagle.

"Oh my God."

"Yeah?"

"Here." I took the brush from him and did his arm.

"That's amazing."

"I know." I brushed him again.

He gazed at me for a long moment. "What?"

"What's what?"

"You have a weird look on your face."

"Nothing. I'm just excited for this."

He took the brush. "We're really doing this?"

"Unless you're chickening out."

"Chickening out of victory? When have I ever?"

I grinned. This *was* gonna be a victory. And I was gonna show my friends that even though I wasn't around as much for meetings, I was still totally loyal to the Subs Club. I was prepared to do us the ultimate service: defeat our arch-fucking-nemesis. "We could get some brushes here. Right? And then just shop online for the other stuff?"

"Let's do it."

We took the rubber mitt, a currycomb, a stiff bristle brush, and a soft brush up to the checkout. Plus a riding whip Ryan had found that was long and straight and black, with a silver cap on the handle, and a tiny, thin lash about two inches long.

The cashier rang us up without a word.

I nodded at her. "I think for now our niece is just going to groom her horse. And maybe whip it, but only to give cues."

She didn't answer. Handed our bag to us with a flat stare. "Have a good day."

I was pretty fucking sure we would.

We ended up going home and shopping for human-pony stuff online. We used Ryan's laptop this time so we could sit on the couch. We found a website that was really helpful in terms of telling us about pony gear. But there was so *much* gear, and we had no idea what we actually needed.

"Bridle." Ryan made a note. "Definitely. And I guess just a regular bit? We don't need the kind that, like, pushes your tongue down, right?"

"Why would we need that?"

"It's for bad ponies."

"I'm not a bad pony!" I rested my chin on his shoulder and stared at the screen.

"Aww." He leaned his head against mine. "Are you the best pony?"

"Yeah." I yawned and made *nyop nyop nyop* sounds afterward. Settled my chin back on his shoulder. I turned my head slightly and stuck my tongue up and to the side until it touched his earlobe.

He laughed and swatted me away. "Pay attention. Here's the form we have to fill out about your pony persona. See?"

Breed. Name. Age. Height. Weight. Coloring. Distinguishing marks. Temperament. Past owners. Cart pony or riding pony? It went on.

"So what kind of horse are you?" Ryan asked.

"A Friesian," I said immediately. D loved Friesians, and D was one of the coolest guys I'd ever met. He'd shown me some pictures, and Friesians really were literally the most beautiful horses ever.

"A what?"

"A Friesian. It's a giant black warhorse. Here." I took over the laptop and Googled Friesians. Pulled up a picture of a huge black horse with a long, wavy mane and tail.

"Pretty sure my sister had that exact perm in high school." Ryan cocked his head. "That's a gorgeous animal."

"Right? Now imagine I'm that."

He looked at me. "If you were a horse, you would totally be that."

"I know. Look at that *tail.* People spend, like, hours putting conditioner on that shit, D said."

He went back to the form and typed in Friesian. "And what's your name?"

I thought for a moment. "It needs to be something really powerful. Like Thor."

He made a face.

"You don't like Thor? What about, like, Storm . . . Trooper? Fire Hawk? Lightning Cloud King Flame-Wreath?"

"That's a little long."

"Thunder Canyon."

"Isn't that a ride at Cedar Point?"

I nodded. "It is. The *best* ride. I want my name to be Thunder Canyon."

"Are you serious?"

"Yes."

"Thunder Canyon the Friesian." He filled it in. "How old are you?"

"Um, how long do horses live?"

"Like, thirty years or something."

"Can I be seven?"

"Sure." Ryan typed it into the form. "Aaaand . . . sex?"

"Yes, please."

"Don't be an idiot. What's your sex?"

"Man horse."

"That's not a choice. Stallion, gelding, mare, colt, filly."

I looked at the choices. "What the hell is 'gelding'?"

"It means you're a boy horse with your balls cut off."

"Hell no! I'm a stallion."

We went through my temperament and training. I was playful and friendly. I listened most of the time. I knew how to walk, trot, canter, and gallop on cue.

"What are your preferred treats?" Ryan glanced at me.

"Wings."

"Horses can't eat wings. That's sick." He looked at the screen again. "The examples are carrots, apple slices, peppermints, sugar cubes, and oats."

"What about . . . wings?"

"Still not an option."

"Jolly Ranchers?"

"I think Jolly Ranchers would work." He filled it in.

Eventually we moved on to the list of beginner pony gear. We found a fetish shop that sold bridles. Very expensive bridles.

"Ooh, I want the feathery thing on top!"

Ryan looked at me. "You want a plume?"

"Yeah. I gotta stand out, right?"

"Hell yeah."

I pointed at another bridle. "I like that gold bit. And what are those things?"

Ryan enlarged the picture of the bridle. "Blinkers. They keep the horse focused on what's straight in front of him."

"Let's get that blinkers one, with the gold bit."

"It doesn't have a plume."

"We can make a feathery thing to put on top. It'll be cheaper that way."

"That shouldn't be too hard to rig." Ryan put the bridle in the cart, and I got a thrill in the pit of my stomach. I was gonna wear that fucker. On my *face*.

We found a harness that said it was good for beginning ponies. A lead rope. Some hoof gloves. An information page that explained the difference between riding ponies and cart ponies.

"I'm not gonna be naked at this show thingy," I said, gazing warily at the photos of naked ponies. "Okay? Can I be one of the ponies that wears black clothes under the harness?"

"Sure. Except you've got a really good chest. I'd vote for shirtless."

It was a fair point. My chest was fucking amazing. Plus abs. "But Friesians are all black," I pointed out.

"All right." He paused. "*Tight* black T-shirt, then."

"Done." I clicked on another link. "Look at *this shit*." This page had rows and rows of hoods. Some had ears and noses; some were like leather gas masks. "These are demonic." I clicked on a full leather horse head with terrifying eyeholes.

"Ewwww!" Ryan grabbed for the computer. "Get rid of it!" He clicked back to harnesses, then breathed a sigh of relief. "Just use your regular face for this, okay?"

"Agreed."

"Do we need riding reins or long reins?"

"Long reins, right? Because we're doing carts."

"Shit, we're up to three hundred and thirty dollars already."

"Oh, fuck."

"And we don't even have a cart yet."

I looked at him. "What do we do?"

"I think I can get us a cart, actually. If you don't mind waiting a week or so."

"Dude, the less time we have, the sweeter the montage."

"Ooh, here's a really nice black tail. Do you want the butt plug tail? Or the one that attaches to a harness?"

I stared at him. "The tail goes up my butt?"

"It can."

"Shit just got real." I turned back to the screen. "Get me the butt plug one."

"You sure?"

"I don't want some wussy harness tail. Mine's gonna be up my ass."

He added it. "Oookay, and we already have a whip, so—"

"No! I don't wanna be whipped." I slung my arm around his throat and pretended to choke him.

He played along, making strangled noises for a moment, before batting my arm away. "Look what the pony play site says on this subject: 'For dressage, the whip is a vital cuing device. It is not used to hit or punish the pony. It takes the place of leg cues.' See, if we're doing this dressage thing, we need a whip." He paused. "What do they mean, takes the place of leg cues?"

"I dunno."

We looked it up and found a video of a ponygirl doing dressage. The human wasn't riding the pony—she stood on the ground holding long reins and was using a thin, straight whip, like the one we'd bought, to tap different parts of the pony's body. She never hit the pony—like, almost everything she did with the whip was so light and quick you'd miss it if you blinked.

"So wait, do I have to prance like that?" I asked. The ponygirl was, like, seriously lifting her legs up. And doing some crazy sideways movements.

"Uh, yeah. Look at the video description. Dressage is the highest form of horse training. It balances obedience, flexibility, and elegance."

"How does that equal prancing?"

"Haven't you ever seen the horse stuff at the Olympics? The dressage horses have to do all kinds of prancy stuff. They, like, jog in place." He stood. "Like this." He jogged in slo-mo, lifting his legs high without actually moving forward.

I raised my eyebrows. "Maybe you want to be the pony?"

"Hell no. This is all you." He sat again.

"I want a mane. So everyone knows I'm a Friesian."

He thought for a moment. "I might have an idea."

I rested my head on his shoulder. "What?"

"I was Slash from Guns N' Roses for Halloween a few years ago. I think I still have the wig."

I stared at him. "*You* went as Slash?"

"Why not?"

"Hey, rock on."

Slowly, things began to take shape. We ordered the gear and promised we wouldn't worry about the price. And over the next few days, while we waited for the stuff to arrive, I watched videos. Not just pony play videos, but real horse videos too. Man, people did some weird shit with horses. Like, what was the point of making a horse run around you in circles? And what the crap was "posting"?

The human ponies were hilarious. Some of them wore the demon hoods, and some had fancy bridles or latex suits or crazy boots designed to make their legs look like horse legs with hooves on the end. But some just had black clothes and bit gags with reins attached. Nothing fancy. I watched a lot of dressage videos and studied the prancing. I wrote down the names of different gaits and transitions. Walk, trot, canter, gallop. Halt, back up. Dressage: half pass. Full pass. A bunch of French words I couldn't pronounce. I read about what horses liked to eat, and how they communicated with their ears and tails and stuff.

One night I made the mistake of clicking on a link about burdizzo clamps. "Ryaaaaannnn!" I called.

He emerged from the bedroom. "Yeah?"

"Sometimes pony players have pretend vet examinations and sometimes they use these clamps that get used on real horses to crush their balls and make them fall off, except they don't actually crush the human ponies' balls, but they pretend to with the burrito clamps and it's horrifying."

He didn't quite catch all that, so he came to read over my shoulder. He made some faces as he read. "Those are not called burrito clamps."

"Bur-donka-donka whatever clamps. I don't care."

"So are you saying you want to get fake gelded?"

"*No*. I am saying that if you ever even think about gelding Thunder Canyon, he will trample you."

Ryan put an arm around me. "I vow to keep my pony intact."

"Forever," I said.

"Forever," he agreed.

Later, when he was locked away in the bedroom again with his drawing program, I was looking online for more pony play info.

That's when I found the Pegasus Sheath.

A seven-inch sheath shaped like a horse penis, which could be worn with or without an erection. The idea that Thunder Canyon wouldn't have one was unfathomable to me. Plus it was on sale. Plus it was black, so it matched Friesians.

I glanced at the bedroom door. How freaking surprised would Ryan be? I put it in my cart and ordered it, and then spent the next fifteen minutes repeating the words "Pegasus Sheath" in my head and snickering.

CHAPTER TEN

Dave assembled Miles and me at the duplex for a top-secret meeting on Tuesday while Gould was at work. "I wanted to talk to you about Gould's birthday, which is now two weeks and six days away."

Shit. I'd forgotten. And from the expression on Dave's face, he knew I'd forgotten.

"He doesn't want anything big," Dave went on. "But I was thinking maybe we could throw him just a medium-sized turning-thirty party."

Miles narrowed his eyes. "But he's not turning thirty."

"I know. But he's been getting a lot of crap from his parents lately about how if he's not married by thirty, his ancestors are gonna start, like, rotating in their graves like rotisserie chickens, and I think it's getting to him."

"Do they know he's gay?" I asked.

"He's not. He's bi or queer or whatever he's going by now. And I don't think they care if he marries a man or a woman, they just want him married."

Miles sighed. "He should know better than to listen to that nonsense."

Dave shook his head. "It's not that easy, dude. My mom tells me about all her friends who are becoming grandmas, and it, like, makes me want to instantly have a baby just so she won't stop loving me. Anyway, he thinks his thirtieth birthday is gonna be completely miserable because his family's gonna be judging him. So I thought we could throw him a really fun thirtieth two years in advance, without his relatives around, to counteract the real thing."

"That sounds awesome," I said.

"What if he *is* married by thirty?" Miles asked.

"Then you can never have too many pleasant thirtieth birthday parties." Dave slid a card across the table to us. "I got this for us to sign."

The card was for a special bar mitzvah boy.

Miles frowned at it. "Classy."

"I know, right? He gets me 'For the world's best grandma' cards every year, so this is only fair."

Miles signed the card, then passed it to me. "Drix and I can make a cake." He took out his phone. "I'll let him know."

I looked up from the card. "I can sing him a Marilyn Monroe happy birthday."

"Cool." Dave nodded. "I haven't decided on the exact theme, but I figure we'll go to dinner somewhere that serves gluten-free beer. And obviously, everyone's welcome. Partners, friends. Friends of partners." He looked at me and grinned. "Even Ryan, if he can behave himself."

That kinda gut-punched me, but by the time I even got my thoughts together, Dave was talking again.

"We're gonna plan the greatest non-thirtieth birthday ever for one Mr. R . . ." He stopped. Squinted. "Oh my God. What is Gould's first name? Robert or Roger?"

I hesitated. I'd never called him anything but Gould. And yeah, pretty sure some drunken night years ago I'd asked him what his full name was, but hell if I could remember. "Uh . . ."

Dave's mouth hung kinda open. "This is ridiculous. He's our best friend. His name is on my lease. I *know* what it is. I'm just having this epic brain fart."

Miles raised his eyebrows and continued typing on his phone. "They say your memory begins to deteriorate after age twenty-five."

Dave waved at him, frustrated. "Miles, you have a beautiful mind. Is it Robert or Roger?"

"I think it's Robert, but I'm not sure. He was introduced to me as Gould. Even Hal called him that. Who's his mail addressed to?"

"Mr. R. Gould."

Dave glanced at each of us. "Seriously, nobody knows his first name? And we've been friends with him for how long?"

"Forty-seven years." I tried to draw a nice heart next to my message on the card, but it looked like a butt.

"Nobody has been friends with him for forty-seven years."

"If you count past lives."

"Nothing you're saying is real."

"I think it's Robert," Miles said.

Dave sighed, drumming the table. "It's either Robert or Roger. How can his last name be so Jewish when his first name is so something you would name your cat to be ironic?"

"What about his parents?" Miles tried. "We've definitely heard them say his name. Right?"

Dave shrugged. "I don't know. His mom used to take us shopping at Kohl's and be like—" he put on a British accent "—'Robert, do you need any drink-specific glassware?' Or maybe it was 'Roger.'"

I slid the card back to him. "Dude, his parents aren't British."

"I know. A lot of people are British in my mind, though. Like Miles."

Miles rolled his eyes.

"I'm gonna call him." Dave took out his phone and dialed. I could hear the ringing on the other end, and then, faintly, Gould's hello.

Dave leaned forward, elbows on the table. "Hi, R. Gould?" he said, in a fake polite tone. "It's your friend David. Yes, David Holbrook. I live with you." He listened for a moment. "It's okay—I'm told I'm not very memorable." Another pause. "What am I wearing?" He glanced down. "Uhhh . . . your clothes. I dress in your clothes while you're gone and have tea parties with myself, pretending to be you."

He listened some more. "Wonderful. Anyway, I wondered if you could solve a dilemma we're having. And please don't think I'm a bad friend. But what the fuck is your first name?"

A pause. "Is it Robert? Or Roger?"

Another pause.

"Miles and Kamen don't know either."

I couldn't quite make out what Gould was saying, but I could tell he was laughing.

Dave slumped. "Pleeeaaaase just tell us?" He made a face at Miles and me as he listened. "Rathbone? That is *not* a real name."

He placed a hand over the mouthpiece and whispered, "He's being difficult." Into the phone, he said, "It's Robert, seriously? See, now I can't tell whether you're screwing with me, or . . . I see. Well, I can't wait until you come home and hold me until deep in the night."

He laughed at whatever Gould said next.

"Gould! I don't even— What does that even *mean*?" His jaw dropped. "Oh dear God. Is that seriously a thing people do? Okay. Then yes. You can do that to me when you get home."

Dave hung up slowly. Glanced at Miles and me. "He pretends he's all innocent, but he's the craziest mofo of us all. Anyway, he says Robert, but he may be fucking with us, since he seems to think it's highly amusing that we don't know."

I remembered something all of a sudden. "It's Robert."

Dave smoothed a hand over his hair. "You're sure?"

"I saw it on a document."

It had been on Gould's hospital release form, which I'd seen when I picked him up. I remembered watching Gould sign it and thinking his wrist looked weirdly skinny. His face too. He'd been so worried about being overweight for as long as I'd known him that it was surprising to realize he must've lost a lot really fast. I remembered thinking I should hug him, but not doing it because . . . I don't know. He seemed delicate. Like he'd fall apart if anyone touched him. And I was pissed at him, a little, I guess. Which wasn't fair, but I was.

"Ah well," Dave said after a moment. "I guess it doesn't matter much. We're just gonna call him Gould forever." He paused. "But it's nice to know."

That night while Ryan was in the shower, I looked online for any local pony info or events in the area besides PetPlayFest. It would be really cool to get to watch some other people do pony play before I had to do it. But all I found was some pony munch thing through a Fet group, and it turned out to be a couple of hours away.

Since I was on Fet for the first time in months, I stalked my friends to see what they were up to. Gould had joined some poly group, so hey. Dave had nothing new in his feed. D had put up some quote about the power of silence. Miles had written some wall post about true love that was full of fancy words. Maya had recently commented in, like, eighteen discussion groups.

And Ricky . . .

Ricky's profile said he was in a relationship, which had been the case last time I'd checked a few months ago. Except now his status read: *Belongs to: SayImADreamer.*

It took me a sec to register. 'Cause I'd heard that username before, but I couldn't think where. And then a memory came to me of the Subs Club's earliest days. Gould telling us that Bill Henson was back on Fetmatch under a new name.

"No pictures of his face, no mention of who he is. He's SayImADreamer. I thought people should know."

I stared at the status for a while longer.

"What the fuck?" I whispered. Then I said it aloud to Collingsworth, who was snoring in a corner of the room.

I grabbed my phone and called Dave. It rang a bunch, and I started to worry Dave was at work. But he finally picked up. "Hey, buddy."

"I think Ricky's playing with Bill."

"What?" It was a "what" like he hadn't heard me, or hadn't processed what I'd said.

"Get on Fet. It says he's in a relationship with SayImADreamer."

"Did you say Ricky's playing with Bill?"

"Yes."

"That's ridiculous."

"Look," I insisted.

I listened to the click of the keyboard. Eventually Dave came back on. "It's on Bill's profile too. It says Ricky *belongs* to him." His voice was kind of . . . annoyed, almost, which was not what I'd expected. I'd expected him to go apeshit. Or maybe, like, cry or something.

I scrolled up and down through Ricky's profile, like maybe his status would change if I kept doing that. "So this is why he didn't want to tell us who he was seeing."

Dave was quiet for a few seconds. "I'm going to hang up with you and call him."

"Hold on. We can't just jump on him about this."

"Why the *hell* would he do this?" he snapped. "He knows what Bill did. He *knows* Bill's not safe!"

"I don't know."

"Last year he was all, 'Oh I'm so scared I'll die if I do BDSM, and now he's fucking *playing with Bill*?"

"We should definitely talk to him. But we need, like . . . finesse."

"Bullshit. I'm calling him."

"*No*," I said firmly. "You're not his dad. You can't forbid him to date someone you don't like. Think first. Isn't that what you and D are working on? Thinking first?"

All I heard for a moment was Dave's breathing. Then: "Could you talk to him?"

Whuuut? "Me?"

"I'm overbearing. But you're very innocuous, and he loves you."

"I don't . . . Dave, I seriously don't know if this is any of our business."

"What are you *talking* about?" he asked coldly.

I heard the shower turn off, and I took the phone into the front hall. "Ricky's an adult. And like you said, he *knows* the risks."

"Clearly he doesn't."

"He told you he was seeing someone almost a year ago. We gotta assume that's Bill, right? So he's survived this long."

Except what if Bill was abusing him or something, and Ricky was afraid to leave?

The thought freaked me out, but at the same time, I didn't actually believe it. Which was maybe stupid, since I knew how dangerous Bill could be, but I'd always been, I think, more willing than the others to consider the possibility that Bill had made one huge mistake and learned from it.

Obviously, killing someone was way too huge a thing to be called a mistake. And yeah, I'd seen Bill around Riddle before the night he played with Hal, and I thought he was arrogant and, like, sloppy. But I'd known other people who'd played with him and liked him.

"I cannot believe," Dave said slowly, "that you think there's anything remotely okay about this."

"I didn't say *I* approve. But it is Ricky's choice. Not ours."

"Kamen." He sounded scary. "I don't care if you're in a new relationship, if you're busy with other shit—whatever. You can't just abandon your obligations to the group."

"Since when are my friendships obligations?"

"Responsibilities, whatever you want to call them. Because we *do* have responsibilities to one another. And you can't just bail."

"Bail on what? Who am I responsible for? Ricky? He and I aren't even that close." I paused for a second as it dawned on me. "You mean to you. You mean I have a responsibility to do what you want, and help *you* make things the way you think they should be."

"Where the hell did you get that? Ricky's our *friend*."

"So's Ryan!" It just burst the fuck out of me.

Silence. "What does that have to do with anything?"

"It has to do with—with you thinking I have a responsibility to look out for people in our group, but you don't think *you* have any responsibility to care about Ryan."

"Whoa, dude. Can we get back on topic?"

"No. You *know* this is on topic, at least sort of. You liked Ryan when you met him. You were fine when I started hooking up with him. And then I don't know what happened, but you and everyone else turned against him, and—"

"Oh my God, so now this is a conspiracy?"

"Sometimes it feels like one! I see the way you look at him, and the way you look at me when I'm with him, and you don't like him. It's *not* in my head."

"Buddy, I can't make myself care about Ryan as much as I care about you, or Miles, or Gould, or even Ricky. Okay? I can't flip a switch and make myself feel something that isn't there."

He actually said that the quietest and gentlest of all the things he'd said so far. But it hurt way worse than anything else.

Why, though? Why would you even need to flip a switch? Why wouldn't you just care about him because he's important to me?

He sighed. "Look. If you don't want to talk to Ricky, I'll do it myself."

But before I could figure out how to reply, he'd hung up.

I spent the next few days anxious, wondering if I was wrong about Ricky. Maybe we *did* need to stop him from doing stuff with Bill. I just didn't understand how we hadn't found out before now. Gossip traveled fast in our community. Especially among the gay guys.

Then around Thursday, it hit me: Cinnamon. That was probably the fucking secret she'd wanted to tell me. And Mom, at the housewarming party, asking about Ricky. Saying, *"He seems very happy,"* but in that pleading voice.

What the hell? Why hadn't she just *told* me?

Because it's not your business. Seriously, dude, it's not.

By Friday, I'd made the decision to put it out of my head. I needed to focus on my pony studies. Ryan and I had been reading up on the rules for the dressage competition, and there was a lot to figure out. We had to choreograph a dressage routine set to music, and it had to incorporate certain movements, gaits, and transitions. We had just over three weeks until PetPlayFest, and I'd never even worn a bridle.

Saturday morning, the first wave of pony stuff arrived. Ryan and I tore that shit open like it was Christmas.

"Awww, yes." I pulled out a jumble of leather. It smelled fantastic.

"Are you huffing the reins?"

"Kinda." I took another sniff and passed the reins to him. Then I ripped open the plastic bag containing the bridle, and the one containing the hooves.

The hooves were pretty stiff, but they were padded around the wrists. I held them up. "Can I try this stuff on?"

"Does it look like I'm stopping you?" He picked up the bridle. It had the bit attached with clips to the cheek pieces—I'd been studying my Parts of the Bridle diagram—but the blinkers were in a separate packet.

I eyed the bit, with its rubber coated mouthpiece and bright gold rings. It looked different than it had on the website. Bigger, kind of. "I just have to put that in my mouth?"

"Uh-huh." He looked at me. "You ready?"

I nodded, nervous and excited.

He held the straps in one hand, bit in the other, and guided the bit into my mouth. My dick got sort of hard as he tightened the cheek straps, pulling the bit back until it stretched the corners of my mouth.

"Owmugerhh, thiff ithff weey-uvd."

He laughed, tugging a strap. "What's that?"

"*Wyy-unhhh.*"

"Sorry, you're just a little garbled . . ."

I rolled my eyes at him. He unsnapped the bit from the cheek pieces and eased it out of my mouth. The leather straps dangled from the sides of my face. "I said it's weird." I wiped my mouth. "How am I supposed to not drool all over myself?"

"Suck it back in, I guess." He set the bit aside. "We can leave that off until everything else is in place."

I held out my hands. "Put on my hooves."

Collingsworth was watching us suspiciously from the corner, his head nearly touching the ground.

Ryan put the hoof mitts on my hands. I concentrated on the smell of leather, the warmth of his hands on my wrists as he fastened the straps. I was getting, like, floaty just from the brush of his knuckles on my arm as he buckled me in.

"Nice," he said quietly.

I flexed my hands inside the mitts. Put them on the floor. Craaazzyyy. I couldn't pick stuff up or scratch my face or anything.

"How's it feel?" he asked.

"Um, good. Kind of ridiculous, but I like it."

"Harness next. Want to take your shirt off?"

"Do *you* want me to take my shirt off?"

"Every minute of every day."

I tried, but I'd already forgotten about the hooves. "Can't."

I held still as he eased my shirt up and pulled it over my head and then over my hooves. As soon as it was off, I felt cold, which made no sense, because the apartment wasn't cold at all. He ran his fingertips down my side, and I realized I wasn't cold, exactly—more like extra sensitive. Like just the feeling of the straps on my head and not being able to use my hands was making all my other senses overactive.

He grinned. "You wouldn't be able to do anything if I called upon Gay-Skull and launched a tickle offensive."

I jerked my arms close to my side, knocking his hand away. "Don't you dare."

He laughed. "What would you do?"

"Use my pony power to subdue you."

He stroked my shoulder, but it didn't feel like the prelude to a tickle offensive. It was really gentle, and I closed my eyes for a few seconds. Flexed my hands inside the hooves again.

You won't be able to do anything. Once you're hooked to a cart and your hands are tied behind your back and you have a bit in your mouth, he can touch you however he wants, lead you wherever he wants, and there's nothing you can do.

That kinda hit me all at once, and I started breathing faster.

He stroked all the way down my back, almost to my ass. Made a circle with one finger around the small of my back, then traced up again. I arched like I was trying to follow his hand.

I sat there on my heels while he sorted out the harness. He put it over my shoulders and around my waist and adjusted the straps. My dick got harder each time he touched me. "I'm gonna be the worst horse," I whispered.

"Why's that?"

"Because I'm getting a boner and all you're doing is putting my tack on."

He laughed. "You have the strongest reactions to *wearing* things. How do you get dressed in the morning?"

I grinned. "I think it's only when I'm wearing things I'm not supposed to be wearing." I rubbed my nose with the back of my hoof. "Seriously, what if I go to this show and I have to prance around with an erection?"

He tightened a shoulder strap. "You're a stallion. You're supposed to be horny."

"Good, because I'm getting tack-related carnal stirrings."

"Talk to your doctor about TRCS. There *is* a solution . . ."

I laughed. "Do I look weird?"

He studied me. Shook his head slowly.

"You don't have to lie."

"You look different. But I'm getting TRCS too."

"Really?"

"Oh yeah. It's, like, the leather smell and seeing you all . . . covered in straps." He buckled the last piece of the harness. "You are tacked up, my friend."

"Do I need the tail?"

"Do you want the tail now? Or is this enough for today?"

"Um . . . it depends. What are we gonna do?"

"Well, I found this site." He got on his phone and pulled up a website that was like, "10 Things to Do if You're New to Pony Play."

The first one was "Take your pony for a walk."

"I thought we could do that," he suggested. "We could go up to Berry Park. They have that creepy trail that goes to the cell phone tower. No one's ever walking there. And there's plenty of bushes to hide in if we do see anyone."

I glanced at him uncertainly. "What if people *did* see?"

He shrugged. "They'd live. Right?"

I thought about it. "I guess so."

"If you don't want to, we won't."

I tried to scratch my chest with a hoof. "I want to."

He checked the screen. "It says to not overwhelm your pony with too much tack the first time out. So, like, we could leave the bit off, so you can talk to me. And the tail and blinkers. Sound good?"

I nodded, relieved. How weird was it that I actually *did* feel kind of overwhelmed? This was supposed to be a joke. Just a dumb thing I was doing to show Cinnamon up.

I read the rest of the list. "'Give your pony a bath.' Ooh. I wanna do that."

"Where would we do it?"

I looked out the window, the bridle straps sliding against my face and the back of my head. "In the yard."

"People would definitely see."

"I can take off the pony stuff and just wear shorts. But I'd secretly be a pony."

He laughed. "Not sure what the neighbors are gonna make of me washing you, but okay."

He took off the bridle and hooves and had me put on my shirt over the harness. Then we packed our gear in our reusable Geegs bag and drove to Berry Park. I was too nervous to talk much. I wanted to do this, but the closer we got, the more I realized that this whole PetPlayFest thing was *not* something I'd thought through. If I felt this weird about the idea of wearing a bridle where people *might* see but probably wouldn't, how was I gonna do horse ballet in front of a whole bunch of people?

We walked a good ways into the woods, to where the trail was overgrown and gnats were flying around our heads. Ryan stopped. "Here, you think?"

"Sure." It didn't look like a place that anyone would be walking unless they were planning to have outside sex.

Ryan set down the bag and opened it. Pulled out the bridle. "Blinkers on or off?"

"Umm . . ." I stared at the bridle. "Off."

He left the blinkers off and tried to untangle the mess of straps. "I already forget how this goes."

"Here." I took it from him and adjusted it. "Try it like this."

He grinned. "You're not supposed to have hands. You're a horse."

"Shert errrrp. I'm helping you." I handed it back to him. "I feel like you should have a horseman name too. Something that sounds good with Thunder Canyon. Like 'Rafael Charmant, riding Thunder Canyon.'"

"Uh-huh. Bend your pretty face down."

I bent down, and he slid the bridle over my head. I swallowed as he fastened the straps.

"There." He stood back.

It felt . . . like no big thing. I mean, I was standing in the woods with straps all around my head, but I could live with that. I was glad we didn't have the bit yet, though. I was trying to imagine having to take orders from him without being able to talk, and it made my spine feel like a bunch of mice were running up and down it. We never played with gags or anything, because I basically never shut up, and we both liked it that way.

"Okay?" he asked.

"Yeah."

"You look good."

"You're lying." I pushed at the bridle. "I look dumb."

"No." He shook his head. "You'd be surprised."

I looked down at the front of his pants, because his dick never lied to me. I couldn't see anything, so I reached out and groped him. There was moderate hardness.

"Hey, Secretariat." He pulled back. "Save it for the broodmares."

"My name is Thunder Canyon," I reminded him.

"Do I call you Thunder for short?"

"If you want."

"Or Canyon?"

"Whatever you want, dude. You're my owner."

He brushed a gnat away from my face. Paused with his hand out, then petted my forehead. I half closed my eyes and bent so he could reach me better. Then I snickered.

"What?" he asked.

"Nothing."

He reached back into the bag. "I'm gonna put your hoof thingies on."

I held out my hands one at a time while he put the gloves on. I got TRCS again. I also started laughing so hard I couldn't stop.

"What?" he asked.

I just made little squeaks in my throat until I could talk again. "It's just . . . so . . . *weird*." I held up my hoof-hands. "Look at this! People actually do this shit."

He laughed too, shaking his head at me. "I *know*. And you're gonna do it in like three weeks. So you'd better take this seriously."

I looked at him, my lips pressed together. The laughter was mostly under control except for a couple of snorts.

He hooked the ends of the reins to the clips on the cheek pieces. "We're gonna take a walk now."

I took a deep breath and shook off the last of the chuckles. "What do I have to do?"

"Um, just walk."

"Do I have to prance?"

"You can just walk."

"Do you want me to make horse sounds?"

"Seriously, Kamen, all you have to do is walk." He paused. "Though if you do want to make horse sounds, that would be amusing."

I tried a whinny.

He pretty much peed himself laughing. So who was the one not taking this seriously now?

"That sounds nothing like a horse," he said between gasps.

"You do it, then!"

He did. It sounded pretty good.

"Well, it's easy for you to make horse sounds. You have a cartoon voice."

"I'm sorry. You're the pony. I didn't mean to insult your sounds."

"I'm never gonna neigh again."

He gazed at me for a sec like he was trying not to smile. "Guilty hooves got no rhythm?"

"Shut up."

We walked along the barely existent trail, and I got used to the quiet, and to not having to concentrate on anything but staying in step with him. I looked down at my hoof hands a couple of times. Tried to be as at home in my pony gear as Cinnamon clearly was. Tried to imagine learning how to, like, crab-trot sideways like the dressage ponies, and pull a cart, and not feel stupid when I did it.

"Whoa," Ryan said softly at one point. He stopped, and I did too. He patted me, like he was totally cool with the idea that I was a horse. "Walk on." He started forward, and I followed.

Next time we stopped, I took a deep breath, then did that thing horses do where they blow out air and make their lips flutter.

Ryan glanced at me in surprise. "That was good."

I grinned.

He clucked, and we walked on.

The next day, Ryan went to Geegs before I even woke up, so we didn't get to have wake-up sex. It was just me in a house full of stuff that reminded me of him—panties, dresses, a bridle, a harness. That fucking whip and the butt plug tail.

I decided I wanted to know what the tail felt like, so I got it out and washed the plug part. Lubed it up and spent a few minutes working it in. It took a while, because the flared part of the plug was pretty wide, and the neck really narrow—I guess so it wouldn't fall out when you were cantering or whatever.

I walked around the house with the tail swishing against my legs. It felt pretty good, actually. I made some coffee and drank it and checked baseball scores on my phone. Then I wandered into the bedroom and got out my computer. Brought up Ryan's megalodon drawing and studied it. Dude was talented. I wasn't an art expert or anything, but I knew what looked cool and what didn't. It bummed me out that he hadn't pursued art professionally.

The plug was getting me hard, so I started rubbing my dick—just casually, not with any real intent. Then I got Whitney Houston stuck in my head, and I started swaying a little to the imaginary music. So that thing totally happened where I didn't hear Ryan come in, and then suddenly he was in the bedroom and looking at me all *What the fuck?*

"Hey." I glanced over my shoulder at the long black tail, then back at Ryan. "It's not what it looks like."

"It looks like you're dancing and touching yourself to my drawing of a megalodon while wearing a butt plug horse tail, but I don't want to assume anything."

"No, you pretty much got it. But I was also humming 'How Will I Know' under my breath."

He nodded. Watched me for a moment, like he was trying to figure something out. Then he said, "I actually have something I've been wanting to show you."

"Oh my God. What?"

"I was gonna wait until I had a little more done, but . . ." He crossed to the bed and got his tablet. Brought it over to me. He shook his head as he approached. "I almost want you to take the tail out, because I'm trying to be kind of serious, but it's just too perfect."

I swished it for him. Took the tablet when he handed it to me.

"I did some illustrations. You can swipe through."

"Illustrations of what?"

"Just look."

I looked at the screen.

Holy shit.

I stared for what felt like fifteen minutes. Then I swiped. Swiped again. They were illustrations of "Snow Wanderer." Four paintings of, like, this arctic suburbia, done in the same style as the megalodon painting, but a thousand times more . . . just *more*. Snowflakes blowing around, houses with vinyl siding and snow on the roofs, snow-covered trash cans on the curbs—and this kid removing snowmen's faces. The paintings were the kind of sad that makes your stomach drop for a minute.

There was one where the kid's hat had gotten snagged in a tree and pulled off his head, but he was too busy eating a snowman's raisin mouth to notice it was caught on the branch.

It sounds silly, but it wasn't. Not to me, anyway. These paintings made the whole "Snow Wanderer" idea look nostalgic and strange, and—not nightmarish, but you know those dreams you wake up from knowing that you had something amazing in the dream that you don't have in real life, like the ability to fly, or a huge house? These drawings gave me that feeling.

"These are beautiful," I told him.

He shrugged, but his lips were pressed together like he was nervous.

"How long have you been working on this?"

"A couple of weeks. I like listening to you work on the song, and I just thought maybe this would be cool to go along with it."

"Dude, Ryan, this is incredible." I couldn't stop swiping through, noticing new things about the drawings each time—the way the branches of a tree made, like, a cage around the moon. The dog pee stain at the base of one snowman. A little girl's silhouette in the bedroom of a neighbor's house.

"Glad you like them."

"I want these under the song."

"What?"

I turned to him. "I'm gonna post the song on YouTube when I have a final version. I want these to be the images for the video. If you'd let me. Is that okay?"

"Uh, yeah." He smiled quickly. "Of course. I didn't think you'd . . . I mean, that's awesome that you want them."

"You really have no idea, do you?" I cupped his face in one hand and kissed him long and slow. He let out a breath into my mouth and clutched me almost too hard with one hand until we were done.

I glanced back at the tablet. "Ricky has this animation program—we won't turn it into a cartoon or anything—but he can add just a little motion, so it's like a wind is blowing those snowflakes around. We can make this, like, insane."

"Okay. I can do more, if you want."

"That would be— I can't even."

When I turned to him again, I couldn't figure out what was going on in his head. So sometimes when that happened, I just stayed quiet, which was what I did this time.

He leaned his head against my arm. I raised my arm so he could get under it, then crushed him with it. "Thank you," he whispered.

My chin scruff dragged along the top of his head. "For what?"

"For making me feel like I can do stuff like this, and it's not . . . childish."

For a second, I thought *this* was the Ryan I wanted my friends to see. This incredibly sweet guy who was kinda insecure, but, like, amazing and willing to try anything and funny as shit. Then I was like, no, it's not two separate Ryans. I wanted them to love even the guy who argued with them and told jokes they didn't like. Wanted them to love the whole package, like I did. "Dude, how can being a genius be childish?"

He sighed, leaning harder on me. "You don't even know. I've done a lot of things because of what I thought I was supposed to want, instead of because of what I actually want." He paused. "So thanks for, I guess, taking me seriously."

I just held him after that without saying anything. Because I *got it*, man.

I got it.

CHAPTER ELEVEN

Ryan and I spent the morning watching some pony play videos together. He studied the handlers—their long-reining techniques and the ways they interacted with the ponies—and I tried to study how the ponies behaved and moved. Except they were totally inconsistent. Some of them walked on two legs, some on four. The two-legged ones either had their hands cuffed behind their back, or else they moved them through the air in time with their actual legs. Most of them were really well behaved, to the point where they were kind of boring to watch after a few minutes. But my favorite one was a pony named Belle who'd won "best personality" in some New York competition a few years ago. She was, like, knocking buckets over, freaking out about a set of wind chimes, trying to grab the reins in her teeth . . . She never did what she was told, but somehow she managed to be cute about it rather than annoying.

Ryan didn't say much about the videos. I had to talk through my thoughts during each one, but he just kinda quietly took them in. We went to Berry Park after lunch and tried the blinkers. And the tail. We had to cut a hole in a pair of my shorts so I could wear the tail and still be decent. Having a tail coming out of my ass was pretty okay, but the blinkers were another story. At first I was like, *Cool, this'll be no big deal.* But once they were on and I realized how little I could see, I was kind of freaked. I walked forward when Ryan clucked, but stopped almost immediately.

"Come on," Ryan urged.

I tried to swipe at the blinkers, but my hands were trapped in the hoof gloves.

I turned my head back and forth. "I can't see out the sides!"

Ryan came around to my front. "That's the point."

"I'm gonna trip over stuff."

"You'll still be able to see the ground. I'll be leading you."

I lowered my head and stared at the ground. Okay, I *could* see it fine. But . . . "This is not cool. I feel like I'm gonna run into something." Man, I felt for bio horses. Blinkers were bullshit.

"You won't." He snapped his fingers in front of me. "Hey. Hey, look here."

I looked at him, not sure how I felt about this.

"You won't trip," he repeated. "You know why?"

"Why?"

"Because you're my pony. And I'm not gonna let anything happen to you." He patted my shoulder real solid, then offered me his fist for a fist bump.

I pounded it with my hoof and smiled slowly.

"Thunder Canyon? What are you?"

"I'm your fuckin' pony."

"That's right. And we're gonna go out there, and we're gonna do some long reining. Because we've got three weeks to prepare, and we need a serious fucking montage."

We fist-bumped again, and then he took the reins and led me out onto the trail.

He left the bit out for the first few minutes, as I tried to get used to wearing the blinkers. He stayed beside me, and he definitely didn't let me trip. I got familiar with the different pressures of the head straps depending on where he was steering me. Then we stopped, and he put the bit in my mouth and clipped it to the bridle. I started drooling within, like, two seconds. "Grooofffhhh." I was trying for "Gross," but talking only made it grosser.

He ran his hand up and down my back, and holy *shit* that felt good. He gave my harness a light tug. "Hey. You okay?"

I nodded.

"I'm gonna get behind you. Stay there." He gathered up the reins and went to stand behind me. My stomach flipped. It was crazy to me how different things felt when I couldn't see him.

He shook the reins lightly over my shoulders and clucked. I walked forward. Easy enough. I was breathing kinda loud and slurpy-ish around the bit, but whatevs.

He tugged the right rein. It stretched the corner of my mouth. "Can you feel that?"

"Yehhh," I said around the bit.

"Is it too hard?"

I laughed. "Nhhhoo."

He pulled the left rein a little lighter. "How's that?"

"Pehw-hehhh."

"Perfect?"

He totally understood my pony-talk, so that made me feel better. "Yehhh."

He pulled back on both reins, and I stopped. He walked up right behind me. I could feel him, but I couldn't see him, because stupid blinkers. He petted me again. Like, just the way you would a real horse down the neck and over the shoulder. "You're doing so good," he said.

I hadn't actually done much of anything, but I still felt awesome when he said that.

"Can I ride you?" he asked.

I swung my head toward him. "Yewannuhryyymehhh?"

"Yeah." He gathered the reins into a shorter loop.

I nodded again. "Ohhkhharrr."

I crouched. He climbed up on my back. I hooked my arms under his legs. I wanted to point out that we were finally *Freak the Mighty*-ing it, but I had the bit in.

I groaned as I got to my feet, and he slapped my shoulder. "Shut up. I'm not heavy."

I mock staggered back and forth, while he laughed. "Kamen!" He kicked at my sides. "Thunder Canyon! Go forward. Go, pony!"

I shook my head and snorted, then started jogging.

"Oh God." Ryan clutched my shoulders, then slung his arms around my neck as we headed down the trail. "This was a terrible idea."

I hitched him up higher on my back and jogged a little faster.

"Yeehaw!" Ryan yelled.

Suddenly I tripped for real, and wiped out.

We collapsed in a heap, laughing and groaning.

"Okay." Ryan rolled himself off of me. "We are definitely not riding anymore."

"Wooo huff hoo guuhh buikhh ern vuuh fa-uhww."

He laughed and unclipped my bit. "What was that?"

I moved my mouth, wiping away the spit. "You have to get back in the saddle."

"You're a cart pony. We need to stick to carts. Once we have a cart, that is."

"Yeah, what's going on with that?"

"Patience, patience." He looked around. "And we have to find somewhere better to practice."

I thought for a minute. "Our apartment has a long hallway. If the cart's small enough . . ."

He shook his head. "We need to be outside. I'll check around on Fet. See if anyone has any private property. Or find out where other pony people go, at least."

I considered this for a moment. "Actually, I might have a better idea."

I met D for lunch on Monday at a place called Ham on the Corner. It served mostly ham. On buns that were toasted in a skillet full of bacon grease.

I bit into my sandwich. "Dave says that you have land. Outside of the city."

He nodded, paunch rising slightly as he inhaled. "Yes. But if you would like to build on it, I must decline. I have—" his gaze shifted "—plans for it. But if you'd like to camp with your very small partner, that is acceptable."

"I don't want to build. Or camp. Ryan and I just need a place to practice something. Is it private?"

"Very much so, and I am surprised you would even need to ask." His eyes narrowed. "What, may I ask, are you practicing?"

"It's just a thing we have to rehearse."

"It's not a . . ." He leaned forward and lowered his voice. "It's not a flash mob, is it?"

"What?"

He sighed deeply and ate some more ham. "David recently told me about flash mobs. I'm not judging. But I am troubled."

"I promise it's not a flash mob." I stared at my sandwich for a second, then decided to go with the truth. "Ryan and I are trying pony play, man." I hadn't really meant for the "man" to slip out. It was just me trying too hard to be casual. I even added a shrug.

D brought his sandwich slowly to his mouth. Without taking his gaze off of me, he bit and chewed. Those blue eyes were *intense.*

He swallowed. "Pony play."

"Yeah, like where a person pretends to be a horse." I shrugged again. "You know."

"Yes. I know." He took another slow bite.

"I, uh . . . I know you like horses."

He didn't comment.

I cleared my throat. "A Friesian."

"Pardon?"

"That's the kind of horse I am. A Friesian. Because I remember you telling me how great they are."

His expression softened. "I'm not sure whether I am honored or disturbed." He paused. "I will go with honored."

"Please don't tell Dave. It would kill him."

A strange guzzling sound came out of his throat. I thought for a sec he was crying. Then I realized he was laughing. *Hard.* "Ohh. I'll try. I really will. But . . ." He wiped under his eye with one finger. "I'm not laughing at you. I'm just . . . imagining David . . ."

I tried to glower at him, but I couldn't keep a straight face. "If you don't tell him about this, I promise I won't tell him you enjoyed the renaissance faire."

D hesitated. Licked mustard off his thumb. "David is aware that I enjoyed myself at the festival."

I raised my eyebrows. "Really?"

"We are practicing a greater degree of honesty in our relationship. Have some fries." He motioned to his plate.

"Fine." I leaned over to grab some fries. "But still don't tell him."

D was staring at my midsection. I realized my T-shirt had ridden up, and my jeans had ridden down. Which left a little bit of red lace exposed. I sank back into my seat, pulling my shirt down.

He met my gaze again. Nodded briefly. "Your secret is safe with me."

And I knew it would be.

That afternoon, I got "Snow Wanderer" pretty much set. I made a couple of recordings on my shitty laptop recorder, but wasn't totally happy with either of them. So I called one of the other guys I knew who played at Pitch sometimes. He worked in the Hymland College library, in their media center. The media center had installed a recording booth a couple of years ago. He said it was booked pretty much till the end of the semester, but he could try to get me a spot.

So that made me happy.

Then the Pegasus Sheath arrived, which made me double happy. I walked around with it on and, like, swung it around in circles and stuff until it was time for work.

And then that night, Ryan's friend Dan came over in an SUV and dropped off a pony cart. We parked the cart on our deck. It was kinda patchworkish—bicycle tires, what looked like a piece of a workout bench, and one of the shafts was slightly longer than the other.

"Where'd this come from?" I demanded.

"Dan works in a bicycle shop."

"How does that explain anything?"

"Maybe some evenings when I was 'working late' last week, I was actually at the cycle shop with some guys who like to build shit."

I stroked the left trace. "You made this?"

"I had a ton of help."

I looked up at him. "What'd you tell the guys it was for?"

"I said my mom had just gotten a Shetland pony."

"That's one of those stories that sounds so fake it might be true."

"Knowing my mom, it could be true. Speaking of which . . ."

"Yeah?"

"My parents want us to drive up there for brunch on Sunday."

"Awesome!"

"We'll lose a whole day of practice," he warned.

"Dude. There is time in the montage for brunch."

"Good." He looked relieved. Had he honestly thought I'd be upset about missing practice to go see his family?

We carried the cart up the back steps and put it in the laundry room. And then I showed him the Pegasus Sheath.

He was literally speechless.

We had sex with me wearing it, which was a little weird, but hey. This house was a judgment-free zone.

Ryan took Tuesday off work. I mean, no kidding, called in and did the fake cough and everything. We went out to D's property to practice. The cart didn't exactly fit in my car, so we had to do some creative things with tying the trunk half-shut so the shafts could stick out. But I was feeling awesome, and Ryan let me blast "Man in Motion" from *St. Elmo's Fire* on our way there.

The property was just a few acres on the edge of a suburb, off a dirt road. D had given me GPS coordinates, since there wasn't a technical address. I had a feeling he'd expected me to find it by compass or something, but I just plugged the coordinates into my phone, and it worked out okay. There was a meadow surrounded on two sides by woods, and the grass looked like it had been mowed recently. I wondered who D got to take care of his land. And whether Ryan and I risked running into, like, the caretaker one of these days.

We parked along the edge of the dirt road. Unloaded the cart and the gear, dragged it into the meadow, and tacked up.

This time, Ryan put the hooves on, then hooked my wrists behind my back with padded leather cuffs.

I shifted. I felt a little off-balance, but nothing horrible.

He stepped back. "Looking good."

If you say so.

He spent a while hitching me to the cart. He had to pull up videos on his phone a couple of times, but eventually he got the shafts secured to my harness. He led me around in a circle so I could get used to pulling the cart. It creaked a lot, but it wasn't heavy or anything.

He picked up the reins and whip, and went around to get in the cart. It was actually easier to be a pony with my hands cuffed—like, it really hit home to me that I didn't have to make choices. I just had to follow cues.

I was aware of every tiny sensation—the tail brushing my bare legs, the plug pressed deep in my ass. The harness straps rubbing against my T-shirt, the bit pushing down on my tongue. Sweat trickling under the bridle and drool running down the sides of my chin. The slight tension in the reins as Ryan gathered them. The fucking Pegasus Sheath hanging out of my pants. The fact that I couldn't see anywhere except right in front of me, thanks to whatever ass lesion had invented blinkers. I pulled nervously against the wrist cuffs, but they didn't give.

I held my breath as I waited.

He flicked the reins lightly over my shoulders and clucked. I jumped forward into a brisk, half-panicked walk. Was jerked back by the cart's resistance, but then I leaned forward and got it moving across the grass. The tail swished against my calves, and the plug shifted inside, making my dick try to rise in its sheath. *Stallion power, motherfuckers.*

"Easy." Ryan tugged gently on the reins. "Where's the fire?"

I smiled around the bit and slowed down. I still didn't really get what this game did to me. I knew it made me feel really self-conscious, which was weird, because self-consciousness had never been my thing. I'd always liked making people laugh, and the best way to do that was usually to make a complete idiot of myself. But now I was doing probably the most ridiculous-looking thing of my life, and for once, I didn't want anyone to laugh. Even though I totally understood why they would.

Ryan had asked if I was gonna tell my friends about the pony play, and I'd been all like, *Duh*—but then I'd made D keep it a secret. And I got kind of terrified whenever I imagined doing this in front of an audience. So what was up with that?

But the people who go to a pet play thing probably aren't there to make fun of the pets.

Probably.

He tugged the left rein, and I turned, careful to make a wide arc so the cart didn't tip. My skin vibrated the way it used to sometimes at tennis practice when it was hot out and I didn't hydrate enough. This should have been easy. This was just Ryan telling me what to do and me paying attention. But I felt like I was treading water in the middle of the fucking ocean. Like, how could it be as simple as turning left when he pulled the left rein? Didn't I have to act like a horse? Make my stupid horse noises or something? Fight him once in a while?

And how fast was I supposed to be walking? How high was I supposed to be lifting my legs?

He'll tell you.

But maybe Ryan was as nervous as I was, because he hardly said anything to me.

We made a circle, and then I stopped suddenly.

"You okay?" Ryan asked.

"Ahhh Erhh dohhhn ihh riiiihhh?" I asked around the bit.

He dropped the reins, jumped off the cart, and came around to stand in front of me. He unclipped the bit and eased it from my mouth. Held it, slobber and all. "What was that?"

"Am I doing it right?"

"Sure. I mean, I think so. Why?"

"I feel weird."

"Weird how?"

I couldn't explain. And he didn't try to make me. He just stood there patiently and waited.

"Embarrassed," I said finally.

"You? Embarrassed?"

"I know. But at first pony stuff was funny, and now I actually want to be good at it."

He grinned. "Me too. And we will be."

"But I feel awkward."

"You're wearing a butt plug tail and a bridle and you're hooked to a cart. Of course you're gonna feel awkward at first."

"I'm also getting a boner. Again."

He laughed. "Aww."

"It's from the tail. I don't even like it, but it's turning me on."

"You want me to take it out?"

"Hell no." I angled my hips toward him. "See it? See my giant stallion boner?"

"Gross. Do you want to take a break?"

"We barely did anything. I want to keep going."

"You sure?"

"Yeah. Really, I want to do this." I pulled against the cuffs again. "Can you, um . . ."

"Yes?"

I shifted my weight. "Talk to me more? I know it sounds dumb, but, like, I don't know how much to turn or how fast to walk. And that one time you told me to slow down, that was great for me."

He nodded. "Okay."

"Is that . . . Does that work for you?"

"Yeah."

"You don't look sure."

He laughed again. "This is all new to me too. I'm just trying to figure out what to have you do, and what to say to you and all that."

"We can just go in circles for a while. Like those people in the video."

"Okay. Let's try it."

"Sweet."

He fished in his pocket. Produced a small, wrapped candy. "Here. Have this." He unwrapped it.

"You brought Jolly Ranchers?"

"Of course." He put the Jolly Rancher—blue—on his palm and held it up to me. I leaned down and took it with my mouth.

He gave me a minute to eat it, then held up the bit. I opened my mouth, and he eased it in, clipping it to the bridle once more. He patted my shoulder, picked up the reins, and stepped behind me again.

Nothing happened for a moment.

"Sorry," he said. "Lost my whip in the grass."

Okay, so Cinnamon had like years of experience and the grace of a thousand ballerinas, and her handler probably never lost his whip in the grass. But that didn't mean Ryan and I couldn't go to this pony show and trample her—goddamn pun intended.

"Found it." Ryan picked up the whip and got up on the cart. I felt him adjusting the reins, shifting on the seat. Finally he flicked the leather over my shoulders. "Walk on."

I walked on. He tugged on the right rein, and I turned until he stopped pulling, trying not to walk too fast or too slow. "Good," he said.

Some of my tension eased. We made a wide circle. Then he tugged both reins. "Whoa."

I stopped.

"Good boy."

Crushing it.

He clucked. "Trot."

By the second circle, I was bored. I tried throwing my head forward a little, pulling on the reins. He took the hint and snapped the reins again, clucking.

We made a faster circle.

I had just turned to make a third circle when I became aware he was pulling on the left rein. I changed direction, and we made a figure eight.

I was ballin' at this. Also, I hardly noticed the tail anymore, and my hard-on had gone down a little, so that was helpful.

He started steering me in all kinds of patterns: snakes and zigzags and spirals. He made me slow down or speed up or stop every minute or so. I tried to think like an actual horse, which was tough, because who knew what they actually thought about? Food, probs. Which, hey, me too. And they probably thought about the barn, and how much they wanted to go back there and sleep. And maybe they thought about other horses they found sexy?

I remembered a video that said they got spooked easily. So possibly they spent a lot of time thinking about how freaky everything looked. Birds and trees and whatever. I thought about Belle, the human pony who'd freaked out about the wind chimes.

I totally didn't feel nervous or awkward anymore. But I was getting tired. I could have been nice and just stopped moving. But I was, like, having horse thoughts. I looked over toward the spot where we'd left our stuff. Turned and started jogging toward it.

"Whoa! Hey!"

Ryan pulled on the reins, but I kept jogging, trying to ignore the plug shifting inside me. I reached our stuff and whoa-ed abruptly.

He hopped off the cart came around in front of me, shaking his head, clearly trying not to laugh. "Bad Thunder Canyon."

I glanced meaningfully at the car.

"You're checking out for the day?"

I nodded.

"Fine, then. But no more Jolly Ranchers for you."

I blew some snot on him.

Because that was how horses rolled.

He glared at me, and I grinned around the bit.

He unhitched me. Took my bit out and held it by one ring while he wiped it off. He clipped the lead rope to a ring on my chinstrap. Then he picked up our bag and led me over to the trees. I didn't talk, even though I kind of wanted to.

He stripped off my harness and my shirt. And my shorts—it was an ordeal getting them off without disturbing the tail—leaving me, um, naked. Except for the tail. And the sheath.

Well, this is new.

He wrapped my lead rope around a branch.

Then he put on the spiky-rubber-mitt thingy and started rubbing my back. Hard. I groaned, trying to press into the glove as he circled it across my shoulders and then down my lower back. "Oh God." I sighed as he scrubbed the small of my back. "Oh *God.*"

"Horses don't talk," he reminded me.

"Mr. Ed does."

"You are not Mr. Ed." He moved to my front and did my chest and abs, using a gentler pressure.

"Thunder Canyon is way awesomer than Mr. Ed. Thunder Canyon would eat Mr. Ed's heart in a death match."

Ryan smiled. "Shhhhh." He used the mitt to pinch my stomach. Tossed the glove aside and picked up the soft brush.

The soft brush was slightly less fun, because hi, ticklish. I kept jerking away, until he did the backs of my legs. Then my stallion hard-on came back.

He whistled a jaunty little tune and nudged my legs apart. Then he brushed the insides of my thighs. I shifted my weight from foot to foot, trying not to air hump. "Good boy," he said, like he knew exactly what he was doing to me. He patted my ass.

The situation got worse when he swapped the brush for a comb and started combing my tail. Even though he held the tail by the base, each stroke of the comb pulled on the plug, making it shift inside me.

I started bouncing back and forth a little as the boner sitch went up to DEFCON 1.

"You could be more famous than Mr. Ed." He tugged hard on a stubborn knot. "Thunder Canyon, the dancing horse."

"You're an asshole," I said, which earned me a slap on the butt.

I watched him put the comb away, feeling suddenly very quiet and warm inside.

He wasn't an asshole. He was the guy who went on all the adventures with me, who had my fucking reins in his hand, and so who even *cared* if I didn't know what submission "meant," or whatever, because it probably meant different things to everybody. This guy. *This* guy . . .

I'd already earned all the reward I needed.

"Why are you smiling?" he asked suspiciously.

I just shook my head and horse-snorted.

He rubbed me down with a rag. Including, briefly, between the legs. I groaned and tried to move my hips in time with his hand, but he pulled the rag away.

Offered me a Jolly Rancher.

Which I almost choked on when he reached behind me and started pulling on my tail plug. It had been in so long that he had to work on it for a while—twisting it and thrusting with it—until it popped out. He wrapped it in the rag and set it aside. Untied the lead rope, took off the bridle, and looked at me. Got up on his toes and kissed me in a way that was definitely not approps for human and horse. "You can get dressed."

If I was going to talk to Ricky about the "Snow Wanderer" illustrations, then I pretty much had to talk to him about the Bill thing.

This was gonna suck nasty sweaty sumo balls. I invited him to lunch at Mel's, and he didn't seem suspicious about my motives, so that was a plus. He also didn't look tired or scared or anything that suggested he was in some kind of traumatic relationship he couldn't escape from. In fact, he looked damn good—he'd filled out a little and was wearing his hair shorter. His guns were, like—the show probably wasn't sold out, but you wouldn't want to wait much longer to buy tickets.

I tried the usual *What have you been up to?* shooting-the-shit kind of stuff. He told me about his job, and about Cobalt's owners sending some weird email to all the members basically blaming them for the club going under, and about some cartoon show about a pigeon who gets a job teaching British lit at a high school, which I apparently needed to start watching yesterday.

He sipped his Coke. "Dave was supposed to talk to me about being on a panel at the kink fair, but he hasn't answered my texts in days." There was a hard note in Ricky's voice, almost a challenge. I was so used to him sounding like a giddy schoolkid, even if he was just talking about, you know, someone stealing his parking spot at work, that I was a little surprised.

"Oh."

Ricky didn't quit staring at me. "So you guys found out, huh?"

I nodded, trying not to look judge-y or anything. "I saw your status."

He picked at his sandwich, finally dropping his gaze. "So are you here to lecture me?"

"No," I said honestly. "I believe you're an adult and can make your own choices."

He looked up. "You hate Bill." It wasn't a question.

I didn't answer at first. "I . . . have a hard time with him."

"This isn't because I don't care about Hal," he said sharply. "But Bill *is* a human being, whatever you guys think. And he honestly feels terrible about Hal. He pretty much never stops thinking about it. You guys think he's some kind of monster, but—"

"We don't think that. Seriously." I mean, maybe we did. I wasn't sure anymore.

He took a bite of his sandwich, then put it down. "I met him almost a year ago, at Riddle. I knew who he was, because everyone kept whispering about him. And a couple of people warned me to stay away from him. So I was sitting on the sofa in the lounge, and suddenly he was in the chair next to me. It was like being in the ocean and looking behind you and seeing a shark fin, you know?" He slid a tomato to the side of his foil and glanced up at me. "But he looked so . . . sad. I mean, just *defeated.* And a couple of other people in the lounge moved to another room when he sat down. So I said hi, because I thought someone should."

"That was nice of you." I meant it.

Ricky didn't talk for a while. "He treats me like a prince." His voice was kinda ragged. "I didn't know anything when we started out. I'd never really played before, and I remember thinking if I got killed, it would be my own fault. But I trusted him. You probably think I'm an idiot, but I did."

"I don't think you're an idiot."

"He's been so, so good to me." He looked like he wanted to beg me to understand. "He's careful. He really is. He's been to classes, since Hal, and you can tell he's really into what he's learning." He ducked his head again. "But I know it's betraying you guys. So I've tried to stay out of your way."

"Ricky. We don't think you're betraying us."

"Dave does. Or why won't he answer my texts?"

"You know how Dave is. He kinda thinks everything is his business. He just needs time to get used to this."

"I'm sorry."

"Don't be."

He looked at his sandwich but didn't eat any more of it. "Bill just doesn't fit anywhere. You know? He lost almost all his kinky friends after Hal. And he's so, like . . . dealing with so much shit now, that he doesn't really make new friends. And it's hard sometimes to care so much about someone no one else seems to connect with."

No kidding.

"I know," I said. "And you know what? I really didn't ask you here to talk about this."

He didn't look convinced. "You just wanted to hang out?"

I winced. "Okay, I did ask you here for something. But it's got nothing to do with Bill."

"Then what's up?"

"Ryan did some drawings. And I want to use them to make a video that I can put under a song I'm writing. And I thought it'd be cool if there could be some animation. Nothing major, just—"

"Oh my God!" Ricky was off on a whole thing about this new animation program he had. I couldn't follow any of it, but the more he talked, the more awesome I felt. Because we *weren't* here to talk about Bill. Bill and Hal didn't need to be part of everything I thought or discussed. And yeah, shit had changed after Hal died, and it was still changing. I wanted to be allowed to change too. It was just like I'd told the well-dressed hare: different wasn't bad.

I figured I should write that shit down, but I didn't want to be rude and take out my phone, so I just listened to Ricky instead.

That night, Ryan and I discussed show attire. I wanted him to get some friggin' breeches and riding boots, because he'd look hot. We were thinking my board shorts with the hole in the back weren't gonna cut it for the competition, so we shopped online until we found some awesome leather pants that were made for pony play and had space in the back for the tail, and space in the front for . . .

"The Pegasus Sheath!" I said happily.

"Yep." Ryan clicked on them. "I think we need these."

In the corner, Collingsworth yawned.

Ryan looked over at him. Stared for a few seconds. "He has something weird in his teeth."

"Really?" I glanced over, but Collingsworth's mouth was closed. "What?"

"I dunno. Here, Col! C'mere, boy."

Collingsworth got up slowly and lumbered over. Ryan checked his mouth. "I *believe*," Ryan said, "this is a remnant of one of my socks." He held it up.

"Uh-oh."

Ryan looked meaningfully at Collingsworth, who glanced away.

"He's never chewed our stuff before," I pointed out. "He must be missing Amanda."

I comforted Collingsworth while Ryan finished ordering the pants. Something smelled weird, like rotting fish. I sniffed the air. "What's that smell?"

"Huh?"

I sniffed again, closer to Collingsworth. "He smells gross."

Ryan leaned over and sniffed, then focused on the screen again. "That's probably his anal glands."

"His what?"

"Anal glands."

I rubbed Collingsworth's head, staring up at Ryan. "What's that?"

"You know. Dogs' anal glands sometimes get full, and then they have to go to the vet or the groomer's and get the . . . stuff squeezed out."

"What stuff?" I was alarmed. "Poop?"

"No, it's not poop. It's just, like . . . I don't know, butt juice."

I stopped petting Collingsworth, who turned his giant head to stare mournfully at me. "What's it made of?"

"Uhhh." Ryan didn't look away from the screen. "I don't know."

"How does the vet get it out?"

"I told you. They reach in there and squeeze the sac thingie."

"Reach in there?"

Ryan glanced at me. "Why are you so upset? I reach in your butt all the time."

"Yeah, to do good things."

Collingsworth moved closer to me.

I was still trying to process all this. "What happens if you don't squeeze the butt sac?"

"Then I guess it's probably kind of uncomfortable for the dog. And it leaks a little."

I slowly scooted away from Collingsworth and turned my attention back to the computer, but I did not stop being perplexed by anal glands.

"What else?" Ryan asked. "I think we've got just about everything we could need."

I got the brilliant idea to order some of those black fuzzy boots to imitate the feathering Friesians have on their ankles.

"We're headed for the poorhouse," Ryan said as he clicked Submit Order.

"Totally worth it, though."

After that, I played him the recordings of "Snow Wanderer," and he gave me some advice on the lyrics. Then we tried to do a scene with the military costumes we'd gotten at the party store recently. We were supposed to be soldiers who took cover together during enemy fire, but we had a little trouble getting our visions to align.

I made the sound of a grenade exploding, and Ryan collapsed on the living room floor.

"Oh, help. Yeah, oh my *God*, Kamen, my leg."

I looked at his leg, imagining it mangled and covered in blood. "Oh, Jesus!"

"It's gone!"

"No, it's still there," I whispered.

He raised his head. "It was blown off by the grenade."

"No, but I want you to lose it later to gangrene, so can you just—"

"It's *my* leg."

"I knowwww," I whined. "But can it please stay attached? Just for now?"

"Fine."

We took it back a few lines. "Oh, Jesus!" I yelled.

"I've got a butt-load of shrapnel in my flesh."

I stared at him. "A butt-load? Really?"

"Well, what'd they call it back in world war times? Fuck-ton?"

"I don't know. Just say you were hit by shrapnel."

"Okay, but after this, can we not interrupt anymore?"

"Fine."

He tipped his head back and moaned. "I've been strafed!"

"You weren't strafed, dude. That was a grenade."

"Oh my God, just *go* with it, Kamen."

"Don't worry! You're gonna be fine. I'll take you to the hospital tent." I started to pick him up.

"Owww, my leg!"

He was a good goddamn actor, because I got startled and dropped him. He moaned again, frealz this time. Collingsworth ambled over and licked him. I pushed Collingsworth away, because I really didn't want to smell butt juice while I was trying to save a life.

"Look . . ." I leaned down and kissed Ryan, then gazed into his little brown fuckin' bunny eyes. "It's gonna hurt when I lift you, but then we'll get you fixed up."

He looked up at me. Lolled his head around a little. "I see the most . . . *beautiful* light . . ."

He closed his eyes all dramatic.

I tapped him. "But don't die yet, because we haven't even fucked."

"I know, I'm just passing out."

"Okay, now can we fast-forward to three weeks later and your leg is gone and, like, you're afraid you'll never be able to have sex again, but then I have sex with you in the hospital?"

"Okay."

We made it through the role-play, but it was a little hairy. Afterward we had a couple of beers, and then suddenly it was 3 a.m.

"Oh fuck." Ryan moaned. "I have to get up in three hours. Maybe I should be sick again tomorrow."

"Dude, I wouldn't stop you."

"I can't believe it's 3 a.m."

I sang a little Matchbox Twenty wearing just my military jacket and no pants, which led to some serious nineties nostalgia. Which led to us checking the internet to see if Matchbox Twenty was on tour. We discovered the band no longer played together, but that Rob Thomas toured on his own. *And* on the twenty-second he was playing a venue only two and a half hours from us, which, in our sleep-deprived and slightly drunk state, seemed like a sign from the universe. So we ordered tickets.

"We're getting bad at adulting," Ryan mumbled when we finally got into bed.

"What do you mean?"

"I mean we're, like, out of control with our spending. And we're being pulled in a lot of different directions."

"Different directions?"

He just laughed. A few seconds later, though, he said, "Would you seriously consider moving? When our lease is up?"

My stomach felt funny. I'd really been hoping we'd never have to have this conversation. "Maybe. I guess we should wait and see?"

"Yeah." He fidgeted. "I just keep thinking I want to be doing something different than I am. But I'm not sure what. I think it'd be cool if we just set off to, like, find ourselves."

I lay there for a while, thinking about that.

"Moving's gonna cost a lot of money," I said finally.

He didn't answer. Possibly he was asleep. From the floor near the bed, Collingsworth's tags jingled as he scratched his ear.

"Do humans have butt juice?" I asked, poking Ryan.

"Mmrrpphh?"

"Do humans have anal glands and butt juice?"

He sighed. "No."

"Are you sure?"

"I don't . . . Probably not. Not like dogs do."

"Can you Google it?"

"You have a phone."

"Yours is closer. Please?"

He sighed again. "Go to sleep."

I lay there a little bit longer. Then I leaned over to the nightstand and grabbed my phone. Miles would know. Miles knew everything.

I texted him. *Do humans have butt juice like dogs do?*

He texted back a few minutes later: *It's 4 in the morning.*

I know. But you're awake.

Zac had a nightmare.

Aww. :(

I waited a few seconds, then tried again: *Do humans have butt juice?*

What are you talking about?

Like when dogs need their anal glands squeezed.

He didn't reply for a while. Then I got: *Humans have glands located along the walls of the anal canal. They secrete scent fluid into the canal through pathways that open into the anal crypts, and while obstruction is rare, it is possible.*

Hahahahahahahahaahhahaah ANAL CRYPTS! :-D :-D

Please go to bed.

I felt kinda lonely and didn't want to go to sleep. *New Indiana Jones movie. Anal Crypt of Doom.*

Please.

Secretions of the Lost Glands.

I will pay you.

I don't need mine squeezed, right?

No.

Ok. Love you.

Love you too.

I put down my phone and lay there another moment. Then I rolled onto my side and gently tapped Ryan's shoulder. "Hey, Ry?" I patted him a little harder. "Ry?"

"Mmmmmnnnn." He pulled the pillow over his head.

"We have anal crypts."

He didn't answer.

"I just thought you should know. We all have secrets in our butts. Like Egyptian tombs."

He didn't answer. That was fine. I'd make sure to tell him again over breakfast.

CHAPTER TWELVE

There were a couple of days where we didn't have time for much pony stuff because of work. I wore the garter belt to work one of those days and had fun texting Ryan pics from the bathroom. Ryan dug out his Slash wig from our storage room, so I finally had a mane. And I texted Dave to ask if we could have all the craft junk that was left over from us trying to decorate the duplex for Christmas last year. I wanted to do some crafting with my bridle and harness.

Friday my friend Alex at the Hymland media center called to say their eleven-o'clock recording studio appointment had canceled. So I ended up taking my guitar out to Hymland and spending two hours in the recording booth. I only got a couple of solid takes, but I could work with that. Alex let me stay on afterward to use the center's editing software. I didn't get anywhere near finished before I had to head to work, but Alex said I could come back anytime to edit.

That evening, Ryan and I were practicing long reining through the apartment—weaving around the furniture, halting, backing up. It was going well until we heard a low rumble from Collingsworth, who was staring at the front hall.

Dave stood beside the well-dressed hare, his mouth open, a plastic box in his arms.

I shook my mane out of my eyes. "Daaaffff!"

Dave's mouth worked, but no sound came out for a few seconds. "I, uh . . . I just wanted to drop off the Christmas stuff. I'm sorry. I didn't realize . . ."

Ryan stepped beside me, reins in hand. "We thought you'd text if you were planning to come over. Or at least knock."

"I did text. The door was unlocked, so . . ." He glanced at my tail, then back up at me. "Believe me, I will knock every time I come over from now until the end of time."

I tried to reach for my bridle to take the bit out, but my hands—hooves—were cuffed behind my back. I made a frustrated noise, and Ryan reached up to unclip the bit.

"Dude." I wiped my mouth on my shoulder. "We're practicing for a thing. I was gonna tell you before, but—"

"No." Dave shook his head, looking pained. "I knew you had to be into something weird. I just never thought . . ." His voice dropped to a whisper. "I never thought any friend of mine would be a goddamn furry."

"I'm not a furry, Dave. I'm a pony. There's a difference."

Dave looked at Ryan, who nodded.

"There is a difference," Ryan said.

I nodded too. "Also, you should quit hating on furries, because there's nothing wrong with them."

Dave let out an exaggerated sigh. "I know. I'm trying to get better. But something about people acting like animals just makes me so uncomfortable. But you," he added quickly. "You look . . . um . . . good."

Ryan looped my reins in his hand. "We started doing pony play because we wanted to take down Cinnamon at PetPlayFest at the end of the month."

"Cinnamon?" Dave looked confused.

"Yeah," I said. "She and I got in a fight at Riddle, and she was going on about how pony play was so hard, and I could never do it. So I wanted to prove her wrong."

"Are you serious?"

"Plus she's always harassing you on Fet, and, like, I just think this is a really good way to get her back." What was crazy was this didn't feel totally true anymore. Like, yeah, Cinnamon was why the pony play had *started*. But now it was about more than that. It was about how I wasn't afraid to try new things, and about how I didn't need to think of Ryan as some guy I had to listen to because he was my dom. He could just be my friend and my favorite person in the universe and the guy I wanted to try new things *for*.

Ryan shrugged. "We're a ragtag team of misfits. And we want to come from behind and win this competition."

I snickered. "Come from behind." I wanted to put my hoof up for a high-five, but handcuffs.

Ryan explained a little more about PetPlayFest. Like about the five competitions we had to do, and the horse ballet and shit.

Dave was looking back and forth between the two of us, but he was kind of smiling now. "You're going to defeat Cinnamon."

Ryan and I nodded.

"Publicly?"

"Yeah," we said together.

"Goddamn it." He set down the box, stepped forward, and hugged me. Kissed my cheek strap. "You beautiful beast you. This will be a Subs Club victory like no other."

I grinned. "I know."

He turned to Ryan, and I was nervous for a second. I remembered what he'd said about not being able to make himself care about Ryan, and it hurt, but I reminded myself Dave was allowed to have his feelings.

Dave leaned forward and gave Ryan an awkward hug. "Go," he said, stepping back. "Put that bit back in his mouth and ride the fuck out of him. You've got a competition to win."

Ryan and I smiled at each other.

Dave took his phone out. "What day is this thing? And what time? I'll tell the others immediately."

"Uhhh . . ." Even back when I'd considered telling my friends I was doing pony play, I'd imagined, like, *telling* them. As in, coming home from PetPlayFest with a trophy and giving them all the deets. Not having them watch me. "You really don't have to be there."

He looked up. "Don't be ridiculous. You think I'd miss you trotting around with a tail up your ass? Date and time."

I told him.

My phone blew up that evening with horse puns from everyone, from Gould to Miles and Drix to Maya to Ricky. *I heard they're actually moving the competition*, Maya texted. And I freaked for a second that she was serious. But when I asked her *WTF*, she was like. *Yeah, to Pennsylvania. Up near Filly, I think.*

Just promise you won't bale if the going gets tough, Dave said. *That wouldn't be farrier to the rest of us.*

This went on for a while. But amid the puns, there was a lot of support too. Ricky and Drix weren't gonna be able to make the competition, and Maya would have to arrive late. But Gould, Miles, Dave, and D would be there. And though I was still pretty embarrassed at the idea of them seeing me in my pony gear, struggling to prance, I decided I was fucking glad they'd be there to cheer me on.

Cinnamon didn't stand a chance.

Saturday Ryan and I slept in and arrived at our practice spot late in the afternoon, ready to tackle dressage. It was hot out. Ryan and I hauled the bag of pony gear out into the meadow. The grass was getting longish, and right from the get-go I barely had the energy to pick up my feet. We were so sweaty that all he did was give me a brief rubdown with a cloth and put some sunscreen on us both before we got started.

"So I guess we just need to start practicing the moves." He pulled up the list on his phone. "Here, I'll leave the bridle off for now, and you just face me and try to do the thing I describe. All right?"

"Okay." I took a few steps forward and turned to him. "Hit me with it."

"You're gonna have to enter the arena at a working trot. Which is just like the trotting you've been doing, except your hands aren't gonna be behind you. In dressage, you have to move your arms like they're legs. So each time you lift a foot, you move the opposite hand forward, like in the videos."

"So, like, left hand at the same time as right foot."

"Exactly."

I gave it a go.

"Not bad. Your legs and arms are a little out of synch. And maybe lift your knees a little higher."

"Easy for you to say. You just get to stand there and watch while I die of heatstroke." I got my arms and legs synched, and then we worked on the extended trot, which was the same thing but with longer strides. My T-shirt was soaked through, and the idea of having to put hooves and tack on eventually was making me want to die.

"The extended trot needs to be like a glide," Ryan called, glancing at the phone and then shielding the screen with one hand so he could read it. "Really throw those legs forward and imagine you're floating."

I imagined I was drowning in a sea of my own sweat.

We practiced the salute, which was like a horse curtsy that took place at marker X. Dressage rings had a bunch of posts with letters, and I guess marker X was something special. "We need to make some letter posts," Ryan said.

I rolled my eyes. *Yep. Maybe we should've brought our craft shit so we could sit here making letter posts in the blazing-as-balls sun.*

Next we tried a *passage*—which, according to Ryan, was pronounced "*pa-sahhhge.*" The *passage* was a collected trot with very little forward movement. So it was almost like jogging in place, but you still moved forward a little. "I do not feel graceful," I complained.

"Shh. Work on keeping your arms moving with your legs."

I grumbled under my breath. Shushing me? Really?

We kept going. Cantering with lead changes—*tempi.* Piaffe. Pirouette. I was terrible at everything. Though I did kind of like the pirouette, since it involved spinning around. He put my bridle on and tried to practice cuing me with the whip for all the different moves, but all I could think about was AC. A cold beer. Curling up in front of the TV with Collingsworth.

"Prance when you trot," he urged me. "Lift those legs."

I seriously tried to prance, but it was exhausting. He kept tentatively tapping my calves with the whip and telling me to lift my legs higher, which was pissing me off. So then I started pulling away whenever the whip came near me, and finally I yanked the reins right out of his hands and bolted. I hadn't planned to do it, but it felt pretty great. There wasn't really anything I could do with all my gear on, so I just stopped a few feet away and stared at him.

"Thunder!" he shouted. "Not cool."

I backed up a little as he approached, since he was still holding the whip. When he got too close, I turned and jogged away again. What was interesting was that even though I was irritated with him,

I felt as close as I ever had to slipping into a pony headspace. To communicating as a horse rather than a person.

He tossed the whip aside.

Reached into his pocket and took out a Jolly Rancher.

Game changer.

"C'mere," he said. "Come on over here. No more dressage today."

For a second I thought maybe it was a trap. But the Jolly Rancher was green apple, so I walked forward until I was right in front of him. He took my bridle off and set it on the ground. Unwrapped the Jolly Rancher and fed it to me. Then he helped me drink half a bottle of water and poured the rest over my head.

"You worked harder than I did today. I think you've earned something when we get home."

"Is it wings?" I asked hopefully.

"It's better than wings. If I do my job right."

We took my tail out, and walked over to the trees. Sat in the grass together, under the shade. He picked a blade of grass and spun it between his thumb and finger. I watched him.

"What if we lose?" I asked after a while.

He turned to me. "What if we do?"

"Will it all be for nothing, then? Like, the hundreds of dollars we spent, and all the drives out here, and the guys building the cart for us . . ."

"Kamen." He shook his head and kinda huffed, smiling. "It's not for nothing. I'm having, like, the best time ever."

I nodded. "I mostly know that. I just wanted to make a dramatic speech because it's, like, that moment in the movie when we have a crisis of conscience right before the big day."

"You mean crisis of confidence?"

"Sure." I took the piece of grass from him. "And I also wanted to make sure you feel like I do. This is really fun. Even though I hate dressage."

"Look, we're probably going to win. Because we're awesome. But if we don't, it's fine."

"Because we're still awesome?"

"Exactly."

I twirled the grass against his forehead. "I really want to win, though."

"Good." He slapped the grass out of my hand. "Then let's get home and get your reward. And we'll be back at this in a couple of days."

He took me home, and we showered together. And I guess he did his job right, because everything that happened that night was better than wings.

We took off early the next morning to have brunch at Ryan's family's house, leaving a key under the matt so Gould could walk Collingsworth. We spent the drive there singing along to the radio, and I tried to teach Ryan how to harmonize.

"Are you nervous?" he asked as we got close.

"Are you kidding? I hung out with your parents that one time. They were awesome."

"Yeah, you hung out with them for, like, two seconds. This is your first experience spending any significant amount of time with them. And meeting my sister."

"I am one hundred percent looking forward to it." Parents freaking loved me. Especially moms.

We had an awesome time. Ryan's mom was a weatherwoman for a local station, so I got her to do the weather voice for me. His dad was charming as fuck, and just super chill. Ryan's sister, Jacey, was all breathtakingly beautiful and wickedly sarcastic, and even though during brunch I saw her put her finger in her ear and then look at it, she made my list of favorite people ever.

The meal conversation sort of turned into embarrassing stories about Ryan's childhood, which I loved, even though Ryan looked like he wanted to drown himself in his OJ.

"One time—" His mom laughed. "Ohhh, God. Ry was six, and I took him with me to the grocery store. We passed this *really* tall black man in the produce section, and Ry goes, loud enough for the whole store to hear, 'Look, Mom! It's Michael Jordan!'"

Everyone got a kick out of that.

Ryan's mom rubbed her temples. "I thought I was going to die of embarrassment."

I took more crepe thingies. "Dude, that sounds so much like stuff I did when I was little."

Jacey flashed Ryan a grin. "That's what I remember most about you as a kid. You never knew when to shut up."

Ryan flushed but grinned back. "That hasn't changed."

Ryan's mom shook her head. "What *I* remember is Ryan had so many interests. School and drawing and sports and clubs . . ." She looked at Ryan. "And you would work *so* hard to do things perfectly. But then always, right before you finished something, you'd stop."

"Thanks, Mom."

"It's true!" She turned to me. "We have all these unfinished drawings of Ry's. And then school, you know, he studied and studied for the ACT. He was so determined to get into the college he wanted. But then once he'd taken the ACT, he didn't do anything to prepare for the SAT, and—"

"So I ended up going to my second-choice college." Ryan didn't sound like he thought this was funny anymore. "Big deal."

"And you had all these ideas about what you were going to do for a career. We couldn't keep them all straight."

"Until I stepped in." Ryan's dad raised his OJ glass like he was toasting.

We all looked over at him.

Ryan's dad took a swig of juice. "I said, 'Ry, you're gonna have to make a decision and stick to it. You can't go your whole life jumping from job to job. Hobby to hobby.'"

Ryan's expression was strange. He didn't look upset, exactly, but he definitely didn't look happy. "Yeah," he said quietly. "You told me to be a paralegal."

"I didn't tell you to. You did the research on practical careers, and you made a decision. And you're doing great. Your mom and I are very proud of you."

Jacey was staring at her plate. Ryan's mom looked about to say something, but she didn't.

Ryan's dad laughed. "You see these shows and movies glamorizing people in their late twenties and early thirties who are so self-absorbed. Who still haven't settled down and are, you know, playing video games and bitching about their love lives. And I always think, 'This is not as complicated as you're making it.'"

Ryan's mom served herself more salad. "Young people have a lot more options now than we did." She'd bought a massive bag of croutons in my honor, and there was an awkward silence as she shook some onto her plate.

"It's like—" Ryan's dad settled back and turned to me. "You're in the restaurant business, right? You can enjoy many different foods. You can like lamb and beef and pork and chicken. But when it comes time to cook a meal, you have to decide what's gonna be your main course. People don't trust a leader who can't make decisions and stick to them."

I was kind of surprised I'd thought he was so chill. He definitely had a dickish side to him. I wiped my mouth with my napkin. "I don't actually eat a lot of meals with main courses." I watched Ryan's dad take a long swig of OJ. "I eat a bunch of different foods for each meal. And, like, a lot of people I serve send their meals back because it turns out they don't like them, or they think it needs more seasoning, or whatever." I wasn't sure I was, like, rocking the correct metaphor here, but hey. "I don't think I'd trust a leader who wasn't willing to provide a wide variety, or consider a lot of different paths to deliciousness. Or admit they were wrong about a choice they made."

I glanced at Ryan, who shot me a grateful look.

His dad went on. "But I think that amount of choice is what's hurting young people today. Why not pick something practical to do with your life and take pride in doing it? Instead of puttering around from endeavor to endeavor." He shook his head. "Young people don't have any concept of hardship. They think hardship is not being able to buy the newest iPhone."

"Anyone who's alive knows what hardship is," I said, pretty loud.

Silence. So great, Ryan was probably never going to let me near his family again.

But his dad shrugged. "Maybe so."

We all went back to eating.

We played Cranium after the meal, which was insanely fun. Ryan was real good with the Cranium clay. We watched TV, then got all the food out again around dinnertime for round two.

Ryan and I had planned to leave by eight, but it was nine thirty by the time we started home.

Ryan leaned against the passenger window. "I should've taken tomorrow off work. I am *not* gonna want to get up."

"Aw. I'll switch places with you."

"You'll walk around hunched over, and no one will know the difference?"

I grinned and started singing "Short People" by Randy Newman.

He shoved my arm gently. Looked out the window. "I always do this."

"Do what?"

"Stay at my family's longer than I mean to."

"Yeah, 'cause your family's awesome. Except for your sister who picks her earwax."

"I know. We've never been able to do anything about her."

"You all are so cute."

"Yeah. We're like a family of meerkats. We're all tiny and blond, and we turn at the same time if you say something to one of us."

"I love you all."

"Except my dad?"

"Your dad's cool. I'm sorry if I should have kept my mouth shut."

He shook his head. "I really appreciated that. My dad's great. He just has, like, really strong ideas. And feels these random urges to express them."

I drove for a moment in silence. "You wish you saw them more?"

"Yeah." His voice was soft. "I know why you spend so much time with your friends. When you get around the right people, it just . . . changes you from the inside. And you forget about the robot you are at work, or the dick you are when you have to wait too long in line at the store, and you're just totally you, and it's perfect."

I nodded. "You nailed it, man."

"That's how I feel about you."

I smiled at him quickly, then looked back at the road. "Me too. About you, I mean. Not about me."

He got really quiet after that, and I figured I was missing something. This was a thing that had been happening most of my life: People around me would get sad—not just *I really wanted to eat at*

Thai Spice but I forgot it's closed on Mondays sad, but *deep* sad—and I'd understand sort of what they were feeling and why. But I didn't get there all the way. It was like we were snorkeling together, but the other person had an oxygen tank and that thing that goes in your mouth when you scuba dive, and suddenly they'd just dive down into the sea, and I'd be left up at the surface with my snorkel, wishing I could follow them.

I was the right guy to go pick Gould up at the hospital, because I wasn't gonna judge and I could keep a secret and I knew the best place to get a milkshake afterward. But I was the wrong guy to figure out exactly what Gould was feeling and help him deal with it.

We were approaching the exit for Silverton, and suddenly I had an idea.

I turned to Ryan. "Can we make a stop?"

"Uh . . . sure."

I saw him trying to peek at the gas gauge.

"Just for fun," I said, pulling into the right lane. "There's nothing wrong."

"What's fun in Silverton?"

I didn't answer. I took the exit and headed toward the state forest. "Do you like stars and stuff?"

"Um, at 10 p.m. on a Sunday night, when I have to work in the morning? I suppose."

"Come on. I just want to stop for a few minutes."

He laughed. "Okay."

We reached the entrance to the forest, and my mind was still on people's sadness. Even my grief when Hal died hadn't seemed to match my friends'. I *had* watched news about the trial—the others were like, *"No, we can't even stand to hear about it."* I'd been the first one to go back to Riddle. Whenever we were hanging out, I'd wanted to tell funny stories about Hal, but for a while, the others gave me weird looks if I was like, *"Hey, remember that time he tried to make a frozen Slip'N Slide?"*

Dave had said recently that the way he remembered it, the four of us hardly spent any time together after the funeral. He remembered the group almost falling apart—like we all just diverged and left each other alone.

I didn't remember it like that. Maybe we hadn't spent a lot of time together as a group, but I'd still seen each of them pretty regularly. Except Gould—Gould had been hard to contact. And he hadn't lived with Dave at the time, so it wasn't like I could just go pound on his bedroom door when I visited Dave and force him to come out.

I really didn't think I missed Hal any less than they did. My mom kept telling me people dealt with grief differently. I used to have nightmares about Hal that I only told her about. Not really nightmares about his death, but nightmares that he had survived the rope scene but was badly injured, and we'd just gone on with our lives, thinking he was dead and never knowing better.

I turned into the picnic area of the forest.

"Is this some kind of Lovers' Lane?" Ryan asked. "Makeout Point? Tail Trail?"

"Sort of." I parked in a gravel lay-by and shut off the engine.

We walked past picnic benches and dark shelters, to a grassy area with a few scraggly bushes. I took off my hoodie and spread it on the grass, and we both sat on it. The sky was cloudy, so not that many stars. But I always liked night clouds even better than day clouds. And, man, you could *breathe* out here without feeling like you had your mouth around a car's exhaust pipe.

"Sorry," I said after a while. "I shouldn't be keeping you out late."

"It's fine. I hardly ever get out of the city."

"I know. I was just thinking how awesome breathing is out here." Now that we were sitting here, I felt weird about the reason I'd made this stop. So I waited until we'd shot the shit for a while and then brought it up, clumsily as Collingsworth trying to walk from his bed to his food bowl.

"This is where we scattered Hal's ashes."

He turned to me so fast I kinda flinched.

"Sorry if that's a creepy thing to spring on you. But I love this place, and, I mean, the wind carried him off, so it's not like we're sitting on him or anything."

"Oh." He nodded, like he was trying to figure out what to say.

"I know it's a little weird."

"It's not. I just didn't know."

I wasn't sure why I'd done this. Taken him to this place that was maybe technically supposed to be a sad place for me—just because I thought *he* was feeling sad. But this wasn't a sad place, and I guess I wanted to show him something that really *confused* me.

Because when I thought about Hal and the forest, sometimes I felt like Hal definitely wasn't alone. He had, like, trees and birds and hikers and the air and all the seasons. And the rest of us were tied to this place by him, and he got to spend forever in this badass forest that was way better than a roached-out apartment in the city.

But then I thought about this one night a few months before he died. He'd been crashing at my place for three days, and I kinda needed him out because he kept leaving his weed stuff around the living room, and my landlord was the type of guy who'd come in every week to look at the wiring or comment on the tub rust or whatever. And one night Hal had harder stuff than weed, so I was like, *"No, man. You gotta go home."*

That makes me sound shitty, like I knew my friend had a drug problem or something, and all I could think was, you know, don't get me in trouble. But the others and I had talked to Hal a million times about, like, *"Hey, are you sure this is just once in a while, or is it becoming a problem?"* And as far as I could tell, he really wasn't crazy addicted. He was just a dude who did what felt good in the moment, and once in a while what felt good was illegal. But always drug-illegal, not, like, murder-illegal.

I told him I'd drive him home, and he was doing the whole, *I don't feel like going home* thing. And I was just like, *"Why? Tell me why. I'm listening."* But he wouldn't give me a reason, so I got him in the car, and I played his favorite music, and I asked if he needed to stop for food, and I tried to talk to him about this guy at work he'd been trying to get with, but he was just kind of a prick about all my efforts.

I got to his apartment and took him inside. At least four roaches scattered when I turned on the light, and the place smelled like tar and macaroni salad. There were dishes piled in the sink, the microwave was open and looked like someone had barfed in it, and I thought, *Dude, no wonder you don't feel like being here.* I tried to get him into the bedroom, but he said it was too hot in there and he wanted to sleep on the couch. So I helped him onto the couch and pulled a blanket over him. Rinsed out the least gross cup in the sink and brought him some water. All this mom stuff. He was quiet through all of it.

And as soon as I started to say good-bye, he wanted to talk about the guy at the drugstore where he worked.

Then he wanted me to play him a song.

"I don't have my guitar."

"So just sing."

I sang.

He said he'd go sleep in his bed, if I'd come in with him and see if I thought his mattress needed to be flipped.

What twenty-four-year-old had ever fucking flipped a mattress for any reason other than spilling beer or puking on it?

But I went to the bedroom and got him resettled in there. He had these *sheets* that were, like, jersey cotton, with tiny white sheep all over, and every once in a while, one dark-blue sheep. I was pretty sure my grandmother'd had those same sheets. I told him I had to go, and he just stared at the wall. Eventually I patted his shoulder and left, but I had this bad taste in my mouth for the rest of the night. I imagined him lying awake, feeling totally abandoned.

Which was ridiculous in a way, because he was an adult man who could figure out options if he was lonely. But wasn't ridiculous at all if you thought about just . . . humans.

So sometimes now when I left the forest, I thought I was leaving Hal someplace peaceful, someplace where he was laughing at me for having to go back to the city and the noise and the roaches.

But sometimes I worried I was leaving him somewhere he didn't feel like being, somewhere lonely.

Last year, Gould, Miles, Dave, and I had gone to see some movie where a young guy lived in a gross house and drank and did drugs and, like, hired a hooker and cried in her arms instead of having sex with her. At the end, he drove his car into a pole, and you weren't supposed to know whether it was suicide or an accident. Gould had been *pissed.*

"I hate that. Everyone who dies young in movies is either this perfect innocent or this tragic douche bag."

I'd kind of liked the movie. *"What do you mean?"*

"I mean if someone *living* is in their twenties and drinks or experiments with drugs or fights with their partner or spends hours lying on the couch feeling sorry for themselves, then we're just like, 'Yeah, that guy's in his twenties.' But if they *die* and they did all that, then it's like they were always in some metaphorical fast car careening out of control, destined for tragedy."

I'd thought a lot about that afterward, since I knew he was talking about Hal. Some of the news articles about Hal had done the *He had his whole life ahead of him* thing. But I'd also heard people from the kink community talk about how Hal had been on poppers and high as fuck that night and how he'd always taken a lot of risks. That was when I'd started learning Tracy Chapman's "Fast Car" and playing it at Pitch.

"Hey." Ryan nudged me. "You okay?"

I glanced at him. "Yeah. I'm thinking about Hal, but it's not bad or anything."

I thought suddenly about how D and Drix and maybe GK and Kel would have had to do this too: figure out how to be there for Dave and Miles and Gould when they were grieving. I wondered how they'd reacted. I could see D being awkward in the face of strong emotion. But Dave had tons of strong emotions, so maybe D was actually good at dealing with that. I bet Drix had handled Miles's Hal-baggage like a pro. I still couldn't even picture GK and Kel with Gould, period, so I had no idea how they dealt with the fact that Gould was still kind of a wreck.

Ryan looked uncomfortable.

I scooted closer to him. "I don't need you to do any big thing to show me you love me."

"What?"

I didn't have a clue how to explain this. "Dave told D he wanted to do domestic discipline, and that was, like, a turning point in their relationship. And Drix told Miles he'd help him raise the kid, and Miles was like, 'Holy fuck.' I just want you to know that I don't need anything huge from you. All the stuff you're doing is perfect. Megalodon stories and pony competitions and helping me with my music."

He seemed to relax a little then. "So it doesn't bother you that I'm . . ."

"What?"

"You don't mind half-finished drawings?"

At first I was confused, because I thought he meant literally. Then I figured maybe he meant the whole thing with what his mom had said, and the *I wish I had a different job* or *I wish I lived in a different city* or *Let's get a cat instead.*

"Hey," I said. "We don't need to finish the drawings until we're, like, ninety-eight."

After a few minutes, he said, "Come here, Kamen."

He held me. Tiny little Chihuahua dude just took me in his arms like I fit there. And then I started singing "Fast Car"—softly—and I

figured he wouldn't think I'd gone off the rails or anything, since I randomly burst into song all the time. So I just sang it because it made me feel good, and because I wanted Hal to know fast cars didn't mean tragedy and for Ryan to know that he and I were gonna keep exploring and that we didn't have to end up with a life that made perfect sense—just one we'd built together.

CHAPTER THIRTEEN

In the final two weeks before PetPlayFest, the montage got intense. Pretty much every chance we got, we were up at D's property, practicing. Dressage sucked. I still couldn't remember the difference between *passage* and piaffe, and I got the cues all mixed up. If he used word commands, I got confused. If he gave only whip and rein cues, I wasn't quite as confused, but I still struggled.

"I'm never gonna beat Cinnamon," I said after a particularly rough practice. We'd brought handmade letter signs and set up an arena. We'd started working to music—I'd chosen Survivor's "High on You" as my performance piece. It was a fast song, and neither of us was a great choreographer, but it gave me a chance to do a lot of pirouettes, which I was actually pretty good at.

"Hey, don't talk like that. Your pirouettes are looking great. Your half pass is, at the least, entertaining. Your prancing is getting better."

It had been getting better. Mostly because Ryan had found, in our gear bag, a curved plug designed to rub the prostate. He'd started having me wear that instead of the tail when we practiced dressage. In some ways, it hindered us, because all I could think about was coming, and not piaffing. But Jesus Christ did it get me lifting my legs.

He put his hands on his hips. "I do think your biggest issue is headspace. Like, you've got to let go and believe you're a pony."

I sighed. "Sometimes I believe I'm a pony. But sometimes I believe I'm a guy prancing around in a leather harness, looking ridiculous."

He cupped my cheek. "You're only as ridiculous as you let yourself feel. And if you want me to cross-stitch that on a throw pillow, I will."

I threw myself into the montage once more. The leather pants arrived, and I started working in those, and tried to get used to having my balls and sheathed cock exposed. I even started shaving my balls, because let's be honest, if they were gonna be on display in my crotchless pants, I wanted them to look good. We also incorporated the furry boots and the Slash wig. We didn't practice bobbing for apples, or the balloon pop, since we figured those competitions were pretty self-explanatory. But we did buy kneepads so I could practice running on all fours, since all pets in the balloon pop had to be on their hands and knees.

The cart pulling, I loved. We timed ourselves each practice, and I got better and better. We didn't really have a way to measure the oval we'd marked out in the meadow and compare it to the size of the course we'd be racing at PetPlayFest. But whatever. I was athletic, and Ryan was light, and I felt confident I could win a race.

I got a bunch of texts from Dave about Gould's party, which was gonna be in the poolroom of a sports bar downtown. Something was niggling me about the date, and I couldn't figure out what until Ryan and I were singing "Bent" one night to get us in the mood for the Rob Thomas concert that weekend. And then it hit me.

Gould's freaking fake thirtieth birthday was the same night as the concert.

I thought about it for a moment. Then I called Dave.

"Hey." Dave sounded like he was chewing.

"I'm not gonna make it to Gould's party."

Silence on the other end.

"I, uh . . . There's this concert. Ryan and I were talking about Matchbox Twenty last week, and we thought it would be funny to try to see Rob Thomas in concert. And I was drunk and bought tickets and forgot that was the night of Gould's thing. So I'm just gonna drop by Gould's work at lunch Friday and wish him happy birthday. And then maybe we could all do dinner sometime soon?"

I expected some protest. Expected Dave to rant about how we'd been planning this for two weeks, and it would suck without me. But he just said, "Fine."

"I'm really sorry."

"You do what you gotta do."

"You really okay with this?"

"Yeah," he said shortly. "We'll still have plenty of fun. You go do your thing with Ryan."

That kind of hurt my feelings. "I'm sorry."

"What? No big deal. We'll live." I didn't like how he said that. I was pretty sure he was gonna bitch about me to Miles as soon as we hung up. Plus there was a part of me that wanted my friends to be devastated at the idea of having a party without me.

"Well, anyway . . ."

"You talk to Ricky?" he interrupted.

"Yeah. He was . . . I mean, he likes Bill. I don't know if I can do anything about that. But I warned him to be careful."

"Did you tell Gould? About Ricky and Bill?"

"No."

"Well, he found out somehow." More chewing.

"Oh."

"So Ricky's not speaking to us. And, for once, it wasn't me with my loud mouth who ruined things. Gould, like, went *after* him about it."

"Went after him?"

Dave swallowed whatever he was eating. "I just don't get how Gould can play with GK and Kel but hate Bill so much."

"I know, man. But you know . . ." There was a thing I wanted to say, and I wasn't sure if I was gonna say it right, or if it was even the right thing to say. "Maybe we all need to move forward." Not just me. And not just where Hal was concerned. But, like, all of us needed to keep going, keep growing up.

A pause. "He's going to the drugstore again."

"What?" Gould had gone through a period after Hal's death where some days he'd go to the drugstore where Hal had worked and just sit there in the car. Dave had been super creeped out by it, but I'd thought maybe it was pretty normal for someone who was in shock and grieving and all that. But if he was doing it again . . . "Did you talk to him about it?"

"No. He told Miles."

"Shit."

I could *hear* Dave shrug. "Anyway, I've got to go."

"No, hold on."

He sighed. "You tell me, Kamen. You tell me what to tell Gould about moving forward."

"It's not just Gould. It's like what Ryan said about thinking of the Subs Club as, like, bigger than our personal tragedy."

"Please, don't quote *him* on this. I can't handle—"

"Well, learn to handle it, because he's not fucking wrong!" I didn't really mean to interrupt, but it was already happening, and sometimes words are like a fart—you can't stuff 'em back in. "You like it. You like being stuck in the past. We all do, probably, in a way. Because who's gonna blame us if we don't know where to go from here? All we have to do when regular adult shit gets hard is, like, point a finger at Bill, or Cinnamon, or GK and Kel, or whoever, and— You know? And Ryan's got a different perspective, and that actually *helps* me with moving on."

"Yeah, you're drinking his Kool-Aid."

"What Kool-Aid? The Kool-Aid where I actually have a life now that's not just being sad about Hal or mad about BDSM injustices or whatever?"

"He doesn't even understand about Hal, or us, or anything! He wasn't *there*. He's just another person who thinks this is some sensational thing that happened that they can fucking tell their friends about, or whatever. 'Cool story, bro.'"

That was such unbelievable hypo-fucking-critical bullshit I couldn't even wrap my head around it. "Maya wasn't there. Neither was Ricky. Neither was D."

"Maya fucking cried when I told her about Hal. Ricky was scared shitless. They *get* why it was such a big deal. And D— Fuck, yeah, he *wasn't* there, but he never asked to be part of the club. Okay? Ryan asked to be part of our group—part of *our* group. And then he comes in with his having-no-fucking-idea, and talks about—about Hal being stupid—"

"That's not what he said!"

"He said subs need to take more responsibility, and he *was* talking about Hal, and I don't get how it doesn't bug the shit out of you that he's completely insensitive to people's feelings."

"You." I jabbed my finger furiously, even though he couldn't see me. "*You* are blunt. *You* say shit without thinking, and it hurts people's feelings. Maybe this is just a taste of your own medicine, dude."

"I don't—"

"You do."

"But I'm not—"

"Just listen!"

"*You* listen!"

"To what? I listen to you all the freaking time, man. You tell me how to feel about political issues or how I should feel about my own relationship, and I'm sick of it. I'm sick of *listening* to you."

"Then hang up the fucking phone!" he shouted.

So I did.

"We should move," I said to Ryan that night.

Ryan looked up from his latest "Snow Wanderer" drawing, surprised. "What?"

"Not right now. But we ought to pick a city, and then, in a year, move there. I've been thinking about it. And I do want to try it."

"*Really*?"

I nodded.

Moving forward. I'm fucking moving forward. Look at me doing that.

He set the tablet aside. "Kamen, that's . . . awesome."

There was way too big a pause there, and he didn't look like he thought it was awesome. So what the fuck was that about? Why didn't people just say what they fucking meant? *Except Dave. I don't want him to say what he means ever again.*

"Is it?" I demanded. "Is it awesome?"

He looked startled. "Sure. Yeah. Where do you think we should go?"

I forced myself to breathe. "Maybe Austin, since it has a good music scene. Or Nashville." I was having a really hard time making my voice sound pleasant.

"Or Seattle."

"Or Seattle."

He leaned back and stretched, chewing on his lip. "Well, we've got some time to think about it."

"For sure."

"You're being really weird right now."

"I'm just hungry. We should make dinner. Pasta Boat? What about juice? You want juice? I could juice some shit."

He was staring at me like I'd grown a microwave-sized Collingsworth head. "I don't think you should be around the juicer right now. It has sharp things."

"I can handle sharp things."

I got the juicer out and juiced the fuck out of some apples and some kale and a star fruit, just to prove a point.

I was a lot like that for the next couple of days, as my panic about the idea of moving fought with these random bursts of *Yeah, I do want to do this. 'Cause maybe my destiny is waiting for me in some city I've never thought about, and maybe I* will *become a famous singer. Maybe I've been holding myself back for a long time.*

The day of the concert, I threw myself into a city search. Ryan was at work for a half day, so I spent five straight hours on the computer, only getting up to walk Collingsworth.

I looked up Austin. *Holy elephant fuck*, no. Shitty apartments were, like, thousands of dollars. Seattle, I decided, was too rainy. And Pittsburgh was too . . . Pittsburgh.

"What about Cleveland?" I asked when Ryan came home at lunchtime.

He walked to the back of the couch and leaned down to kiss the top of my head. "Cleveland?"

"Yeah. It used to be a joke, but I've been reading about it. They've made tons of renovations over the past few years. And now they have a good music scene."

He paused. He'd been kind of skittish around me since that vigorous juicing session. "I'd be down for Cleveland. It's not too far away. And probably, like, half an hour closer to my family than I am now."

Not too far away.

It was like four hours from my friends. But that was okay. Because the whole point of moving was to find out who I was when they weren't, like, factoring into everything I did in life. And if I needed to see them, I could make weekend trips. Take a couple weeks off in the summer and visit for longer—if the guys even still wanted me around, since apparently I'd fallen in love with a monster who failed to weep every time we brought up Hal.

"I even found some places near Cleveland State that are pet-friendly. So we could get a dog. Or a cat, whatever. And I could work at one of the restaurants that does mad student business. And if you decide you want to go to law school, there's Case."

He patted my shoulder, staring at the screen. "This is awesome. Get ready, Cleveland."

"You don't sound excited. Why aren't you excited?"

"No, I'm excited. I'm just surprised you suddenly want to do this."

"Well, you're the one who gets freaking alerts on your phone about apartments." I couldn't keep the irritation out of my voice. "I'm just getting on the train. The moving-forward train."

"Did something happen?"

"*No*. Nothing happened. God."

"Well, this is gonna be a fun concert, huh?" he said dryly. He went to shower, closing the bathroom door way too hard. I stayed at the computer, staring at the tabs for Cleveland apartments.

The concert was a fucking bust. I couldn't really focus. I imagined the others eating gluten-free cake downtown, and drinking beer, and then going back to Dave's to watch whatever stupid shit was on Netflix. Imagined them being fine without me.

Ryan was in a freaking great mood. He sang the whole way home. But I think that was less of a for-real great mood and more a way of digging at me, since I was being a dick.

I went over to the duplex the next day after pony practice, where I'd managed to get actually zero dressage moves right. I wanted to wish Gould a happy birthday and apologize again for not being there, since it wasn't his fault that Dave was a bastard and that I'd gotten myself into a whole big moving-way-too-far-forward mess.

Gould was gone, but Dave was there, and we were super cold to each other, which— Good. Just a few more months of not talking, and then I wouldn't even have to worry about him anymore.

Except I couldn't exactly keep my mouth shut. "Ryan and I are gonna move to Cleveland," I said, with an I-give-zero-fucks shrug.

He gave me a real kind of, you know, death stare. "What?"

"We've been thinking about it a lot. And when our lease is up next year, we might want to try something different." Dave was looking at me like he wanted to put a grappling hook through my face. "He wants to be closer to his parents. I want a change of pace. So we're moving."

"To *Cleveland*?"

"It's turning into a really nice city now."

"Cleveland."

"Yeah."

"River-on-fire Cleveland."

"That was decades ago."

"The city that regularly lets LeBron James jizz on its face."

"That's the one."

"Fucking *West Sixth Street*."

"Yeah, man. Cleveland."

Dave turned away and gave this incredibly derisive snort.

I glared at him. "What do you have against Cleveland?"

"My God, Kamen, Cleveland is the Cobalt of cities!"

Ouch.

Dave took a deep breath. "My Megabus broke down there once, and a tramp tried to take my gas station grab-n-go sandwich."

"Well, that's where we're moving. So deal with it."

He shook his head in disgust. "I've already dealt with it. Like you said: other people's lives are none of my business."

I hated this. But I didn't know how to make it better. So I said something really, like, not at all a comeback, like, "See you around."

And I left.

The next day was even worse. I was doing dishes when Ryan came home from work, and I couldn't get all the damn plates into the dumb-fuck dishwasher. I was getting frustrated enough to want to throw shit.

"Hey!" Ryan called from the living room. I listened to him hang his keys on the key hook, which for some reason made me feel even worse. Why did we have a *key hook*? Who the hell was I?

I didn't answer.

He came into the kitchen. "How was your day?"

I forced another plate into the lower rack. Were we even gonna have a dishwasher in Cleveland? Where would we live? How long would it take me to make new friends? Would my old friends ever call me? Or was it gonna be, like, texts every day . . . then once a week . . . then every couple of months . . . then never?

I tried to keep my voice normal. "Stupid."

"Stupid, huh?"

"Worked the lunch shift. Which is stupid."

"Got ya."

"My car needs new brakes. And I can't fit all the plates in here."

"So leave some in the sink."

I straightened. "It's not that simple!"

"Eaaaaasy. What the hell has been up your ass the past couple of days, buddy?"

That was almost too much, him using names my friends had always used with me. Big guy. Buddy. *Condescending fucking nicknames.* I wanted this life with him. I did. I wanted to be independent and push myself and not always make safe decisions. I wanted to—I don't know—have this relationship be the most important thing to me. Wanted Ryan to be my family.

But I also wanted what I'd always had. Because even if my friends and I weren't perfect, I loved them so much that it, like, physically hurt, and being part of that group was an opportunity beyond what most people were given. Maybe that sounded stupid, since pretty much everyone had friends. But not like mine.

Ryan stepped around me and picked up the stack of remaining plates. Started washing them by hand in the sink. "Sorry about your car."

"It's a piece of shit anyway."

"When we move next year, we can get a new car. One of those tiny ones. With three wheels."

"With what money?"

He turned. "Come on. Don't be like this."

I tossed some silverware in the dishwasher basket. "I might not even want to move to Cleveland."

"It was your idea."

"Well, maybe now I'm changing my mind! Is that okay? Am I allowed to change my mind? You change your mind all the time."

He stared at me. "Dude. What is going *on*? If you tell me, maybe I can help."

"Don't call me 'dude.' We're not sixteen." I grabbed another plate and stuffed it in the rack. "Dave's Megabus broke down in Cleveland and a hobo took his sandwich."

He turned off the water. "What kind of sandwich?"

"Does it matter? Cleveland hobos are relentless. They'll take anything!"

He stepped behind me and wrapped his arms around me. Oh my God. Why was he trying to be nice to me? Why did he not want to throw the plates too? Was I completely fucking alone in my need to just *destroy* something? His hands left wet patches on my shirt. "We have hobos here."

"Not like Cleveland hobos."

"What do you know about Cleveland hobos?"

I shrugged him off and put the plate in the dishwasher. "I'm just not sure we've thought this through."

"You know Dave has a tendency to exaggerate to try to get you to—"

"No. Don't say things about my friends. You don't know them like I do. You don't know what we've been through. You weren't *there*." I was fucking this up so bad. Like, possibly worse than anything had ever been fucked up in the whole history of the world.

Ryan was silent.

I took a deep breath. "Sorry. I just . . ."

He waited a second, and when I didn't continue, asked, "So where *do* you want to move?"

"Maybe nowhere! Maybe I never freaking wanted to move anywhere! But you—"

"So what, it's my fault? I forced you into this? We hang out with *your* friends and go to *your* dungeon and get the painting of the animal *you* want—"

"You wanted the hare too! Don't even act like you didn't want the hare!"

"I wanted a megalodon! You know what I think this is about? Your friends dictating your life. Everything you do, you have to think about how they'll feel or what you'll tell them—"

"They don't dictate my life!"

"Then why can't we do this one thing I want?"

I turned to him and continued, my panic rising. "Do you really want it? Or is this like what your parents were talking about? Where you work really hard for a while to build a perfect life here and then leave it unfinished?"

He stared at me. Not even a glare, just, like, this shocked, almost blank expression.

"Ryan. I'm s—"

"No." He looked away. "Don't."

He stalked to our bedroom. I listened to him slam around in there for a while. I wasn't sure what to do. I pretty much didn't fight with anyone. Like, once in a while I had to check my friends if I thought they were being too dickish about something, but I didn't even *know* how to fight with Ryan. We'd always been best buds.

Best buds was not a relationship.

Best buds was not adulting.

I went to the front hall and leaned beside the well-dressed hare. Collingsworth followed me and watched as I tried to calm down.

I couldn't talk to Dave. Miles would be nice to me, but he was the most likely to secretly judge. I took out my phone. But Gould . . .

One time, last year, I was kinda mad because I thought Dave and Miles weren't taking me seriously. And Gould took me aside and was like, "You know what's up better than any of us. We could all learn a lot from you." And that made me feel way better.

Gould answered on the second ring. "Hey, Kamen."

"Hey, um . . ." I took a breath. "Can I come over?"

"Sure. What's up?"

"I just . . ." I glanced over my shoulder as though I expected Ryan to be right there. "I need to come over. As long as Dave's not there. Please?"

"He's out with Maya. Come on over," Gould said calmly.

When I got to the front porch of the duplex, it hit me that I shouldn't be bothering him with this. If he was really having a shitty time like Dave had said, he probably didn't want to hear about me having a fight with Ryan. Plus I'd bailed on his birthday to go to a friggin' Rob Thomas concert, so I probably wasn't his favorite person right now.

But he let me in and sat on the couch with me and asked, "What's up?"

"Uh. Ryan and me had a fight."

"About what?"

I took another few seconds to try to calm down. "About moving to Cleveland."

He nodded. "Dave said you were moving."

I looked at him and wanted to basically beg him to tell me what to do. Because he had a really nice face—everyone always talked about his nice face and how it made you think he could solve any problem. "I just get so confused sometimes about whether I'm doing adulting right."

He smiled and shook his head. Put his arm around me. "Come here." He pulled me against his shoulder.

I blinked for a moment. "You smell good."

"Thanks."

I tried to look up at him. "And now I'm fighting with Dave because he thinks I abandoned the group because I didn't come to your birthday and I'm always with Ryan and Ryan doesn't know anything about Hal. And I think maybe that's why I told Ryan I'd move, because I was mad at Dave. But now I've got all this shit running through my head, like if Ryan *does* want to move, then don't I have to respect that? We can't just stay here forever because *I* want to, right?"

"I think—"

"But I don't think he really does want to move. I think he just has one of those brains where he thinks that whatever he's doing, he should actually be doing something else. Like he second-guesses all his decisions. Except when we do pony play, and then he's super focused, and he's an amazing handler."

Gould nodded.

"I think he's really happy here. With me. Mostly. But I don't know. And how do I know *I* wouldn't be happier somewhere else? I don't think I would, but I've never tried it."

"So you think—"

"And there's all this stuff I never really thought about in terms of relationships, because I was too freaking in love to care. But what if we *do* break up, and I don't have anywhere to live. And if we had a dog, who would get the dog? And do I get to keep the 'Snow Wanderer' drawings? Because those were a gift, but they're also his greatest creation."

"Slow down," Gould said gently.

I clutched at him, thinking suddenly about my parents. "Gould. Why does anyone get married?"

"Whoooooaaaaa, Kamen."

That was a command I'd gotten real good at responding to.

He clapped me on the back. "No one's getting married. There is no dog. I'm not sure what 'Snow Wanderer' is. Take a couple deep breaths."

I did. Raised my head from his shoulder and looked at him. "I'm sorry I didn't come to your birthday party."

"It's fine."

"I didn't know the concert was on the same day."

"I know."

"I was drunk when I bought the tickets."

"It's cool."

"And then I got mad at Dave, and I hardly ever get mad at anyone."

"It's gonna be all right."

"Are you sure?"

He nodded. "Very sure. It's okay to tell Ryan you don't want to move right now. All you have to do is talk to him, and I'm sure you'll work it out. And then talk to Dave."

"He's pissed at me."

"He misses you. So much. Believe me."

I didn't answer. I believed him a little because of the nice face.

He glanced at the door. "What if I went to get milkshakes? And alcohol? And then we can talk all evening?"

Milkshakes and alcohol did seem like they'd make everything better. But I didn't want to be alone yet, so I made him spoon with me on the couch for a solid half hour.

'Cause everyone needed spooning sometimes.

While I was waiting for Gould to get back, Dave came home. He had a Styrofoam mannequin head under one arm.

He did kind of a double take when he saw me, which made me feel like a trainload of suck, because it used to be totally normal for him to come home and find me in his house.

"You okay?" he muttered. "You look kinda pale."

"I came here to talk to Gould about, um, how Ryan and I had a fight. And he went to get milkshakes."

Dave didn't say anything. He set the mannequin head on the coffee table.

"I don't think I want to move to Cleveland."

Dave shook his head. "You'll probably change your mind as soon as you and Ryan make up. Just like you'll change your plans if Matchbox Twenty comes to town—"

"Fuck off. Gould said it was fine I wasn't there."

"Well, you know he doesn't exactly speak up when something bothers him."

"So you have to do it for him?" I shot back.

"I try to look out for him. Unlike *some* people."

"There you go trying to choreograph other people's lives again."

"*Choreograph*? Where'd you pick that one up? Ryan?"

"I know what 'choreograph' means. You know, I don't want to say this. But you're being a real Kristy right now."

"Yeah? Well Kristy got shit done."

"But she was insufferable about it."

"Insufferable? Seriously, what's happened to you?"

"I know what words mean, Dave! Why do you think I don't know words?"

"I know you know words, I just think that ever since you've been with Ryan, you've been totally different, and I fucking *hate* it."

We both stared at each other for a moment.

I focused on the mannequin head. "This is so stupid. We're not in eighth grade anymore."

"Really? Because you just went to a Matchbox Twenty concert."

I almost laughed.

Dave stepped closer. "I just don't *get* it. You're gonna move? Is that something you want, or something he wants you to want?"

"*I* want it. Maybe. Why is that so hard for you to believe, that I could want to leave here? I've always wanted to see other places."

"So go see them!" Dave's voice broke slightly, and he hesitated. "And then . . . come back." He had kind of a pre-crying face going on, and it surprised me.

"Hey . . ."

He mumbled something and put his hand on the mannequin head.

"What?" I asked.

"I feel like he's taking you away from us. I don't want to feel like that, but I do. That's why I . . ." He let out a long sigh.

I picked at the throw cushion. "I would come back. If I moved, I'd visit all the time. But I have to do some things that are just for me. I know you guys care about me, but you also— You all have this idea of me that's, like, outdated. I know I'm hard to take seriously, but I *am* growing up, and I'm trying to have a relationship, and a career, and—and nobody thinks it's weird for Miles to want those things, but it's like you still expect me to be Kamen from high school."

Dave didn't answer. I wasn't trying to make him cry, but, like, he was an emotional little fucker, and he'd probably feel better if he cried, honestly. He stared at me. "I don't mean to do that."

"You're like, 'Just stand at the kink fair and look pretty, Kamen, because you can't handle actual responsibilities.' 'You don't really want to move to Cleveland, Kamen, because you couldn't possibly know anything about moving or Cleveland or wanting things.' Well, fuck you." I didn't say it angrily—more like kinda tired and a little bit, like, trying to let him know I loved him even when he was being a dick.

He was gripping the Styrofoam head hard enough to leave some serious dents. "That's not how I feel."

"It's okay," I told him. "It's okay to let us all make our own mistakes, or let us, you know, succeed outside of the group. You're allowed to focus on your relationship with D, and on going to school, and not always worry about other people."

He looked down.

I went on. "Nothing terrible's gonna happen just because you can't keep an eye on us all the time." I waited until he was looking up, then smiled a little. "I'm a big boy. A hobo's not gonna steal my sandwich."

He took a deep breath, but then swallowed and nodded instead of talking.

"Ryan was right. And I know you don't like when he's right, but he was. If we're gonna make this group work—and I don't mean the Subs Club, I mean *us*, our family—then it can't just be the easy stuff and the group hugs. It's got to be everything. The—the tough issues and the disagreeing and the trying to see all the sides."

"Okay," he said quietly.

"We got through Hal. We did. All of us, together. Anything else . . . We can do it. Right? Piece of cake?"

"Uh-huh." He tried to smile, but then a single tear fell. And, Jesus Christ, no one can resist a single tear.

"Do you want a hug?" I asked.

He shook his head, but I called bullshit. Dude was a hug-whore.

I stood. He tried to back up so I couldn't reach him, but I grabbed him. Murdered him a little, slowly, with my arms, and also with all the love in the world. After a few seconds of resistance, his hands came up and clutched my shoulders.

"I know," he whispered against my shoulder. "I know all the things you're telling me, and I still act like this, and I'm sorry."

"It's okay."

"It's not. I hate losing people. I hate it. And you . . . You've always been the one who makes everyone feel better. About everything. If you're not around, like, what's even the point?"

"I'm gonna be around. No matter where I am, I'm gonna be around."

I felt him nod.

Gould came in with a large paper bag in his arms. Stopped when he saw us hugging. Raised his eyebrows at me. I gave him a thumbs-up.

Dave took a step back and looked at Gould. "Hey."

"Hey." Gould held up a carton of milkshakes. "I got three."

Ryan was still up when Gould dropped me off that night. He was drawing in the living room. I was a little drunk. Collingsworth started to lumber to the door to greet me, then face-planted.

"We need to talk," I told Ryan.

He looked up and nodded.

I got down on my knees in front of the couch and waited until the room stopped blurring. "I've done a really dumb job of being a friend and a boyfriend at the same time. I know I'm really close with my friends, and it's a little weird, but we've just got to find a way to deal with that. Because I love them."

He nodded.

I put my hand on his knee, then stared at it. "And I do respect what you want. That's an important thing that I want you to know. I can compromise. But . . . I don't know if I'm ready to move to Cleveland yet. I shouldn't have told you I wanted to if it wasn't true. And I shouldn't have implied that *you* didn't really want it just to make me feel better about being a douche. So can we maybe stay here for at least a couple of years, and then reconsider?"

He sighed and leaned back. Set the drawing tablet aside. "I don't need to move to Cleveland either. I just . . . I'm exactly like my parents said. I suck at holding still. I suck at being satisfied. You—*us*—this is the first time I've felt content. And I think it's freaking me out. Because I keep expecting to feel like I need to be doing something different. And I don't feel that."

I squeezed his knee and got a little fascinated watching my fingers move. "But what if you do want other things, and I'm holding you back?"

He shook his head. "If we want other things someday, we can have other things someday. But honestly, I'm really fucking happy right now."

I smiled a little. "Me too."

He rubbed his face. "I can't even tell you how relieved I was when you said you didn't want to move. It was like I didn't even realize until right then that the stuff I'd been telling myself about what I wanted was mostly bullshit."

"I'm sorry I said the thing about your parents."

"I'm sorry I said the thing about your friends."

I climbed up to sit beside him. "I want you to like them. My friends, I mean. I don't want you to think they dictate my life."

"I guess I feel a little threatened by them."

"But *why*? They're such dork skillets."

"They're awesome. It's just sometimes—and I can't even figure out why—I get so scared that I can't live up to . . . what they are to you, I guess?"

I leaned against him. "You're already everything. I mean, seriously—anything I could want, you are that."

"You're right. I wasn't there."

"It's okay. I'm glad you weren't."

We were quiet awhile.

"I love you," he said. "Frealz."

I hugged him. Wanted to keep hugging him forever. I finally got the grunt of agony out of him that marks a successful Kamen hug. "Can we, um, try something tonight?"

He leaned back to look at me. "Sure."

"Not, um, underwear or anything. I was thinking maybe we could talk?"

"Okay."

"I mean, we talk a lot. But sometimes I think because we gelled so well right from the beginning, maybe we never talked about really important stuff?"

He tilted his head. "Like what?"

"Like we have a billion inside jokes, but I didn't know until recently, like, what you talked about in your advocate group in San Francisco. Or that you wanted to be an artist, but your dad made you think you couldn't be creative." I swallowed. "I think maybe we talk so much about what's going on in the moment that we forget to talk about who we were before there was an 'us.' Does that sound like a thing that . . . might have happened?"

He nodded slowly. Kissed me. Knocked his forehead lightly against mine, then sat up.

"Okay. So where should we start?"

We went to the bedroom. And we started pretty much with our births and went up to now. We talked about a lot of random things—first day of middle school. How deep the deep ends were at our community pools when we were kids. The first time Ryan dommed someone. We were still going at 3 a.m. And then beyond.

When I woke up, we were still in our clothes, spooning on the bed. Collingsworth was snoring on the floor. I got up, careful not to wake Ryan, and went to make breakfast. Took a brief trip to the hall to look at the well-dressed hare.

"Adulting," I whispered to that smug, puffy-sleeved fucker. "Pretty sure I'm crushing it."

CHAPTER FOURTEEN

The Girl Scout camp was tricked out. As we got onto the grounds, I could see a bunch of tents and little fenced areas. Food carts, trailers, water stations. There were a lot of people here already, and I was torn between being, like, new Star Wars excited, and what-if-you-woke-up-and-everyone-around-you-had-been-replaced-with-robots terrified.

Ryan glanced over at me. "You all right?"

"Uh, yeah. Just wondering what I got myself into."

He reached over and patted my thigh. "You're my pony."

I smiled at him, and didn't even care about the corniness, because it was true. "Yeah. I'm your fucking pony." I checked the backseat again to make sure our duffel bag was still there. We'd been in kind of a rush this morning, and we'd been practicing in the apartment until late last night. But Ryan swore all the stuff we needed was in the bag. We'd put together a whole emergency toiletries kit too, with lots of wipes in case I got dirt on me before the grooming competition, and a toothbrush and stuff in case I got food in my teeth before dressage.

We pulled up to the wooden office building, which had a huge banner on the side reading *WELCOME TO PETPLAYFEST*, with little silhouettes of a cat, dog, horse, and rabbit. Ryan got out first and then came around and opened the door for me. I was still wearing my street clothes, but we'd decided he'd do the talking when we signed in, so that I could start getting in the pony headspace. I climbed out of the car and stood there, looking around.

There was madness all over. Ponies pulling carts. Pups sniffing each other and pretending to pee on trees.

One dog nearby—huge and barrel-chested, with a rottweiler hood that even had a fake tongue sticking out—was scratching his face with his back foot. How such a big guy could bend his leg like that was impressive. His owner was tall and lanky, with dark hair and a goatee and sunglasses. He was shifting around like he was impatient.

A van pulled into the lot. A woman in a long black vinyl jacket got out. She was thin with short hair, large black earrings. She opened the back door and leaned into the vehicle, emerging a moment later with a smaller woman in her arms. The other woman was a cat, I realized, looking at the small, pointed ears attached to a headband and the long tail sewn to the back of the woman's leggings.

Nearby, the dog went rigid. A growl started low in his throat.

"Goddamn it, Glazer!" The dog's owner yelled. "Yes, it's a cat. We've seen a million cats here. Shut up."

Glazer lunged against his harness and barked. The woman put the cat on the ground, and the cat immediately hid behind her legs, back arched.

"Easy. Eaaaa-sy," Glazer's owner warned. Glazer turned and started humping the guy's leg. The man kicked him off. "Jesus fucking Christ, Glazer, really?"

"Oh my God," I whispered to Ryan. "These people are really good at acting like animals."

A truck pulled up dragging a small trailer. The driver, a big-bellied man, handsome in a goofy way, got out and unloaded the ponies. The first one walked easily beside him and stood quietly. The second snorted and stomped her way down the ramp, tossing her head and pulling on the lead rope.

The skittish pony turned toward the field and let out a whinny. From across the lawn came an answering neigh. I looked.

The pony standing a few feet away was tall and wore a brown bodysuit, long brown vinyl gloves, and brown knee-high boots. Her long, silky tail was red to match her hair, which was in a French braid. A purple and silver plume was attached to the crownpiece of her bridle.

Cinnamon.

"There she is," I muttered.

Ryan stopped "Oh. Wow."

"She looks good." I was more than a little freaked.

"Not as good as you." Ryan patted me firmly. "Don't you ever forget it."

Cinnamon started backing up, and Stan followed, giving sharp tugs on the lead rope. He spoke soothingly, and Cinnamon calmed. She caught my eye and gave me a little smirk.

"She smirked at me," I whispered. "Did you see that? She just smirked at me. She *always* smirks at me."

Ryan slowly stroked my shoulder. "It's okay. Thunder Canyon? You ready?"

I was about to reply I'd been born ready, when I heard a shout, and then a joyous bark. I looked over, and Glazer was barreling toward us, his leash trailing.

"Holy shit." I tried to retreat, but even on all fours, this puppy-man was fast. He jumped up on me, wagging his butt, and almost knocked me over.

Then he started to hump the air right next to my leg.

I pushed at him. "Ew! Ew, dude, no!"

"Glazer!" The owner shouted, hurrying toward us. "For the love of all the fucking fucks."

Glazer crouched, looking guilty.

The guy reached us and grabbed Glazer's harness. "We're putting your shock collar on. You hear me?"

Glazer was slinking back and forth, his belly close to the ground, his butt still wagging. The guy clipped a collar with a black box on it around Glazer's thigh.

The guy pulled Glazer away. "Gonna get you neutered. That what you want? You want to get 'em cut off?"

I looked at Ryan, who raised his eyebrows at me.

But the next time I turned around, the guy was petting Glazer's face. "Who's my boy? Who's my good boy?" He looked up at us. "Sorry about that. This is Glazer. One fucking guess why we called him that. He's harmless, except for the goddamn humping."

"It's, uh, fine," Ryan said.

The man turned back to Glazer, who was trying to get his head between the man's legs. "Take your hump toy!" he shouted, thrusting a stuffed rabbit into Glazer's leather jaws. Glazer carefully set the rabbit on the ground and started to hump it.

"We need to go inside," I whispered to Ryan. "Now."

The sign-in desk woman was super friendly. She gave us a handbook, a program, a gift bag, and my competitor number. Then she assigned us a stall and pointed us toward the barn. "The official PPF grooms will be around the stables to help out with water runs, questions, calming down nervous ponies—whatever you need."

"Cool," I said, trying not to sound like a nervous pony.

When we got back outside, Glazer and his owner were gone. So was Cinnamon. Ryan and I headed for the barn.

Ryan checked the schedule as we walked. "Meet 'n' greet at nine. Grooming competition at ten. Then you don't have anything until bobbing for apples at eleven thirty. Lunch break at noon. Cart race at one. Dressage at two fifteen. Balloon pop at three. Awards ceremony at four."

I nodded. "I'm nervous."

"Aww." He leaned against me. "Don't be. I'm the one in charge. All you have to do is what I say."

That was kinda comforting. But Ryan couldn't make me prance beautifully, or remember how to *tempi*. Only I could do that. All I knew was that over the past week, our dressage routine had sort of come together. Our cart race times had improved. And my friends and I were planning a giant cookout next weekend to say good-bye to summer. So even if I made a fool out of myself today, there was still grilling to look forward to.

The barn was actually a picnic shelter partitioned into stalls. There were cross ties on the walls of each, and a narrow wooden bench.

I removed my shorts and the pair of navy panties I was wearing underneath, and started to pull up the leather pony pants. Paused as I attempted to put my dick through the crotch hole.

"Ryan! I missed a spot on my balls. Look."

He leaned down. "Your balls look fine."

"Look at that hair patch." I pointed.

"No one's gonna notice."

"Fix it for me. Please?"

He looked at me. "You want me to shave your balls? Here? Now?"

I nodded. "We have the toiletry kit."

He started to shake his head, but it was like he was too appalled to even do that. "Nobody is going to see your balls."

"I'm wearing the Pegasus Sheath! My balls are gonna show. And my balls are huge. You can't tell me people aren't gonna look."

"I really think ball hair is fine."

"I won't feel like a real horse unless you shave my balls."

"Oh my *God*. Kamen! There are so many things wrong with that sentence I don't know where to start. First of all, horses have hair *everywhere*."

I lifted my balls in one hand. "I just don't like the inconsistency of smooth and then hair patch."

Ryan sighed. "Why do *I* have to do it?"

"Because I have to mentally start becoming a pony."

He rolled his eyes.

"Please? I'll let you sit on my shoulders so you can see during the awards ce— Ow!" He'd slapped my thigh.

"Watch yourself, Thunder Canyon." He got out the toiletry kit. "Okay. Because I love you and your balls, and want you to feel like a horse." He squirted a little shaving gel onto his finger and rubbed it onto the hairy ball. I started getting hard. He looked up at me, shaking his head but fighting a smile. "Now how are you gonna get your Pegasus Sheath on?"

I horse-snorted on him.

He shaved my ball carefully, then wiped away the gel. We got my junk through the crotch hole and fastened the leather pants. He helped me sheath up.

"Do I look like a Friesian with a huge dick?" I asked.

"You're getting there."

Dave texted to say they were at the front gate. We told them where to find us, and a few minutes later, Dave, Gould, Miles, and D stood in a cluster in our stall, looking both confused and impressed by their surroundings.

Okay, Dave looked terrified. But that was to be expected.

"Is this as bad as you thought?" I asked him.

He shrugged, tight-lipped.

"Remember. They're *not* furries. And even if they were, you should still respect them."

He nodded, a little pale, as a woman in bunny ears hopped by the shelter.

Gould was staring at my sheath. "That's a very large . . ."

"Horse cock," I supplied.

He nodded.

Miles was reading the program. "Ooh, a pretzel stand. And a hot dog cart that's hosting hot-dog eating contests for pets and humans throughout the day."

D's eyes lit up. "This wonderland of oddities knows what it's about."

Miles looked at him. "D? I think I might like to formally challenge you to the hot-dog eating contest."

D turned slowly to Miles. Stared. "Son, I would obliterate you."

I laughed. "Miles. You probably couldn't even eat one."

But Miles looked like he knew some sort of secret. "Still, I'd like to try." He put out his hand. "Let's see how many wieners we can eat."

Dave groaned. "You are both clearly compensating for *everything*."

"I have nothing to compensate for." D shook Miles's outstretched hand. "I merely cherish meat."

"Look at all these events." Dave read over Miles's shoulder. "Blindfolded obstacle course. Steeplechase. Agility trials. And the first place best-in-show pet gets a fifty-dollar gift certificate to the Pleasure Center. I don't know what that is, but I want to go there."

D gave me a once-over. "I believe we are looking at our victor right here."

Dave nudged him. "Look, though—it says everyone's a winner at PPF. They probably have participation awards. Awards. Just for *participating*."

D's gaze went dark, but then he relaxed. "Well. As long as they make some effort to acknowledge one competitor's superiority over all the others, I'll live."

Ryan got out our bag.

It occurred to me that I really didn't want the others to watch me getting ready. But they didn't seem the least bit shy.

"What sort of accoutrements do you have?" Miles tried to peer into our bag as Ryan unzipped it.

Ryan pulled out our pieces of tack one by one and set them on the bench. "Harness. Bridle. Fuck-ton of ribbon. Just in case we need to get fancy."

"That's a nice plume," Gould said, nodding at the bridle.

Ryan didn't put me in cross ties, because I was the kind of awesome horse that could be trusted untethered. He started wiping me down with a rag. I felt a little embarrassed to be doing this in front of my friends, but whatever. I let Ryan put my harness on. Then the bridle, which we had covered with red pom balls and fitted with a large red plume on the browband. We left the bit off for now.

Miles nodded. "You look formidable."

Ryan tapped my left leg. "Up."

I kicked off my sandals and watched him as he put my furry boots on. "Do you have any snacks? Like a carrot or anything? Or J-Ranchers?"

He straightened. "I will get you food in a minute."

I rested my chin on his shoulder. "I love you. Really a lot."

"Awww." Dave made a face. "You guys are nauseating, but it's nice."

I smiled at him, my chin still on Ryan's shoulder. Ryan rubbed my head. Kissed my jaw. "You're gonna be amazing."

He put my hooves on. Then he gave me five Jolly Ranchers. I ate them all at the same time to create a rainbow of flavor in my mouth.

"You guys should probably leave for the tail," I told the others. "Unless you want to see me pop a huge boner."

"Oh *shit.*" Ryan had reached into the bag and frozen.

"What?" I demanded.

"Ummm . . ." He slowly pulled out my tail.

Or what was left of it.

The butt plug was covered in tooth marks, and the tail was a tangled, wet blob of synthetic horsehair. I gaped. "What the . . .?"

"The dog must have chewed it."

"Collingsworth! How did you not notice it was messed up?"

"I don't know! I was in a hurry this morning because *someone* was taking forever in the shower. I threw it in the bag without looking."

"The dog butler has ruined my tail!"

Dave was trying not to laugh. "Dude, Kamen, that is *nasty*."

I started to panic. "I can't compete!"

Ryan gave me a *come on* look. "It's not the end of the world."

"The whole purpose of a Friesian is the tail!"

D stepped forward. Gazed at me with those sharp, serious blue eyes, and placed a hand on my shoulder. "Son, the purpose of a Friesian is *war*. Now put on your mane and prepare for battle." He grabbed the Slash wig from the bag and handed it to me.

I took it. Tipped it forward so the mess of black hair spilled toward the ground, then flung it back over my head. Ryan had to fish the plume out from under the hair.

My friends all nodded.

"You look like a stallion," Gould said.

"Wait," Ryan said. "We could maybe take a section of the wig and fasten it to a different butt plug?" He turned to Dave. "Can it be done? Can we make a tail without ruining the mane?"

Dave hissed. "It's risky. But it just might work."

One of the grooms stopped by our stall. "Everything okay?"

"My tail's ruined," I told her. "Now I don't feel like a Friesian."

Ryan held it up.

"Oh dear!" the groom said cheerfully. "Well, you're still a very handsome pony. Do you need any water or anything?"

We shook our heads, and the groom moved on.

"Quick!" Dave took my mane off. "We don't have much time."

We actually still had like forty-five minutes.

Dave took a deep breath. Handed the mane to Ryan. "Hold on to this. I need to go to the car and get my emergency hairspray and shears."

"I'll come all over your hairspray and shears!" I called as he walked away. The pony in the next stall looked over at me.

"What the hell?" Ryan asked.

"It's our come-on-two-objects game," I explained. He just shook his head.

The others went off to get pretzels. Once they were gone, Ryan gave it to me straight. "All we have with us is a prostate plug."

"Use it. Use the prostate thing."

"You sure? I know you're really, uh . . . sensitive."

"I can handle it. Plus it makes me prance."

"Can you promise me you won't come?" He looked at my Pegasus Sheath. "Do we need to, like, use a dick ring? Do you want to jerk off first? What?"

"Ry," I said gently. "I told you, I can handle it. Trust Thunder Canyon."

"I do trust you."

I nuzzled his forehead. "This is some serious Black Stallion shit right here."

"I know. We have a bond that can never be broken."

Just then, there was a clanking outside our stall. I turned to see Cinnamon prancing by, being long reined by Stan, her handler. Her bridle fucking *gleamed*; her plume was real sparkly; and her reins were studded with red jewels. She lifted each leg high and went along at a perfect, unhurried gait, her wrists crossed behind her back. Her brown boots were so shiny they looked liquid, and her long chestnut tail flowed almost to the ground.

She gave me a head toss as she passed.

I turned to Ryan, panicking again. "Her harness is made of rubies."

"Those are rhinestones. That's all she is—a plastic jewel. You're the real thing."

I wished I could believe him.

He took some scissors out of our bag.

I gasped. "You're going to cut without Dave?"

He nodded. "You told me how long Dave takes to style hair. We don't have that kind of time."

"Why does everyone keep saying we don't have any time? We seriously have almost an hour."

"Shh." He cut a section off the wig, then tossed the wig aside. Wound one end of the rope of black hair around the base of the plug, tying it tightly and securing it with rubber bands. He used ribbon to hide the rubber bands and the knot, then he braided what was left of the tail.

"You ready?" he asked as he lubed the curved plug.

I nodded and spread my legs. A second later, the prostate plug touched my hole. I groaned as Ryan pushed it inside me. I could feel the scraggly tail brush the back of my leather pants.

"That okay?" Ryan asked.

I tried to take a step forward. Stopped when the plug rubbed that magic spot. "Oh, *fuck*."

"Kamen . . ."

"I'm fine," I managed. "How's it look?"

"Um . . . a little . . . weird. But it'll work."

I tried to take a step. "Oh. Oh, it's very stimulating."

"Scale of one to ten, how likely are you to come if you walk around with that in?"

"Eight point five."

"I can live with that."

I shifted. "My balls are a little cold."

"You just had to wear the Pegasus Sheath. Your junk could be all tucked away right now . . ."

"I'm a stallion. I have no regrets."

He laughed and put on my wig. Brushed it out. "Come on, you. Let's go meet and greet."

For the meet 'n' greet, everyone gathered in the main room of the lodge—dogs, cats, ponies, and even a ferret. Several of the dogs were straining to get at the cats and ferret.

There were snacks for the handlers, and paper bowls handlers could fill with dry cereal, pretzels, fruit, and vegetables for the pets.

Cindy Thompson, director of PetPlayFest, stood at the front of the room and introduced herself and her pup Francie. She looked around. "We're still a couple of participants short, but we'll go ahead and get started." She went around the room and had everyone introduce themselves. Pets had the option of giving their own introductions or having their handlers do it for them.

Ryan glanced at me. "You wanna talk?"

I shook my head.

"I'm Ryan," he said when it was our turn. "This is my horse, Thunder Canyon. He's a seven-year-old Friesian stallion. I've only been his handler for about a month. He's pretty much a genius."

There was a chorus of general approval and nice-to-meet-yous. And a lot of staring at my sheath.

The handler with the two ponies went next. The ponies were named Taylor and Bridget, and even though both of them were quiet while they were introduced, Taylor looked anxious and awkward, but Bridget stood proud and confident, shaking her mane on occasion or pawing with one hoof. Her harness was decorated with jingle bells.

After Cindy went over the agenda and general safety guidelines for the day, she led the animals to a paddock outside for supervised playtime, while handlers, owners, and trainers stayed in the lodge to chat. Cindy went over the playtime rules in detail, and also made it clear that while critters could choose to remain in animal mode, this was a good opportunity for us to break character and talk to one another. Pets new to the scene could get advice from more experienced players, and everyone had a safe place to talk about the day's events—hopes, expectations, and fears. There were smaller enclosures for pets who needed to be kept with their own species—pups who didn't get along with cats, for instance. I went into the main paddock.

There were three official PetPlayFest handlers standing at the gate, keeping an eye on us. Cinnamon was at the far end of the paddock. Glazer was getting pretty real with a fence post. Scribbles, the ferret, was playing with what looked like a giant ball of rubber bands and fishing wire. I wandered around, feeling weird that I was on two legs and almost all the other pets were on four. Eventually I got down on my hands and knees and headed toward the other ponies, wishing Ryan would come and get me out of here so we could start crushing Cinnamon.

Suddenly, I heard a "Psst!"

I looked around. Glazer was waddling toward me. I took a wary step back.

"Don't worry, I'm not here to hump you." His voice was low. "I'm here to discuss Cinnamon."

"Cinnamon?"

"Cinnamon," a new voice confirmed. A floppy-eared female pup named Max appeared. "Biggest bitch ever."

I couldn't say I disagreed.

I followed Max's gaze to the end of the paddock, where Cinnamon was tossing her head and stamping the ground.

"She won every fucking event she entered last year," Glazer muttered. "And believe me, she's not humble about it—as a human or a pony."

"Well," Max said. "She almost lost grooming, because there was a baby bunny in the ring—a real one—and she thought it was a rat."

"Oh God," Glazer said. "She *hates* rats. If only we could set one loose today . . ."

"Hold on," Max said. "We need Scribbles here for the planning."

She barked twice, loudly. A moment later, the ferret ran over, batting his rubber-band ball in front of him.

"We're talking Operation Hot Tamale," Max told him. "Put down your stress ball and listen."

Scribbles chased the ball in a circle, then flopped over on his back and looked up at us. "What's the plan?"

Glazer glanced at me. "You in?"

"Uh . . . in what?"

"We're gonna make sure Cinnamon doesn't win."

I was intrigued. "How are you gonna do that?"

"By making sure one of us wins every event she's entered in." Glazer coughed. "I'm not worried about dressage. There's a new pony, Holly, who's way better than Cinnamon."

"I'm also in dressage," I said. "I could beat her there."

They all looked me up and down, but didn't say anything.

Max cleared her throat. "So we'll count on Holly to take dressage. That just leaves grooming, which Cinnamon's a shoo-in for, so we'll cut our losses there. But the cart race and the balloon pop . . . that's where we could really use your help."

"Mrrriyyooouuuuu!" The high-pitched cry startled us all.

I looked up. "What the hell was that?"

"Mittens." Max was staring in the direction of the sound.

A tiny cat was pacing the fence. She wore a white spandex suit with a white fluffy tail and little leather ears. Her face was painted white, and her nose was pink, and she had very realistic whiskers attached to her cheeks. "Mrrriiiyouuu," she cried. "Meeeyeeeewww."

"That cat doesn't sound like a cat at all," I said.

"I know." Glazer nodded. "But this is a judgment-free zone. So whatever sound a critter makes, hey, we're cool with it. I mean, Scribbles here—do your ferret noise."

Scribbles made an ungodly sound.

"Mrrriiiiyouyouyouuuu," Mittens wailed back.

Max rolled her eyes. "Fucking Mittens."

"She was here last year," Scribbles explained to me. "Never did anything much but roll around on the ground and make noise. She's a delicate little flower."

Glazer barked loudly, but Mittens ignored it. "Anyway, we'll reconvene during the lunch break. We have some plans for making sure Cinnamon doesn't win the balloon pop. You think you can win the cart race, Thunder?"

I nodded. "I know I can."

"Good."

An old pup with the muzzle of his hood painted gray limped over to us. Max yipped. "Excellent! Barkley's here."

"What's up?" Barkley asked in a hoarse voice.

"Operation Hot Tamale," Glazer said.

Barkley groaned and sat slowly in the grass. "Has the secret weapon shown up yet?"

"Not yet," Max said. "But we have Thunder Canyon on our side."

Barkley and I exchanged nods.

"What's the secret weapon?" I asked.

Max grinned at me. "Oh, you'll like him. I don't know if you've checked the official lineup in the lodge, but he's your first bobbing-for-apples rival."

"I didn't even know I could see who I was competing against."

"Oh yeah," Scribbles said. "Just go to the lodge and ask Cindy where the boards are."

"Holy shit," Glazer said suddenly. He was staring at the fence. "Guys, the secret weapon's here."

I looked where he was looking.

A very tall, broad, twentysomething-year-old man in orange pants and hipster glasses walked along the fence at a gait I could only describe as a drift. He had thin, dark curly hair and a slack face, and was carrying a messenger bag. As he passed my section of the fence, a strange smell wafted from him. It wasn't bad, exactly. Just . . . earthy. Two giant orange and yellow cardboard tentacles were strapped to his arms, and six more sprouted from his back like nightmarish butterfly wings.

Fucktopus.

"I need you to take me to my friends," I whispered to Ryan as he clipped a lead to my bridle. The meet 'n' greet was disbanding. There was no sign of Fucktopus, who had been drifting toward the lodge last time I'd seen him.

"Okay." Ryan glanced at me. "Is everything all—"

"We have a *situation*."

It didn't take us long to find the others. They were at the hot dog table. D had three empty paper cartons stacked in front of him, and a hand on his belly. He looked like he was about to hurl. Miles, meanwhile, also had three empty cartons in a stack plus a fourth in front of him, and was calmly, slowly, eating a hot dog with neat little stripes of ketchup and mustard on it.

The others were crowded around watching. Gould was filming discreetly.

"Kamen!" Dave called. "Miles is about to beat D in the hot dog contest."

"He will do no such thing." D groaned and flinched. "I'm only resting."

Miles swallowed his mouthful. "Really? Because I barely feel full."

D glowered at him. "This is the devil's work. No man so slight of build can consume four hot dogs without consequence."

Dave clapped a hand on his shoulder. "He tried to tell you. Slow and steady. But you wolfed three down and now look at you."

I stamped impatiently. "I need to talk to you guys."

Dave and Gould came over, then Dave glanced back at Miles, who said, "I'll join you in a minute."

Dave faced me again. "What's up?"

"He's here."

"Who's here?" His jaw dropped suddenly. "*Bill*?"

"No. Fucktopus."

"What?"

Gould stepped closer. "Are you serious?"

I waved my hoof at them. "*Yes*. He's my bobbing-for-apples rival!"

Dave's mouth was still hanging open. "Holy *shit*."

D walked over, still clutching his belly. "Everything all right?"

No one answered.

"What's he look like?" Gould asked me. "Have you seen him?"

"Yes! He's as big as a house and his tentacles are fucking *ter-i-fy-iiiing*."

Dave shushed me gently. "It's gonna be okay."

"No, it's not. You know how sometimes you meet someone online, and you, like, get such a vivid picture of what they must look like? And it's so vivid that you start to figure the person must not actually look like that, because that would be too crazy of the universe? And then you get a chance to meet the person face-to-face, so you're expecting to be surprised by how they look?"

"Sure. I had—"

"I'm not done yet. And then it turns out they look *exactly* how you first pictured them?"

"Okay."

"That's Fucktopus."

Gould's eyebrows scrunched together. "Sooo . . . you pictured him as big as a house?"

"Kind of, yeah."

"I feel like he's probably not actually that big."

I glared at him. "Not every house is a mansion, and not every man is a reasonable size."

Dave nodded. "Ah, the classic Ben Franklin aphorism."

"He has black-framed glasses and a messenger bag, and he smells like a food co-op. He's like a human Portland."

"Dude, you can so take him."

"Are his tentacles really robotic?" Gould asked.

I shook my head. "They're cardboard, I think. And orange."

Dave squinted. "So why are you even scared?"

"You guys, he seriously freaks me out. I don't want to fight Fucktopus. Please don't make me fight Fucktopus!"

Gould gave me a strange look. "I . . . don't think you have to physically fight him. You just have to bob for apples."

D crossed his arms. "What is the approximate girth of the tentacles?"

Dave elbowed D. "You're totally getting off on this. Fucktopus is like one of your Syfy movie creatures."

"I am doing no such thing."

"No, you definitely like Fucktopus. You want to plant your seed inside him and parthenogenetically create little tentacle b—"

"What was that?" D wrapped his arms around Dave, turned him slightly, and gave his ass a quick, light swat.

Dave pushed against his chest. "Oh my God, get off of me, you free-thinking mountain."

D swatted him again, keeping the movement quick and subtle. "I want to do what with your Fuckto-what-o-gon?"

"It's a fucktopus!" Dave growled and kept pushing, trying not to laugh. "Somebody help me!"

Gould grinned. "No. This is delightful."

"Ugh." Dave struggled without much luck. "He calls it secret spanking, but it's not a secret." He twisted to face D. "Everyone knows what you're doing, and any Good Samaritan at this function would happily notify PPF security on my behalf."

D kissed Dave and released him. "So the security staff can thank me for my service to the community?"

Dave batted at him. "Go away, hot dog breath. We're trying to solve a crisis." He reached for my lead rope, then stopped and looked at Ryan. "May I?"

Ryan handed him the rope. Dave gripped it just under my chin and tugged lightly. "Kamen? Sorry—Thunder Canyon? Look at me. It's time for you to make us all proud. And that means fighting Fucktopus. In a totally nonviolent children's game."

I sighed, staring at the hot dog table. "I feel really weird right now."

"That's because you're dressed like a horse and afraid of a fake tentacle monster. But look at me. *Look* at m— There you go. You're a fucking champion."

I pulled slightly on the bridle. "I don't know."

"What would Rocky do?"

I wrinkled my brow. "Lose?"

"Only in the first one, buddy. This is *Rocky IV*. Fucktopus is your Drago. And this isn't just about you, this is about America. And Russia."

"I thought Cinnamon was my Drago."

"She's more like your Clubber Lang. The important thing is, we'll be proud of you no matter what. As long as you win."

Gould nodded. "Amen."

D gave me that soul-piercing look. "Remember. You're a Friesian."

Dave patted my shoulder again. "But you're also Rocky."

Ryan nudged me. "You're the love of my life."

Gould cleared his throat. "You're a total dork skillet."

I couldn't even talk for a minute on account of the lump in my throat. So I nodded.

Miles stepped over to us. "Finished with hot dog four. D owes me thirty bucks. What did I miss?"

"There's no time to explain." Dave started tugging me forward. "Kamen has to get to his first event."

"Once again," I said, "we have plenty of time."

Dave glanced at Ryan. "Can I lead him? Because this is hilarious."

I didn't move. "I want Ryan to lead me."

Dave looked at me. "Please? It would mean a lot to me."

I let him lead me to the barn to prepare for the grooming contest. He actually only made it as far as the soda cart. Then he handed me off to Ryan so he could buy a drink.

Ryan took me to the stall and gave me a final tack check and wipe down. My nose started to itch. I swiped it with the back of my hoof, but I still felt uncomfortable.

"Ryan?" I whispered.

"Yes?"

"I have a booger."

He stared at me. "No. Absolutely no."

"Ryan. It's *grooming*. They're gonna take points off if the cave has bats."

"I already shaved your ball."

"So this should be a snap." I moved my head toward him. "Get it."

He went to our bag and got a tissue. I bent lower so he could put it up to my nose. "Blow," he ordered.

"It's not the kind you can blow out."

"Try."

I tried, but all that came out was air.

"Which nostril?"

"Right?"

He pushed on the left. "Blow again."

I did. "It's not working. You have to get it."

He sighed and put the tissue over his finger. "You owe me *big time*."

"It's the hard, pointy kind, so don't make it stab me," I warned.

He rolled his eyes and gently stuck his tissue-covered finger into my nostril.

"Oh my God," said a voice nearby. "I am *not* seeing this."

Cinnamon. I glimpsed her red hair off to the side. "What are you doing here?" I demanded. "Go back to your stall."

"I actually have to agree with Cinnamon," said Dave, who had appeared behind Ryan with D and Miles. "What are you *doing*?"

"I have a situation," I told them.

Dave grimaced. "And you're making *Ryan*—"

Ryan turned to them, finger still up my nose. "Listen. There is nothing in this world like the bond between a man and his horse. And if you all can't respect that, then get out."

D closed his eyes for a few seconds, nodding wisely—like, if you went to visit a talking owl that was going to send you on a quest, it would probably nod like that. "He's right. Let them be."

He guided the others away from Ryan and me. Cinnamon was still lurking. She smirked at me. "Good luck with dressage, Boogs."

"Yeah, good luck to you too, you stuck-up ginger bitch!" I yelled through the tissue.

Her eyebrows went up. Ryan's did too. "Get the booger out," I told him.

He did, and went to toss the tissue into a trash barrel. When he came back, I was staring at Cinnamon. "I am going to wipe the freaking pasture with you, okay? You have been rude to me and my friends *forever*, and it stops now."

She laughed, and not in a nice way. "You don't stand a chance."

"I'll kill you in the cart race."

"If you do, it'll be a hollow victory." She glanced at Ryan. "You won't exactly be pulling any significant amount of weight."

My gaze snapped to Ryan. He jammed his hand in his pocket like he was trying not to make a fist.

I scowled at Cinnamon. "Okay, I think you're a sad person with self-esteem issues. But here's a deal for you. If I do better than you overall today, you lay off my friends and me. For good. You politely ignore us if we see each other in a club or in public."

"And if I win?"

"Then you can keep being a biotch."

She shook her head. "That's not enough."

Ryan stepped up to meet her. Now his hand *was* clenched in a fist, and I was kinda scared he might punch her. "Get out of here. Or I'm gonna find Stan and tell him you're loose."

She didn't even look at him. She just grinned at me. "If I win, I get back in my human clothes, and you pull me in a cart around the arena. And I get to drive you in front of everyone."

"Done," I said.

"Kamen!" Ryan whirled toward me, hand still clenched.

I flipped my mane. "It doesn't matter, because I'm gonna win."

Ryan walked up to Cinnamon. "It's time for you to go," he said, putting a hand on her shoulder and turning her around. "Get back to your trainer."

She looked down at him over her shoulder. "You're cute. If you ever want to work with a *real* pony, message me on Fet."

She walked away, her perfect tail bobbing. But as she left, I noticed something small and green on her shoulder. I couldn't see what it was, because her braid kept swaying, covering it. I looked down at Ryan's hand, which was no longer in a fist. His palm was green. "What . . .?"

I glanced at the ground. There was a Jolly Rancher wrapper in the dust.

"Did you stick a Jolly Rancher to her?"

Ryan shrugged. “Oops.”

“You old dog. You—”

“Shh.” He patted my neck. “We’ve got a show to win.”

CHAPTER FIFTEEN

The grooming contest wasn't too scary.

I wasn't gonna lie to myself, or anyone—Cinnamon looked good. She carried herself perfectly, her frigging *skin* was basically dewy and flawless. Her tack gleamed and her tail rippled, and the Jolly Rancher was gone. I was dead before it even started. There were three lineups—ponies, pups, and miscellaneous. A judge came down the pony row and checked us all out. Looked at our tack and our bodies and had us walk in little circles. I was pretty sure she snickered when she saw my tail, but she seemed to appreciate my Pegasus Sheath. I had to be really careful when I walked in the circle, because the friggin' prostate plug was really doing its job. I didn't place. Bridget took third, Cinnamon second, and Holly first.

"It's fine," Ryan said as he led me out of the ring. "We're just getting started."

After the grooming, we had some time to relax before bobbing for apples. Maya showed up, and she was, like, super admiring of my horse getup. Except my sheath. She just rolled her eyes at that.

Ryan and I headed over to the apple tubs early, and he started talking to some handler he'd met earlier, while I wandered around, considering my bobbing strategy.

I almost ran into the tentacled hipster of my nightmares.

"Hey," he said.

For a second I couldn't speak. I just stared at his cardboard tentacles in horror. "Hey," I managed warily.

"Is this your first year here?"

I swallowed. "Y-yeah."

"Me too."

That made me feel better. We got to talking, and he was actually pretty cool and smart. We talked about his tentacle kink, and my costume kink, and the Subs Club, which he was slightly mortified to learn I had cofounded. Then we bonded over our love of women's underwear.

"I have all these gender nonconformist urges," he said. "Plus, I know I look like a guy and use male pronouns, but I don't always *feel* like one inside, you know? That's why Fucktopus is third gender."

"I totally get that, man. All my life, people have thought I was a dude-bro because I did sports and I have these muscles or whatever. I mean, I don't know if I'm binary or not. But I want the *option* to explore nonbinary things."

"Exactly!"

We hoof-to-tentacle high-fived.

"All right!" called a ref, waving her arms. "Competitors! We have three apple tubs. You should already have been assigned your tub, so you should proceed there and shake paws or hooves with your rival."

Fucktopus and I went to tub number two. He stared into the water. "The ocean," he whispered.

"Dude, that is not the ocean."

He looked up. "I'm sorry I keep using your club forum inappropriately."

"It's okay. I hope you find a sea captain."

He held out a tentacle. I bumped it with my hoof. "Let's do this."

The refs crouched by their respective tubs.

The bell sounded a moment later, and Fucktopus and I stuck our heads into the water.

Okay, this was a lot harder than it had been when I was a kid. Every time I got my teeth anywhere near a fucking apple, it scooted away. I could hear people cheering, and I could see out of the corner of my eye that Fucktopus was having way more luck with this than I was. Dude was boss at apple bobbing. I stopped for a moment just to see how many he had: Two. And he was pulling a third out of the water.

I stuck my face back in. Chased the apples and got nowhere. Pulled my face out.

"Oh my God! That squid is amazing at bobbing for apples!" I heard someone yell.

Oh, Fucktopus, you tentacled bastard.

I had to win. *Had* to. I'd already fucked up grooming, and I was nervous as shit about dressage. I needed some serious points.

I stuck my face back in and discovered the magic of pushing the apples against the side of the tub with my cheek, then bracing them there while I sank my teeth in. I dropped one apple in my pile. Two. Three. Four. When the bell went off again, I had water in my eyes and didn't know who had won, but suddenly a ref was patting my shoulder and calling me a good pony, and she declared me the winner.

I went on to round robin the other two winners, and emerged victorious.

Fucktopus was the first to congratulate me. Seconds later, I was stormed by my friends, who group-hugged me. Over their bodies, I could see Fucktopus and Maya gazing at each other. Like, the kind of gazing that leads to trouble.

I cleared my throat at Fucktopus. "Dude. She's nineteen. Don't even go there."

Fucktopus looked at Maya and raised a tentacle to wave at her.

Maya waved back.

I puked in my mouth a little.

By cart race time, I was pumped. I'd barely been able to eat anything for lunch—though I had managed another handful of Jolly Ranchers.

I lined up in the three position between Holly and a gray pony called Snowball. I couldn't see my competitors with the blinkers on, so I focused on the white lines that marked the large oval track. The track was situated on a slight incline, so Ryan had warned me to save some energy for the end, since the last half of the race was uphill. He'd taken my tail out too, so I wouldn't be distracted by the prostate plug. But now I was basically going to be running in assless pants.

I tried not to think about Cinnamon, who was in the six position.

You've got this. You're super fast. Faster than she is.

I heard some jingling to my left, and a handler's voice saying, "Easy . . . eeeeaaaassssyyyy."

"False start," called one of the PPF officials. "Back her up."

I hated not being able to see what was going on. I stamped my foot and chewed on the bit, feeling pretty ponyish all of a sudden.

"Good boy," Ryan whispered. I could feel him tense on the reins, and I moved my head forward to remind him to ease up. He gave me some slack.

"They're in the gates!" called a staff member.

Suddenly the bell clanged, and the reins snapped against my shoulders. I bolted forward, listening to the creak of wheels on either side of me and the cheering of the crowd. Snowball was way in the lead—how the hell had he started so fast? I increased my pace, even though Ryan was tugging on the reins. He'd told me to save my energy, but Snowball was so far ahead that I needed to close some of this distance *now*.

Ryan pulling harder, and I almost slowed. But I could hear one of the ponies to my left starting to overtake me, and no way was I gonna let that happen. I clenched my teeth around the bit and jerked my head up, pulling the reins through Ryan's hands and charging ahead.

I'd almost caught Snowball when we reached the turn. Ryan tugged the left rein, and I made a careful arc. But he kept tugging. Hard tugs, over and over.

Dude, Ryan. I've got this.

Snowball was still slightly ahead of me on the inside. I was guessing Ryan wanted me to cut behind Snowball and then pull alongside him so that I was on the inside of the turn. But that would mean slowing down, which was not gonna happen. Instead I sped up, trying to pass Snowball on the outside.

There was a clank and a jolt as the wheel of our cart collided with another. Someone was trying to pass *us* on the outside.

I pitched to the left, nearly slamming into Snowball.

We were in what I believed was known scientifically as a clusterfuck.

Ryan tugged the right rein, steering me away from Snowball, and since I couldn't see to the side or behind me, I had to trust him that the cart on our outside was gone.

I could feel it, just like I had sometimes in practice—the moment Ryan and I stopped fighting each other and started to work as a team.

He steered me wide of Snowball, which meant we lost some ground, but it got us out of the disaster area. I didn't try to turn my head, just paid attention to his rein cues until it was just me and Snowball, racing up the hill toward the finish.

Except we were both running out of juice. I was breathing hard, trying without much luck to make my legs move faster. He was lagging big time—his driver flicked his thigh with the crop a couple of times, but Snowball was done.

Why had the hill seemed so short going down, and now seemed to stretch endlessly? I could see the orange flag marking the finish, but it was still approximately eight billion miles away. Snowball and I struggled alongside each other, huffing while the spectators cheered us on.

Suddenly, the cheering got louder. I thought at first it was because I was starting to pull ahead of Snowball, but then I heard a jingling to my right.

Cinnamon breezed past both of us at a lively trot. Her spandex onesie barely looked sweaty, and the rubies on her harness gleamed.

Oh no you don't.

I surged forward, finding another gear. Ryan let me have my head, and I staggered toward Cinnamon, her red tail swishing in front of me like a matador's cape. The roar from the crowd grew as I pulled alongside her. She quickened her pace.

She's got energy to spare. She's just toying with me.

The reins smacked my shoulders again, and Ryan tapped my right thigh with the whip. I clenched my jaw and tried to speed up.

Stan whooped and called, "Your boy's flagging!" to Ryan.

No, he isn't, I promised silently. *Your boy's gonna win this thing.*

I came up beside Cinnamon again, and once more, she sped up, leaving me behind. But the incline was long, and I could see her trot was getting clumsier. The entire back of her onesie was sweat-soaked now.

I pulled alongside her again, and this time when she sped up, I matched her. It felt like we were going seventy miles an hour, but really, we were barely jogging.

"Geehiihhh toihh-hrrr?" she called to me.

"Yoohhhh gquonnaa loooofff," I called back.

She veered toward me slightly, and the wheels of our carts collided.

"Qwiiihh-ihh!"

"Giihhrff uhhwb!"

"Nehh-her!"

For Jolly Ranchers. For wings. For glory.

For Ryan.

Okay, mostly for me and bragging rights.

But also for Ryan.

She pulled ahead. Then I pulled ahead. Her driver yelled, "Hyah," and there was a slap of leather on flesh, and then she passed me again. A second later, I felt the light sting of Ryan's whip on my thigh, and I jumped ahead of her. Then we were neck and neck.

We could see the finish line now. Dave was there, holding up his phone. At first I thought he was just taking a video, which was not technically legal, but as I got closer, I could hear, over the cheers, the *Chariots of Fire* theme.

Oh hell yes. That was all I needed.

I rallied one more time and stuck my head in front of Cinnamon's, just as the flag flashed by.

An hour later, I stood at the entrance to the dressage arena, my heart hammering. I was trying to go over the routine in my head, but I kept getting distracted by all the people in the stands and the music and the smell of corn dogs. And my tail, which was back in and stimulating the fuck out of my prostate. I turned to Ryan, wanting to ask him a question about the first turn, but I had the stupid bit in my mouth.

It's all about having fun. And destroying Cinnamon. But mostly having fun.

And Ryan and I were gonna have fun. I mean, we'd fucking owned bobbing for apples and the cart race. Was there anything we couldn't do?

Yes.

Dressage.

I'd just watched Cinnamon in her routine a few minutes before. She'd done it to a suite from *Swan Lake*. And it had been some legit fucking horse ballet.

I glanced at the bleachers. Gould caught my eye and waved, and then the others were waving too.

I lifted a hoof and waved back.

The pony before us halted in the center of the ring to wild applause. She had a cheering section that was whistling and stomping and holding up *TEAM NATALIE* signs. The pony and her handler saluted and then exited the ring, and a moment later, the judges held up their cards: two eights and a nine. Same score as Cinnamon. So really, if I could get two nines and an eight, I'd be golden.

Except every time I thought about Cinnamon's "Swan Lake" thing, I felt a little sicker. Okay, so I wasn't anywhere near that elegant. People loved underdogs. And they loved to be entertained.

And everyone with a soul loved Survivor.

The announcer said my name, and my friends went nuts. Even D whooped, which was a sound so weird I almost forgot to be nervous for a second.

Ryan patted my shoulder. "We got this, buddy."

Sure we did. I was just gonna pee my damn Pegasus Sheath was all.

The intro to "High on You" blared from the speakers, and Ryan flicked the reins. I broke into a trot, tucking my chin as we entered the arena. I headed for the C marker at more of a charge than a trot. Started to turn right as we reached it. Suddenly, Ryan was pulling back on the reins, and I couldn't figure out why.

Salute the judges at X.

I stopped so fast Ryan almost slammed into me. I tried to arch my neck and stand straight, but I was so freaked about screwing up already that I couldn't move. I just clamped down on the bit and waited, slightly off center from C, until Ryan was standing beside me. He bowed, and I horse curtsied, and the prostate plug gave me inappropriate feelings. The judges nodded at us, and the one who'd eyed my sheath during grooming smiled at me. Ryan got behind me and clucked again, tugging the right rein, and I trotted toward the M marker. Jimi Jamison started singing.

The whip touched the back of my neck.

Extend the trot.

I lengthened my stride, trying to make each foot glide just above the ground, reminding myself to move my front legs at the same speed. We were almost to B, and I had a sudden, panicked moment where I couldn't remember if we did a circle or serpentine first.

He'll tell you.

Sure enough, Ryan tugged the left rein just after X, and I turned, creating a serpentine. He was having trouble keeping up with me, because I was basically bolting around the ring. I slowed a little and concentrated on matching my stride to the beat of the song. Passed E, then K.

Don't fuck this up.

At F, he pressed the whip against the right side of my rib cage.

And I could not for the life of me remember what that meant. So I just kinda . . . pranced.

"Half pass, babe," he murmured. "Half pass."

"Shiiihhh," I whispered around the bit.

"It's fine. You're fine."

He was probably gonna get points taken off for talking to me, but I appreciated it so much. I arched my body around the whip and half passed from F to E. *Forward and sideways. Forward and sideways.* Lifting my legs. Keeping my stride even. I started feeling the rhythm of the song, which was awesome, and I lifted my legs higher and punched my arms forward and back. Sassy trot. At E, he switched sides with the whip and stopped me. *Full pass to X—nailing it.* At X, Ryan gave me two quick taps on the right leg. I leaped into a canter, which wasn't super graceful, but I was excited. The *tempi*s were coming up, but it was gonna be fine.

You've got this.

Ryan let out the reins and stood in place, and I made a wide circle around him. He flicked the whip against my calf. *Tempi, motherfuckers.*

I changed leads and moved into the second part of the figure eight. I could feel Ryan moving with me, and it was actually an awesome feeling, to both be so in tune. I leaned into the second turn, arching my neck.

Suddenly, everything went black. My wig had slipped down over my eyes. I shook my head, trying not to break the gait. The wig slipped farther. I shook more vigorously, hearing the laughter from the stands. My mane flew off. I glanced around to see where it had landed, not realizing that I was no longer moving in a circle, and that Ryan hadn't had time to adjust his position accordingly.

I saw what was going to happen about a split second before my left rein hit the side of Ryan's neck and clotheslined him.

He went down like a sandbag.

I slowed, not sure what to do. I started piaffing anxiously, waiting to see if Ryan would get up. Drool was streaming down my chin, and my head felt weirdly naked. The guitar solo raged on as Ryan rolled onto his back.

I made a decision.

I whirled and trotted back to him. Crouched and extended my hoof. He looked up into my eyes, and God, he was beautiful. The most awesome possum fucking pony trainer of all time, and who cared if we were making a mess of this dressage thing? I smiled at him around the bit. He smiled too and grabbed my hoof. And as Jimi Jamison promised to tell us about the girl he met last night, I hauled Ryan back to his feet. The crowd cheered as Ryan took his place behind me. We cantered at a diagonal through the next chorus, changing leads every two strides. At the K post, I moved into a pirouette, then came out of it on a *passage*.

The rest of the routine went by in a blur. We eventually arrived in front of the judges, and I moved into the most collected trot pretty much ever. I was friggin' floating. Piaffin' like I was born to do it.

We stopped, saluted one more time, and then left the ring.

Our crew met us just outside the gate and swarmed me as Ryan was taking out my bit.

"Dude," Dave said. "That was amazing."

I laughed, wiping my mouth with the back of my hoof. "Uh-huh. That was fuckocked."

"It was the very definition of majesty, and I got it all on video."

"I wanna see."

"Hold on." He elbowed me. "Wait for your score."

Yeah, because I really wanted to see every judge publicly give me a zero.

But as I turned, I saw the first judge hold up a five. The second held up a six. The woman who liked my horse cock held up a seven.

My group cheered, and the rest of the spectators applauded.

Ryan patted me. "That's way better than I thought."

"The consecutive numbers are very pleasing from an OCD perspective," Gould said.

"You're totally above average." Dave punched my arm lightly. "Congrats."

D offered me a bottle of water, and I took it between my hooves. Ryan opened it for me, and I chugged it, staring at Dave's phone as he played the video.

"Oh my God." I burst out laughing. "I look so dumb."

"You look hot," Gould said. "Look at your muscles."

"I second 'hot.'" Ryan leaned in to see.

I turned to Gould. "You mackin' on a horse, Gould?" I whispered in his ear. "'Cause I'll give you a ride later, if you want."

He stepped away. "Oh, gross."

I glanced back at the screen. "I do look hot."

"And look at your giant flopping horse dick," Dave pressed. "Ooh, hold on, here's where your wig falls down and you take Ryan *out*."

We watched, and I started laughing so hard I snorted, which made me laugh harder.

Eventually Ryan clipped the reins to the cheek piece and led me back toward my stall so we could regroup before the balloon pop. And so we could take my fucking tail out.

On the way there, we saw Cinnamon, standing by her handler, who was talking to another owner. Her bridle was off, and she wore a green nylon halter instead. She looked at me as I passed. "Cute routine," she said. "Sorry you had some trouble."

There was a loud *thwack*, and Cinnamon jumped about a foot in the air. She put one hoof back to the left side of her ass and turned.

Stan was watching her, crop in hand. "You leave them alone."

It was one of the best moments of my life.

After dressage, we got a break—half an hour. Pets were allowed to hang out in the enclosure where we'd had the meet 'n' greet. Cinnamon wasn't there, but a few other pets I knew were. I didn't see Glazer at first, but then he showed up, hump toy in his mouth. He spat it on the ground. "Everything's set," he told me in a low voice through the rottweiler hood. "All you gotta worry about is popping as many balloons as you can. We'll take care of the rest."

Fucktopus was a few yards down, testing his cardboard tentacles. Across from us, on the other side of the arena, Mittens was rolling in the grass.

"Is she okay?" I asked.

"She's fine," Glazer replied.

Max came up to us, followed by Scribbles and a limping Barkley.

"We're here to strategize about the balloon pop," Max announced.

I looked at Barkley, who slowly lowered his arthritic hips. "You doing the balloon pop, Barks?"

He stared at me, panting slightly. "No," he rasped. "I'm just gonna watch. I'm too old for this shit."

"So," Max said. "We need to make sure Cinnamon doesn't win."

Glazer looked around. "Where's Fucktopus? Fucktopus!"

Fucktopus drifted over, tentacles waving.

"You thought anymore about how we're gonna do this?" Glazer asked Fucktopus.

Fucktopus shook his head.

"I could trip her," Max offered. "But that's all I got."

Barkley let out a hack. We all looked at him. He stared back at us a moment, then focused on me. "That tail you were wearing earlier might come in handy."

"What do you mean?" I asked.

Barkley scratched his grizzled muzzle with his paw. "Get her where her weakness is. She *hates* rats."

Max frowned. "I don't get it."

Barkley leaned forward and whispered to her. Suddenly, Max started wagging her tail. "Oh my God. Oh. My God." She turned and whispered to Glazer.

Then she looked at me. "Thunder? We're gonna need the tail."

"My . . . my butt plug tail? I don't even know where Ryan put it."

Glazer turned to me. The little fake tongue flopped in his leather jowls. The eyeholes of his mask were really creeping me out. "Find it. There's a sanitation station by the blindfolded obstacle course. Go wash that thing off. Wash it good. Then take it to Scribbles."

"Why is no one whispering to me?"

Max smiled. "We want you to be surprised. Listen, Thunder. We're going to set you up as the winner."

"Huh?"

Scribbles nodded. "We're going to try to make sure you pop the most balloons. Glazer, Max, Fucktopus. You work on passing as many balloons as possible to Thunder. As for Cinnamon." Scribbles stared straight ahead, eyes flashing behind his ferret mask. "Leave her to me."

It all came down to this. Cinnamon had, according to the grapevine, completely bombed her obstacle course. She and I now had the same number of points. So whoever won this won the game, set, match, point, and everything.

The other pets and I were led into the small arena full of balloons and lined up on all fours in the middle. A light breeze batted the balloons throughout the ring. There were refs all around the fence, each one assigned to tally the balloons popped by an individual contestant. Cindy went over the rules—stay on all fours was the big one—and then there was a moment of silence.

The buzzer went off.

And all was chaos.

I started blindly lashing out at balloons, but I kept checking to see how Cinnamon was doing. She was a popping fool. She used both hooves at once, slamming them down on balloon after balloon. She even popped one behind her with her high-heeled boot. She could move stunningly fast on all fours. She galloped onto my territory, popping left and right.

"Little slow there, big guy," she called. She was making her way along the fence, taking out the balloons that had scattered along the rail.

I caught a glimpse of Mittens, who was not popping balloons at all, but rolling around on the grass along the fence.

"Thunder!" Max kind of disguised my name as a bark as she kicked a balloon toward me while simultaneously popping one of her own.

I slammed my hoof down on the balloon.

I heard Max yelp, and looked up to see Cinnamon slam her shoulder into Max's side. It did *not* look like an accident. Max limped away, wincing.

So Cinnamon was playing dirty too.

Suddenly there was a barrage of much deeper barking, and I turned toward the source.

Glazer was barreling toward Cinnamon, kicking up grass in his wake. A green balloon floated into Glazer's path. He leaped onto it, and it burst. He continued on and launched himself at Cinnamon, trapping her against the fence. Cinnamon reared back, startled, and tried to kick Glazer off. Glazer arched his back, threw his head up, and began humping the heel of her boot.

"Jesus Christ, Glazer!" Glazer's owner shouted from the sidelines. "You fucking idiot! No!"

There was murmuring from the crowd. Cinnamon whinnied and kicked, but couldn't shake Glazer.

"Disqualified!" A ref yelled. "No humping!"

As I raced for the red balloon, I saw Glazer's owner open the gate and hurry into the ring.

Cinnamon wheeled away and took off down the side of the enclosure as the guy grabbed Glazer's shoulder and pulled him back, clipping a leash to his harness.

As Glazer was dragged from the arena, he raised his paw to the forehead of his mask and saluted me.

Fucktopus was on the far side of the arena, using his tentacles to slap balloons toward me.

And then one of his tentacles fell off. He tried to grab it, but missed.

"Fucktopus is out," I muttered to Max as I passed her. She was sitting, panting, one paw pressed to her ribs as a ref called to her, asking if she was okay. "What do we do?"

"It's all right," she whispered. "He's coming."

Who? I chased an orange balloon along the fence. Passed Fucktopus, who was now staring into the stands, his remaining tentacle limp at his side. I glanced where he was looking and saw Maya gazing back.

Seriously? They were gonna pick *now* for some Romeo and Juliet shit?

I started to call to him, but then Scribbles burst from a cluster of balloons on the other side of the ring, something small and black trailing him. It took me a moment to recognize my mangled tail, wound into a hairy mass and attached to Scribbles with fishing wire from his stress ball. "Rat!" he shouted. "There's a rat! An *actual* rat!"

He sounded pretty convincing.

I saw Cinnamon look up just as Scribbles ran by, the "rat" chasing him.

It didn't look anything like a real rat. And, like, anyone using logic would be like, *Why is a rat chasing Scribbles?* But I guess to Cinnamon, any small, dark, furry thing was cause for blind panic. She whinnied loudly, bolting for the other end of the ring, all balloons forgotten. There was some commotion along the sidelines, but I didn't bother to listen.

I got to work, popping all the balloons Cinnamon had left behind.

"There's no rat!" a ref yelled. "Everyone calm down. It's not a rat."

I popped two more balloons. The arena was littered with colorful latex scraps, and there were hardly any unpopped balloons left.

A moment later, I saw a flash of red as Cinnamon charged by me on all fours, headed for Scribbles. She looked furious. Scribbles started to bolt, but Cinnamon cut him off. She whipped him viciously in the face with her French braid.

Scribbles shouted, clutching his cheek, as Cinnamon trotted away.

With Glazer gone, Scribbles and Max incapacitated, Fucktopus struggling with his tentacles and newfound, totally inappropriate love, and Mittens rolling uselessly on the ground . . . that just left Cinnamon and me.

I looked around but didn't see any more balloons. I was wondering why the refs didn't call the game, but then I spotted it—a single green balloon down at the opposite end of the arena.

Cinnamon spied it at the same moment and threw me a look.

The rest seemed to happen in slo-mo. Fucktopus turned away from Maya and spotted the balloon. He started crawling toward it, but his tentacles were slowing him down.

I galloped toward the balloon, lengthening my stride. Dust got between my kneepads and my leather pants. Grass and dirt filled my mouth. I could hear Cinnamon pounding behind me, and a second later, a glint of red appeared in the corner of my vision.

I looked straight ahead. At Ryan, standing at the fence, calling to me. I couldn't hear what he was saying over all the shouting, but I knew I had to do this.

She might be better groomed and more graceful, but I was fucking *faster*.

Just. Get. The. Balloon.

We both reached the balloon at the same time, and it whooshed into the air as the gust from our combined movement hit it. I didn't think—just rose onto two legs and leaped. So maybe I'd get disqualified for not staying on all fours, but Cinnamon must have done the same thing, because she was in the air too, and we were both reaching, reaching . . .

And then suddenly she was dropping—hadn't been able to get enough hang time in those heels, I guess. I caught the balloon between my hooves and brought it back to the ground with me, collapsing onto my hands and knees. I raised my front hooves, ready to slam them down on the balloon, my mouth open to let out a victory whinny. But before I could stomp, there was a burst of white in front of me, and it knocked the balloon away.

I looked over in shock. Mittens stood a few feet to my left, the balloon between her paws. As I watched, she raised one delicate white paw.

"Mrrriiiiiouuu?" she said.

And popped the fucking balloon.

"I didn't win," I said later in the car. It was nice to be back in regular clothes. Ryan had hosed me down at the wash racks, so I felt clean and tired.

Ryan glanced at me as we waited our turn to leave the lot. "Yeah, the refs could kinda see where you all ganged up on Cinnamon."

"Yeah." I stared out the window, grinning. "But they could also see where she purposely whipped Scribbles in the face. And bowled Max over."

"She was awful."

"You think I did the right thing, don't you?"

"I think the right thing would have been sending her to the glue factory."

I laughed. "Well, at least neither of us got best in show."

"I can't believe you both had the same number of points."

"I guess we're worthy adversaries."

The line of cars inched forward, then was stopped again by the traffic people. "We're never gonna get out of here," Ryan muttered.

"Sure we will." I watched workers pack up the hot dog stand. "You think this is something we're gonna keep doing? Pony play, I mean?"

"Yeah, if you want. I think it's fun."

"I do too." I spotted something out the window. "Hey, there's Cinnamon and Stan." They were standing by a large parked truck a few feet away. Cinnamon was wearing regular clothes, and . . . crying?

Stan was rubbing her back. She seemed way more distressed than losing a pet play competition called for.

"Hold on," I said to Ryan. "I'm getting out. If the line moves, go ahead. I'll catch up with you in a minute."

I hopped out of the car and walked over to her. She looked up, and when she saw me she started crying harder.

"Hey," I said.

"I'm sorry!" She gulped over and over. "I'm so sorry."

"For what?" I asked, confused.

Stan shushed her gently, but Cinnamon shook her head and stared right at me. "I should have noticed. I should have seen."

I had definitely missed something. "Seen what?"

"He died. He died right there in that room, and I didn't notice. I didn't . . . even . . ." She was crying too hard to continue.

Everything in me went cold.

Hal.

"It's okay," I told her. "We know you were— Like, we know it wasn't obvious."

She continued gulping until she choked. "How did I not *see*?"

I walked up to her. She flinched back. "Easy," I said. "It's okay."

She quieted slightly. "I could have saved him. I was the only one there."

Stan looked at me and said quietly, "This happens sometimes. I think she's been wanting to talk to you about it."

Cinnamon wiped her nose on the back of her hand. "I want to say I'm sorry. I can't say it to him, so I want to say it to you. T-two years. And I just keep th-thinking about it."

I held out a hand to her. She eyed it warily. Then slowly put her hand in mine. I smiled at her.

"It was an accident." I thought about Bill. About GK and Kel.

An accident.

Preventable, yes. But I didn't want to do this blame-game bullshit forever.

I squeezed her hand. "It's not your fault."

She squeezed my hand back, then let me go. She turned away. "Thanks," she whispered.

"Good show today," I said. "I mean that."

She turned back to me. Took a deep breath and smiled through her tears. Let out a short, choked laugh. "You too, Kamen." Her smile faded. "I'm sorry."

"Hey. You don't have to say it anymore."

She nodded. "I might still need to say it though. Sometimes."

"That's fine," I told her. "Me too."

CHAPTER SIXTEEN

"Zac," Miles called. "Be careful. That's a choking hazard."

Zac looked up from the tiny piece of plastic he was playing with on the deck.

Miles, Dave, and I were all sprawled in the deck chairs on Miles's back patio. Dave and I had beers. Miles had a glass of white wine. His second.

"Bring it to me, please." Miles held out his hand. Zac ran over and placed the plastic in Miles's hand. "Thank you." He glanced into the yard, where Gould and Ryan were kicking a ball back and forth. "You left Uncle Gould and Uncle Ryan hangin' there. They need someone else to kick the ball to."

"I want a hamburger," Zac said.

"You'll get one as soon as D and Drix are finished grilling. Hey. C'mere." He hugged Zac, then sent him off into the yard with a gentle shove.

Dave peered at Miles from the end of the deck-chair line. "'That's a choking hazard?' Really?"

Miles squinted at him. "It *is* a choking hazard. What are you saying?"

"I'm just saying that any actual human who is not secretly a robot set upon society by scientists who want to test its ability to mimic human feeling would say 'That's dangerous,' or 'You might choke.' Rather than use the phrase, 'That's a choking hazard' to a five-year-old."

"My child is far superior to the weak-minded, babbling offspring of the mortals who surround me. And he can be spoken to like an adult."

Dave looked at me. "Oh my God. I love wine-drinking Dad-Miles."

Miles smiled over the rim of his wineglass. "I'm not the high-collared prude you think I am. I've sampled reefer. I've had sex in a car."

"*You've* had sex in a car?"

Miles shrugged haughtily, taking another sip of wine. "It's really not that uncommon, Dave."

"I'm just surprised, because you once told me fucking in a car was for the proletariat."

"I said that?"

"Yes."

D approached with meat tongs. Stepped onto the deck. "Hello, all. What's going on?"

We shielded our eyes to look up at him. "Heyyyy." Dave held out his hand, and D caught it. "Miles is pregaming the Great Grill-stravaganza."

D turned his gaze to Miles. "I approve."

Miles gave him a thumbs-up and drained the last of his wine.

I set my beer in the chair's cup holder and glanced at D. "Do you have all the meat you need?"

"I do. Drix and I have the grill under control. Though I would like to talk to you for a moment."

"All of us?" Dave asked.

D released Dave's hand. "Just Kamen. Privately."

The others *ooooohhhh*-ed like I'd gotten called to the principal's office. I grinned and stood, following D off the deck and into the yard. We stopped in the shadow of Miles's crabapple tree, and D faced me.

"That was a fine performance the other day. I didn't think I would enjoy humans' pale imitations of the magnificent creature that is the horse. But you did me proud."

"Aww. Thanks, D. You're not disappointed that I cheated?"

He put a hand on my shoulder. "All's fair in love and war. And the purpose of a Friesian . . ."

"Is war," I whispered, clapping my hand over his.

He did the wise-owl nod.

Then he shifted, clearing his throat. "There is something else I wanted to ask you."

"Sure."

He looked like he didn't know where to start. "When . . . when you and Ryan decided to move in together . . . who initiated this? And how did the conversation go?"

I raised my eyebrows. "Uhhh. I don't know. We were just fooling around one night, and I was like, 'I wish I could see you all the time.' And he was like, 'Well, why don't we get a place together when our leases are up?' It just made sense."

He nodded and glanced at the deck, where Dave and Miles were in some kind of slapping war.

"You thinking of asking Dave to live with you?" I asked.

"At some point. Perhaps. Once he's further along with school."

"Oh. My. God."

He turned back to me. "I don't expect word of this to reach David."

I hid a grin. "Your secret's safe with me."

He nodded again. "Good man."

He left to go back to the grill. I took the opportunity to get out my phone and pull up a video. It was about the seven hundredth time I'd watched it today. And now I needed to share it with someone. I headed over to the kickball party and intercepted a kick from Gould to Ryan.

"No fair!" Ryan protested as I kicked the ball to Zac.

I put an arm around his shoulders. "I need you inside the house for a sec."

He excused himself, then followed me through the side door into Miles's laundry room.

"Hi," I told him. "I really love you."

"I really love you too. Are you okay? You have a maniacal grin."

I nodded, not sure how to explain. I thought about how growing up meant more than just a laundry room to me. It meant I was alive and lucky. It meant I could grow old with my friends, and with this man, who made me want to do anything—not *for* him, but *with* him.

I showed him my phone.

He took it. "What's th— Oh!"

"We have seventy views on YouTube and I only put it up yesterday. I thought at least sixty of those were me, but we have a lot of comments from people who aren't me. Twelve likes. And zero dislikes."

"Holy shit." He hit Play, and "Snow Wanderer" came out of the phone's speaker.

We watched the video together. Ricky had animated Ryan's drawings so that the figure wavered a little and the snow swirled, and in one scene, a raisin fell off a snowman's mouth and landed in the snow. He was still staring, slightly openmouthed, when the video ended.

"And it's the drawings people are going nuts about." I took the phone and scrolled slowly down. "Look at the comments. Okay, that one says I sing like a fag, which . . . fair enough. But most of these are about how amazing your drawings are."

"Holy shit," he said again.

Not that YouTube commenters were, like, a gold standard for determining talent, but the word "genius" came up in the comments several times in reference to Ryan's art. Some people actually liked the song too. A few comments were along the lines of *This is so weird* and *Is this for real?* And several didn't make sense because people don't know how to spell.

I looked at Ryan. "Do you think we're gonna go viral?"

"I don't know. Maybe!"

"Maybe we'll be famous."

"Maybe we'll be iTunes best sellers."

"Maybe we'll get to be on a talk show."

He glanced up at me. "Thank you," he said softly.

"Don't thank me. You're the artist."

He slapped my arm. "Shut up."

"Be nice to Pelletor unless you want a tickle offensive."

"Don't forget I have a riding whip at home."

I bent to kiss him. He leaned against me awhile, staring out the window into the yard.

"We ought to get back out there," he said.

I glanced down at him. "Can I carry you out?"

"Oh my fucking God. What is wrong with you?"

"Just once. You can get on my back. Pretend I'm Thunder Canyon."

He rolled his eyes. "Okay. *Fine.* Just. Once."

I crouched so he could mount up.

"I hate you," he muttered, as I straightened. I held on to his leg with one arm and opened the door with the other.

"I love you," I said.

"I guess I love you too."

I hooked both arms under his knees. And waited.

He patted my shoulder. "All right, Thunder Canyon. Walk on."

Explore more of *The Subs Club* series:
riptidepublishing.com/universe/subs-club

Dear Reader,

Thank you for reading J.A. Rock's *Manties in a Twist*!

We know your time is precious and you have many, many entertainment options, so it means a lot that you've chosen to spend your time reading. We really hope you enjoyed it.

We'd be honored if you'd consider posting a review—good or bad—on sites like **Amazon, Barnes & Noble, Kobo, Goodreads, Twitter, Facebook**, **Tumblr,** and your blog or website. We'd also be honored if you told your friends and family about this book. Word of mouth is a book's lifeblood!

For more information on upcoming releases, author interviews, blog tours, contests, giveaways, and more, please sign up for our weekly, spam-free newsletter and visit us around the web:

Newsletter: tinyurl.com/RiptideSignup
Twitter: twitter.com/RiptideBooks
Facebook: facebook.com/RiptidePublishing
Goodreads: tinyurl.com/RiptideOnGoodreads
Tumblr: riptidepublishing.tumblr.com

Thank you so much for Reading the Rainbow!

RiptidePublishing.com

ACKNOWLEDGMENTS

Thank you, as always, to Del. To Brian, for the soundtrack. And to Ken, for Orville Deadenbacher and tales of Bed Bath & Beyond.

The Subs Club Series
The Subs Club
Pain Slut
24/7 (Coming June 2016)

Minotaur
By His Rules
Wacky Wednesday (Wacky Wednesday #1)
The Brat-tastic Jayk Parker (Wacky Wednesday #2)
Calling the Show
Take the Long Way Home
The Grand Ballast

Coming Soon
The Silvers

Playing the Fool series, with Lisa Henry
The Two Gentlemen of Altona
The Merchant of Death
Tempest

With Lisa Henry
When All the World Sleeps
The Good Boy (The Boy #1)
The Naughty Boy (The Boy #1.5)
The Boy Who Belonged (The Boy #2)
Mark Cooper Versus America (Prescott College #1)
Brandon Mills Versus the V-Card (Prescott College #2)
Another Man's Treasure

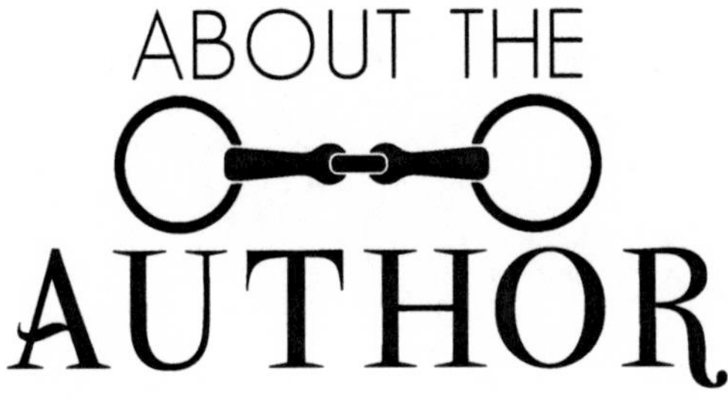

J.A. Rock is the author of queer romance and suspense novels, including *By His Rules*, *Take the Long Way Home*, and, with Lisa Henry, *The Good Boy* and *When All the World Sleeps*. She holds an MFA in creative writing from the University of Alabama and a BA in theater from Case Western Reserve University. J.A. also writes queer fiction and essays under the name Jill Smith. Raised in Ohio and West Virginia, she now lives in Chicago with her dog, Professor Anne Studebaker.

Website: www.jarockauthor.com
Blog: jarockauthor.blogspot.com
Twitter: twitter.com/jarockauthor
Facebook: facebook.com/ja.rock.39

Enjoy more stories like *Manties in a Twist* at RiptidePublishing.com!

The Dom Around the Corner
ISBN: 978-1-62649-325-4

Rules to Live By
ISBN: 978-1-62649-252-3

Earn Bonus Bucks!

Earn 1 Bonus Buck for each dollar you spend. Find out how at RiptidePublishing.com/news/bonus-bucks.

Win Free Ebooks for a Year!

Pre-order coming soon titles directly through our site and you'll receive one entry into a drawing for a chance to win free books for a year! Get the details at RiptidePublishing.com/contests.

CPSIA information can be obtained at www.ICGtesting.com
Printed in the USA
LVOW11s1616210316

480076LV00006B/531/P